WISHING WELLS

Pauline Potterill

ISBN: 9798705051045

Cover design by: Pauline Potterill
Library of Congress Control Number: 2018675309
Printed in the United States of America

To my mother Muriel, for her love of writing, for encouraging imaginative play in my early years and for supporting my endeavours throughout her life.

To my friend Mandy for being brave enough to read my initial draft. Thankyou for your encouragement and enthusiasm. Your support means a lot.

INTRODUCTION

When Emily Hope becomes lost in a snow storm, on her way to the airport, she has no idea how radically her life is about to change. The inhabitants of Greater Blessing are plotting, each with their own little scheme. Emily, it seems, features in every one. Co-incidence? No! As Emily comes to learn, nothing in Greater Blessing happens by chance. Events have been managed for a long, long time. Just ask the cats.

As Emily becomes embroiled in village life and attempts to come to terms with her fate, whatever that might be, she struggles to understand her own needs: assuming of course that the mysterious periapt is just a harmless pendant and she actually has a choice.

WISHING WELLS

December 28th 2013

CHAPTER ONE

E mily could barely see. Tears pricked her eyes. The hurt and anger of a few moments ago displaced. Sleet screeched down the windscreen as the wipers whipped frantically back and forth, packing fear and frustration into one icy ball in the pit of her stomach. With every arc the blades swept a narrower and narrower 'V', her view of the road obscured. She flicked on main beam for better visibility, but this only reflected off the falling snow, ruining her depth of vision. She could barely make out the sides of the road. Only the hedges marking its boundary gave her direction. She dared not stop. She had no idea where she was, and she wasn't dressed to abandon her car. She thought bitterly of the empty flat, and the note on the kitchen table. How could he have done this? He knew how important this contract was to her. She was only going to be away for three weeks and India was an opportunity she couldn't turn down.

Couldn't he see that! So, Grant Dobson would be spending New Year on his own. So bloody what! After all, the privilege of buying and consuming enough over-hiked alcohol in order to tolerate being crushed and 'snogged' by total strangers, as they murdered 'Auld Lang Syne', was a ritual she could do without. There would be plenty more New Years. Why couldn't he just be pleased for her and be supportive? They were going to be apart for three weeks. He could at least wave her off. But no, the bastard, instead of driving her to the airport in his all singing, all dancing BMW, left her a note, couldn't even say it to her face, and a car with a dodgy starter motor!

Suddenly the hedges drifted apart as the road widened. The landscape dipped from view. Tyres crunched for purchase compacting the snow and melting the surface layer like a skater's blade. The car started to slide. Clammy palms gripping the steering wheel she froze and watched a wall of white branches rush to greet her.

* * *

All week Grant had fought with his conscience. India was the final straw. Emily hadn't even tried to get the trip postponed until after the New Year. Every single time it seemed she put her job before him. Yes, he was pleased that she enjoyed her work, but he hardly ever saw her. Some of his friends didn't even believe Emily existed. He tried. How he tried to be supportive, but time after time she broke their plans or made them late. Why couldn't she take life a little less seriously? They were young. They should be out enjoying themselves not sticking to a 'life plan'. Women were having children into their late 30s early 40s these days. He didn't want children yet. Besides, what would she do about work then? Typically, she refused to discuss that aspect. Probably she had a plan but one she knew he wouldn't like. Her friend Louise had just announced that she was pregnant. That could only add fuel to their smouldering argument. And now tonight, when they were supposed to be going to his motor club dinner, something that he had been looking forward to for months, the night when the speeches were made and the trophies given out, she had just assumed that he would take her to the airport. Well, maybe if he just wasn't there when she got home, maybe then she would realise just how angry he was. On impulse he scribbled a note – 'Had to go out. Can't take you to the airport. Have a good trip. Grant' – grabbed his coat and walked out the door.

As he handed the keys of his BMW Z4 to the barman at his club, and the rich smooth Talisker worked its magic, his mood mellowed, and he began to regret his actions. He could have left her the BMW. Emily rarely used her car. He wasn't even certain it would start. Shit!

* * *

With a bone jarring thump, the Clio stopped dead: its wheels rammed against something solid. The engine stalled. Frantically she switched it back on again, afraid to get stuck in the snow. Nervously she put the car in reverse and pressed the accelerator. The car moved backwards slightly. The wheels spun but couldn't mount the mound of snow. She put it in first and rocked it forwards, then backwards, and forwards again. She was going nowhere. Panic rising, she stalled the car. Emily stared at the wipers, which continued to mock her pounding heart. With a shaky hand she switched them off. The hail, which had been angrily slapping the little car, suddenly ceased. In its place, large sticky snowflakes fell. Silence throbbed. Emily was alone in a beautiful but hostile landscape. She fumbled on the passenger seat for her bag and pulled out her phone. Switching it on she stared at the no signal sign. With mounting panic, she switched on the interior light and looked at the map. She had turned off the main road to find a way round an accident that was causing a long tail back. Where she had turned off, she didn't know. The 'A' road had several 'B' roads leading off it or crossing it. It seemed like she had been driving for ages on the country lane, but then she probably hadn't gone that far as the conditions had deteriorated rapidly. She had no idea where she was. Should she stay with the car or get out and try and find help? If she didn't find help, she would freeze to death. The warmest clothes she had with her were the jeans, jumper and jacket she was wearing, and she needed waterproofs for deep snow. As for her feet, they would be wet through in no time in trainers. The alternative was to stay with the car and try to keep warm for as long as it took. Should she leave the engine running to keep the heater going? She didn't think that was a good idea. She was sure she had heard somewhere of people asphyxiating from exhaust fumes when their cars had been buried in snowdrifts. Was it just one of those stupid stories? It was 7.35pm and apart from the reflected glare from the headlamps she could see nothing. She switched them off and let her eyes adjust to the dark. Then she saw it, a light through the hedge.

Getting out of the car she spotted a wrought iron kissing gate set into the hedge about 30ft from the car, which she now saw had come to rest sideways in a lay-by. Grabbing her flight bag, she locked the car and set off unsteadily through the deep snow. The metal gate was icy to touch and awkward to manipulate in the drift. Great dollops of snow fell off it as she forced it away from her and stepped into its semi-circular entrance. Pulling the gate back she stepped out the other side and found herself in a silent wonderland. The snow continued to fall, but not as heavily now. As the clouds thinned, briefly permitting some moonlight, she glimpsed a long curving lane with a thick high hedge on the right and a lower thinner one on the left. Through the latter she could see the light that she had seen from the car, nearer now. Picking her way down the lane, slipping on the buried uneven ground, she found another metal gate. This one was much more ornate, and it took her chilled fingers some time to work out how to open it. As she raised the catch the gate swung open dragging her into the garden. Ahead, light glowed from the mullioned window of a medium sized stone cottage. Wood smoke hung in the frosty air, its seductive promise of warmth drawing her towards the house. Separating her from the charming little storm porch huddled against the building was a starched duvet of snow. With her breath forming small white clouds she trudged forward. With no clue to their existence she stumbled over flower-beds, path and lawn until she arrived inside the tiny porch, stomping her feet to rid them of the snow.

Attached to the wall by the door, was a bracket supporting a bell. With a mixture of hope and apprehension she took hold of the knotted rope, which dangled from its clapper, and shook it. The ring was quite deafening in the tiny porch. It sent goose bumps up the back of her neck. As the sound died away, Emily could just see, through the glass in the door, the dim glow of a light as it danced towards her from the depths of the cottage. A shadowy figure appeared and, awkwardly, a bolt was drawn back, then another, followed by the turning of a very hefty key. Finally, the sneck was lifted, the door opened, and an oil lamp was thrust in Emily's face. A set of delicate bony fingers were curled round the handle of the lamp, holding it aloft. Suddenly the lamp lowered and the smiling face of an elderly white-haired lady with clear skin and lively green eyes greeted her, "Ah, you've arrived. You must be frozen. Come in. Come in. I was getting quite worried." Emily stepped gratefully inside and tried to apologise and explain about being stranded and needing to use a phone. She tried to point out that they hadn't actually met before, but the old lady shook her head, she didn't have a phone, and insisted that Emily, "Go on through, Love. Get yourself warm".

To the sound of bolts being shot back securely into place Emily went through to find a room with a huge open fire. At one side stood a range (complete with bread oven) and at the other, hanging from a bar over the fire, was a large smoke blackened cauldron. Nervously, Emily inspected the rest of her surroundings. Two oil lamps lit the room revealing a stone floor, whitewashed walls, and a table with a green linen tablecloth and a selection of blue and white crockery. In front of the fire stood two old leather armchairs. The lady indicated that

Emily should sit in one and get dry, whilst she got her a hot drink. Soon a mug of hot liquid was placed in her hands. Then, a plate of fresh crusty bread, spread thickly with butter and strawberry jam, was placed on the table beside her. Emily looked suspiciously at the hot drink.

"I 'ope you like herbal tea, I don't 'ave any ordinary," said her host, just a slight hesitancy of speech belying her age.

Emily took a sip and found herself warming to this strange old lady and the gentle informality of her Yorkshire manner.

"That's mainly camomile, very good for stress. You look like you need to relax," said the old lady brightly as she sat opposite and picked up a pile of cards. Opening the first she read aloud, "'Appy Birthday, with all our love, Jack and Sarah. Ninety Four." She then leaned forward and to Emily's surprise put the card on the fire. She watched as its edges curled up and its surface blistered releasing blue and green flame before crackling into charcoal tissue that floated up the chimney. "To Angelica, with best wishes from all a' T Three Wells. Ninety Five." Again, she put it on the fire and watched with amused satisfaction as the glitter on the card sparkled in the flames. "Love and best wishes, Christine. Congratulations, old girl. Ninety Six." Then, looking up at Emily's bemused face, "I am counting me blessings and sharing them wi' t' wind, so that others may benefit, which is only reight and proper." She read and counted the last few cards, the last one being the hundredth. "Oh Love-a-duck! That's just perfect. You see, I am exactly one 'undred today."

"You're a hundred!" exclaimed Emily, "but your face, your skin, you really don't look it. Honestly. I sincerely hope I look as good when, if, I reach your age." The lady smiled and shrugged her shoulders: the look of someone trying to be modest in the face of a familiar compliment. Changing the subject, she said, "What's your name dear? Mine's Angelica."

Emily introduced herself, pondering on the fact that despite her initial comments her host didn't now seem at all confused. As she sipped her tea and ate her sandwiches she began to warm up. Angelica asked her questions and beginning to relax for the first time in weeks, months, Emily answered. She told her all about the sudden snowstorm and getting lost, about her job, and her trip to India. She enthused about what a marvellous thrill it was to be the one chosen to go and how hard she had worked in preparation. Then, under the sympathetic probing of those clear green eyes, Emily Hope started to cry. She didn't know why. Maybe it was the heady smoke from the fire or the effect of the camomile, but she found herself pouring her heart out to this unusual stranger. She told her all about Grant deserting her when she was relying on him, about the rows they had had, about wanting children before it was too late and Grant refusing to discuss it. She told her about Grant, despite his obvious financial acumen as an accountant for a local electrical engineering works, not making any attempt to save for their future, about him refusing to commit to their relationship, about him viewing her career as a pastime. She rambled on about him not growing up, about him just wanting to have fun all the time and not make any plans that didn't involve his beloved MG Midget. He spent hours on e-Bay 'sourcing' bits for it and lovingly polishing it. That wreck got more attention than she did! Finally, she wound to a halt. The fire had died to a smouldering mound of fragile charcoal and Emily suddenly wondered what time it was. She apologised for her emotional outburst and Angelica put another log on the fire. Leaning over to Emily she rested her ancient hand on Emily's knee, "But, do you love 'im?"

Suddenly Emily didn't know. Stunned, she realised that this was a question she hadn't asked herself. She and Grant it seemed had always been together, through school, and then University. Emily and Grant. Grant and Emily. No one had questioned their relationship, until now. She looked at the old lady who just smiled, her soft white hair glowing orangey pink in the glow from the fire. Emily attempted to smile back but then realised that Angelica wasn't smiling at her. She wasn't even looking at her, but past her, to a space just over Emily's left shoulder. Hearing nothing but the soft death of the disintegrating log in the hearth, Emily slowly turned. Acutely aware of the shadows in the corners of the room, shivering in the weak glow of the oil lamps, she nearly leapt out of her skin. There on the back of her chair sat an enormous tabby, still as stone. How it had got there she had no idea. She had heard nothing. How long it had been sitting there, she could only guess. She had a sudden vision of it grinning madly and disappearing, bit by bit, before her very eyes. It didn't though. It remained very solid, just as if it had always been there, exuding confidence and smug wisdom in the way only felines can.

The cat stared appraisingly at her, its large black pupils boring into her soul and weighing her worth. That done, judgement passed, the cat leapt deftly via the chair arm and landed softly on the floor. Briefly brushing Emily's legs, it walked leisurely across the rug and hopped onto Angelica's lap where it settled, purring. Stroking the furry bundle Angelica smiled, "Yes, she's come to stay." Then looking at Emily, "You will stay t' night won't you, you can't possibly go anywhere in this snow? I believe Kevin approves of you, don't you Kevin?"

"Kevin! You call your cat Kevin!"

Both Angelica and Kevin became very still, and stared at her. Angelica raised an eyebrow and Kevin adopted a supercilious slant to his ears.

Emily looked at the cat. Kevin looked back. Kevin was Kevin, and now Emily knew there was no changing that. The cat was Kevin and bizarrely it suited him perfectly. Emily laughed and leaning over she presented the back of her hand to Kevin. He sniffed it gently, and then allowed her to stroke him.

Angelica sat back in her chair and looked at Emily. She seemed satisfied with what she saw. "You know, Duck, I think everything is going to be just fine." Then, reaching into her pocket she pulled out a small object and offered it to Emily in the palm of her outstretched hand. Emily took it and turning it over she saw that it consisted of two interlocking carved stone rings, one slightly larger than the other. Both were highly polished and slightly translucent. The larger of the two had a metal band round it supporting a loop, presumably for a chain. "I kept meaning to get a new chain for it, but never seemed to find t' time. I want you to 'ave it." Then seeing Emily's look of surprise and discomfort at her generosity she added, "I don't 'ave any daughters or granddaughters to give it to. It should go to someone special and well, Kevin doesn't approve of many people...! Please, take it. It is very old, as old as these 'ere hills. It was carved from the joining section of a stalactite and stalagmite cut from the caverns beneath our feet. The carving represents the interlocking circles of life. Our path in this life is never straightforward, Emily. There are certain tasks that we 'ave to undertake and certain responsibilities we 'ave to fulfil. With this, I have now fulfilled mine." Then, the old lady became silent and thoughtful, momentarily forgetting that Emily was there, lost in memories of times long gone. Emily wondered what sort of life those hundred years had contained, and marvelled at the grace and apparent contentment of the human being sat before her that had resulted from it. She noted the straight back and the proud shoulders, the soft white hair tied back in a neat bun that framed the elegant features of a face that was still beautiful. She must have been stunning in her twenties thought Emily and yet she displayed none of the arrogance and disdain that could possess the timelessly beautiful.

Then, Kevin hopped off her lap, and just as suddenly Angelica refocused on Emily. "You go off to India and do what you 'ave to do. Enjoy yourself. India is a wonderful, enchantingly spiritual place and you will see and learn much there. Take the periapt; keep it safe and it will bring you safely 'ome again." She took Emily's hands and squeezed them shut around the carving. Rising, she pulled Emily to her feet, "You'll see. All will be well in t' morning."

Picking up two of the oil lamps she handed one to Emily. She showed her to the long-drop toilet in the outhouse, apologising for the lack of heating, and then when Emily was ready lead her upstairs to a bedroom at the back of the house. Leaving her a lamp the old lady wished her well and then departed.

Left alone, Emily surveyed the room. A small fire blazed behind a brass fireguard in the grate of a neat stone fireplace. There was a high wide bed with crisp linen sheets and an embroidered satin eiderdown. Neatly folded soft pink towels sat on a wooden ladder back chair in the corner of the room. A hand made rug lay on the floor by the bed and a freshly filled jug of hot water stood in a matching floral bowl on an oak dressing table. Alongside it stood a wardrobe with matching inlaid marketry detailing. Emily placed the oil lamp on the dresser and lifted her flight bag onto the bed. The room looked freshly made up, as if a guest were expected. Pulling back the heavy brocade curtains she moved aside the lace curtain, wiped the condensation from the pane and peered through the window into the garden. The snow had stopped falling and all was still. The shrubs bordering the garden hung heavy with snow, which glistened in the frosty moonlight. In the centre of the garden Emily could just make out what appeared to be a well, its pointed roof covered in white. She thought of the carving Angelica had given her. What had she called it? A periapt. Not a word she had heard before. Feeling in her jacket pocket she pulled it out, her fingers caressing its polished surface. How could anyone have carved something so delicate out of something so solid without breaking it? She wrapped it carefully in a wad of tissue and zipped it into a pocket of her flight bag.

Slipping quickly into her nightwear Emily extinguished the oil lamp and climbed between the cool sheets. The pillows smelt vaguely of freshly cut lavender. Lying on her side she stared into the glowing embers of the fire and thought over the things that the old lady had said, about the quickly proffered food and drink, about the fire in the grate and about the bed she was lying in. This wasn't a little used guest room quickly made ready for an unexpected guest, this was a room made ready and waiting for the fully expected. Feeling somewhat apprehensive, as if she had just stepped into the 'Gingerbread House' but being too exhausted and having nowhere else to go, Emily lay awake listening to the sounds of the house as it settled down for the night.

* * *

Grant was frantic. He had tried phoning her several times but each time the call went to 'messaging'. He had no idea where she was. When he had left the dinner, clutching his trophies, the taxi driver had gone on at length about how bad the weather was and that if Grant hadn't booked the taxi he would never have got home. He had tried phoning the airport, but they wouldn't tell him anything. He would have driven out looking for her, but he wasn't fit to drive. He wasn't fit for anything! What an asshole! Horrified by the weather report, he'd watched the lousy night-time news pictures with growing concern. There were cars abandoned all over the Pennines. Freak conditions they were calling it. If only he had taken her to the airport. Emily hated driving at the best of times, but in snow! She'd be terrified, whereas him, he loved it. Driving, it was what he was born for and snow added that extra dimension that required real skill. Driving in snow was an art form and he loved it. But Emily, Emily hated it. Where was she...?

* * *

Sometime during the night Emily fell asleep. She awoke to noise, heart pounding, and orange lights strobing the walls of the unfamiliar room. Slowly, her brain processed the receding drumming sound as that of an internal combustion engine, and identified the source as a 'gritter' lorry rounding the bend at the other side of the garden hedge. As the sound died, she became aware of a weight on the end of the bed, a satisfied purring emanating from its centre. Some time during the night Kevin had joined her; the bedroom door was slightly ajar. A few minutes later car headlights lit up her room shortly followed by another set. The road must be passable again. Pressing the light switch on her watch she saw that it was nearly 5:30am. If she left now, with any luck she could reach the airport by 7:00am and if her flight had been de-layed because of the weather, then maybe she could still catch it. She managed to re-light the oil lamp, dressed, and gathered her things to-gether. Kevin strolled down the stairs with her and followed her into the kitchen. Taking a note pad from her bag she wrote a note thanking Angelica for her hospitality and apologising for leaving without saying goodbye. She propped it on the kitchen table as Kevin rubbed round her ankles. Closing the back door behind her she stepped out into the snow and retraced her footprints across the garden. At the gate she felt compelled to look back, drawn by knowledge long dormant. Kevin was sitting in a side win-dow, his eyes lasering into her soul.

CHAPTER TWO

A s Emily dragged her luggage up the steps to their flat, she wondered what she would find. In the three weeks that she had been away her relationship with Grant had deteriorated from bad to worse. At the airport, before leaving for India, she had received his voice messages but, still angry, she had not replied to his worried apologies. Let him worry. She could have died. When they did finally speak, she hurled abuse at him, rekindling his anger at her disregard for him by always putting her job first. Having flung every piece of grievance at each other from their personal stockpiles of hurt, and no longer able to speak civilly to one another they had resorted to text. This essentially curt form of communication had killed any attempts at reconciliation and as she stepped out of the lift on the third floor Emily realised that it had been at least a week since she had heard from Grant.

* * *

Grant hated himself. If only he had taken her to the airport, none of this would have happened; if he had even just organised a taxi for her, but no he had to abandon her with no notice. If only she had done what he asked and refused to go until after the New Year like any normal person, but no! Why couldn't she see how ridiculous it was? Now, all this! He couldn't believe some of the things Emily had accused him of. All sorts of things! Things he couldn't even remember from years ago. Things he had had no hint of at the time. He remembered the first time he had seen her. How he had been captivated by her crooked smile, the way she shyly bit her top lip to cover the gap in her front teeth. Two years of wearing a brace had cured that but she still affected that same mannerism and it still squeezed his heart whenever she smiled at him. Now though, he wasn't sure he could ever trust her again. The things she had said. The things she had accused him of. She must have been lying to him all these years. How would he ever know if she was truly happy or just putting up with him because it suited her to have a good-looking guy on her arm, a good-looking guy (well he was, everyone said so) with a well-paid job and a car most men would die for. Thinking about it he realised that she just wheeled him out when it suited her, when it was advantageous for her career to be seen with a successful man. Mulling over her accusations of selfishness, telling him to grow up, criticising his money handling – how dare she, he was the one with the accountancy degree – his bitterness hardened until it cracked. He wanted Emily out of his life.

* * *

Her heart in her mouth, she put her key in the lock and tried to turn it. Nothing happened. She checked the key and tried again. Then she noticed that the lock looked new. Stepping back from the door she noticed an envelope taped to the corridor wall above the dado rail. 'Emily' it declared. Ripping it open she gasped at the acid words it contained and sank slowly down the wall until she was sitting on the floor. Staring at the note she started to shake. She could not believe it! He had packed up all her possessions and put them in storage. He had booked her into a motel for three nights to give her time to find another flat. The envelope also contained the 'flats to rent' page ripped from the local paper. Throwing the pages on the floor she got up and pounded her fists on the door. The sound echoed through the empty flat. Furious, she phoned him. The call went to voicemail. She wasn't leaving a message. No way was she giving him the satisfaction of begging him to take her back. She ended the call. After ten minutes of pacing the corridor she phoned her friend Louise. Twenty minutes later she was sitting in Lou's car sobbing her heart out.

Lou was completely at a loss. She had

known Emily and Grant for a good six years now and she couldn't understand how in the space of a month such an apparently solid relationship could have shattered into such vicious shards. Here was her sensible, rational, always-in-control friend spitting vengeance on the formally mild mannered, affable Grant whom it appeared wasn't so mild mannered after all. How could two people change so much in such a short time? It scared Lou, forced her to re-evaluate her own life. She and Mike were about to have a baby, could she be sure that the pair of them would make it through all that that was sure to throw at them.

Once home, she sat Emily down with a cup of coffee and then went upstairs to prepare the spare room. The 2nd bedroom suddenly seemed glaringly smug with its duck print curtains and lampshade, and its half-papered wall of farmyard scenes with alphabet border. She gathered up the small pile of brand-new baby grows and tiny booties and put them out of sight in a drawer. Then she made up the bed in the most adult bedding and duvet cover she could find.

* * *

On Monday Emily went to work. What else could she do? At Lou and Mike's insistence she had spent the weekend checking the joint accounts on-line. Half the money was gone out of each of them. At least Grant hadn't cleaned her out. She considered getting a solicitor but as he appeared to have split everything down the middle, she just moved the bulk of the money into her own accounts leaving a nominal amount in each to keep the accounts open. When she had had time to think she would consider the direct debits. Beyond that she was too upset to do anything.

Work was a nightmare. For three days she held out. She brightly told them all about India, about how keen the Asian workforce was and how quickly they picked up what she was teaching them. She told them about the food and the sights and the hospitality of her hosts and the sightseeing that they laid on for her. She showed them the photographs and made them watch the mini videos she had taken, and she presented them with the sweets she had bought at the last minute at the airport. For three days she tried to deny that anything was wrong but eventually Jennifer, her boss, wore her down and, over a coffee, Emily explained what had happened. At 3pm Jennifer finally persuaded her to go home, take the rest of the week off and look after herself.

Twice she went by the flat. She didn't know why or what she was going to do. If she had met Grant she didn't trust herself to say or do anything that she wouldn't later regret. In the end she resorted to writing a letter but after several attempts she gave up. Should she be angry,

let him know how she felt? Should she be busi-
ness-like and state her demands? The flat might
be his, or more correctly his parents, but she
still had rights. Should she demand he pay for 3
week's airport parking? Unable to get a taxi at
such short notice she had had no option but to
use her car. She had no idea how she was going to
square that one with expenses. Should she plead
with him to take her back? Did she want that?
Did she want Grant back? Could she feel for him
again the way she used to feel, or was it just her
pride that was hurt? Was it just the humiliation
of being dumped or was it the thought of being
single again and having to fend for herself? She
had gone straight from her parents' house to the
University campus and then into sharing Grant's
flat. She had never actually had to do anything
by herself. Spurred on by this sudden realisation
she decided to take some action, to stop being a
victim and show Grant that she didn't need him.

As it was Thursday, she bought the local
paper and had a look at the rental pages. She
was horrified to see the prices of the flats she
considered acceptable, and she couldn't bear the
thought of sharing with strangers. Very quickly
her new-found resolve disintegrated and when
Lou came home, she found a very fragile and forlorn figure sitting on the floor of her living room,
a splash of soggy tissues failing to mop up the
misery.

Employing thumb and forefinger Louise

daintily cleared herself an island of carpet amongst the sea of tissues and sat down beside her friend. Putting her arm round Emily's shoulder she gave her a brief hug. "Have you thought about sitting in the bath?" As Emily huffed, Lou picked up a tissue, crumpled and twisted it and then stuffed the end up Emily's left nostril. As Lou picked up a second tissue Emily couldn't help herself. She started to laugh. "Oh, Lou, what am I going to do?"

"Em, you need some time. You can't deal with all this in the space of a week. You have not only lost your partner but your home and, well, I suppose, for want of a better word, your status: everything that goes with a relationship. I know he's not dead, but you need some time to grieve for what you had. Once you've both had some time to think and calm down and are able to talk to one another again I'm sure you'll be able to sort this out. You two can't break up! You've got to get back together again."

"No! Never!" spat Emily, the vehemence shocking them both. Surprised by her outburst she stared at her friend. Was that really how she felt? Was it anger talking or denial of her true feelings; the words of the old lady repeating in her head, 'but do you love him?'

Friday passed slowly and the thought of the weekend stretching ahead was too much to bear. Seeing Lou and Mike together, their obvious delight in one another and their impending parenthood, only made her situation that much harder to stomach. That night, alone in the soon-to-be nursery, she thought bitterly of what might have been. For want of something better to do she emptied out her cases and that was when she came across the forgotten tissue bundle, tucked into the pocket of her flight bag. With a strange feeling of hope she pulled out the periapt and carefully unwrapped it.

It felt cool and heavy to touch: much cooler and heavier than she was expecting. Holding it under the bedside lamp she examined it closely. The larger ring was creamy white and streaked like marble and the smaller one was a creamy grey. Both rings were highly polished and shone with a slight iridescence as she turned them. Holding the periapt, she felt a certain comfort. She thought of Angelica and her kind hospitality, of Kevin and the cottage, and how she had been made welcome, and how she had left in the night without even saying goodbye. Suddenly, it was very important to go visit the old lady and thank her properly. This would also get her out of the house for at least part of the weekend.

* * *

On the Saturday morning she set off and tried to retrace her steps to the cottage. It took her several attempts to find a road off the 'A' road that looked vaguely familiar. It was a lovely fresh spring day and in the sunshine the country lanes looked very different to the grey and white tunnel she remembered. Bald brown fields with hints of green stretched into the distance behind the budding hedges that lined the road. Here and there a sycamore stood proud above the haw-thorn but generally there weren't enough trees. The cottage had been surrounded by trees. She wasn't certain but it may even have backed onto a wood. She travelled another two miles before the number of trees started to increase. The road rose slightly and then dipped and ahead she saw the right-hand bend and the lay-by in front of the kissing-gate. She now saw that the lay-by was actually a bus stop. She parked her car there anyway and once again stepped through the gate into the little shrub-lined lane.

Everything seemed much more open, and she was surprised to see glimpses of another building through the tall yew hedge on the right. Approaching the garden gate to the cottage she was embarrassed to see that in the snow she had trampled straight across a flower bed in-stead of taking the cobbled path that wound in an 'S' shape to the cottage door. Winding her way along the path she took in the variety of shrubs and plants that even in late January pro-vided an eye-catching display of colour. She had no idea what the plants were. She loved plants but, if they didn't come in designer pots with instructions from a department store and sit on the windowsill, she didn't have a clue what to do with them. Enough Tiger Lilies, Cheese Plants and Umbrella Plants had been experimented on over the years for her to be confident with their care, especially after her major breakthrough, discovering Baby Bio. She would love to have a proper garden one-day and know all about the different plants, even grow her own vegetables. Garden, huh, she didn't even have her own bedroom!

Once again, she rang the doorbell and waited. This time there was no welcoming light, no welcome at all in fact. After another couple of tries she set off round the cottage. There in the centre of the lawn was the well she had seen. It was about 4ft in diameter and built of stone with a slate roof. Across the opening a wooden cover fitted perfectly, the rope from the 'winch' disappearing through a hole in the centre. Hinges at the sides of the cover would allow it to be opened when the bucket was pulled up. As she approached, something large and brown darted amongst the fruit trees at the back corner of the garden and leapt over a wall into the wood beyond. A deer! Wow! Emily had never seen a deer before. Well, not in the wild anyway. As the deer's startled scrambling died away, into the wood beyond, Emily became aware of the sounds of the different birds in the surrounding trees, and nothing else: nothing else, no cars, no planes, just the sounds of nature. Enchanted, she continued round the house. A large vegetable patch greeted her, a compost heap and a couple of ramshackle outbuildings. Then she stopped dead. There, beyond the outbuildings was a graveyard. Higgledy piggledy stone crosses, angels and cherubs congregated beneath a large Church of England church, its multicoloured jewelled windows twinkling in the sunlight. Here and there amongst the headstones bright bunches of flowers linked the living to the dead, sacrificial tokens to the transience of life.

Turning back towards the house she now discovered that she had actually approached from the back. Here was a faded red front door, nestled inside a porch, with an arched trellis supporting some sort of climbing plant. Either side of the door were long low mullioned windows with leaded lights. Looking up she saw more mullioned windows on the first floor and a couple of tiny windows in the roof. The property was much bigger than she had realised. Stepping back, she inspected the building as a whole and noted that the central part had been added to bit by bit over the years, in a ramshackle but not unpleasing way. She tried knocking on the front door but again got no response. Disappointed at having had a wasted journey she walked down the path to the front gate beyond which she could see other buildings. Opening the gate her eyes were drawn to a garish board atop a post nailed to the fence. 'For Sale' it declared. A wave of dismay engulfed

Emily. No, the old lady couldn't be dead!

Looking round she took in the village green. At its centre stood three oak trees under which sat three benches, their wooden slats supported by green painted cast-iron paws. Surrounding the green, on the far side of the road, stood a variety of stone buildings housing a bakery, a pub called 'The Three Wells', a Post Office-cum-store and, just disappearing through its door, Emily spotted Angelica. With a huge feeling of relief she skipped, half ran across the green.

Entering the store, she did a circuit of the two aisles before bumping into the old lady. "Angelica, remember me, Emily? I'm so sorry I left without saying goodbye."

The old lady stared at her and then a great smile spread across her face. "Ah, you're the one. She said you'd come. Yes, you're perfect!" Then seeing Emily's puzzled expression, "I'm Angelica's sister, Ruby. Oh, you probably don't know. Angelica died...quite peacefully in 'er sleep. It's all right. Don't be sad. She'd done all she needed to do in this life."

Emily couldn't believe how sad she felt. She had only known Angelica briefly, but she felt a sudden great affection for her. "What happened? When did she die?"

"Oh, it was the night of the snow and the power cut. Kevin came all the way over to my 'ouse the following morning. So, I knew. That's when I found 'er, and your note."

What! Emily was horrified. Angelica had died the night she was there! She was probably dead when she left the house. She'd been sleeping with a dead woman!

"Can you 'elp me dear? I've never done this before. I like to do somat new every year. Stops the spirit from stagnatin'." When Emily refocused, she saw that Ruby was holding up a lottery ticket and a pen. "Do you know 'ow to fill these in?" Emily explained and Ruby filled it in. She then took a second ticket, filled it in and handed them both to the shopkeeper who smiled weakly at Emily, slid the tickets in the machine and then, with undisguised disdain, handed the receipts to Ruby. Ruby, apparently oblivious of the shopkeeper's snub, paid, put one ticket in her bag and handed the other to Emily. "I want you to 'ave that for being so 'elpful." Walking towards the door she turned to Emily and smiled, "It was 'er time to move on dear. 'Er life was complete and yours dear…yours, is just beginning." With a smile and a wink and a 'Wishing you well' she walked out the door.

Turning to the shopkeeper Emily asked her if there was anywhere in the village that she could get something to eat. The shopkeeper was in her early 60's. She had a head of very black tightly permed hair which neither matched her eyebrows nor complimented her complexion, which was paler than the cream twinset she was wearing. Her lips, however, matched the large red stone hanging on a long gold chain round her neck and the myriad of rings forming knuckle-dusters on both her podgy hands. With a set, but limited smile on her face, she leaned over the counter and peered over the top of her bifocals. She looked Emily up and down slowly and then, even though the shop appeared to be empty, said very quietly, "You wanna watch yoursel'. There are those what don't approve. Those Wells sisters..." At that a shrill ring announced the entry of another customer into the shop. "Let's just say you've been warned. There's The Three Wells pub or the Little Teacups Café. Have a good day."

Emily was glad to get out into the fresh air. Looking up and down the street there was no sign of Ruby, but she spotted the Little Teacups Café on the other side of the road.

Peering through the window she saw several small square tables with gingham tablecloths and silver cruet sets. Around the room a picture rail shelf sported a collection of multi-coloured teapots of different shapes and sizes. There were animals, buildings, vehicles etc., a veritable collector's paradise. Below the shelf hundreds of little teacups hung, each with a different design. Emily stepped inside and walked up to the glass fronted counter. The fare consisted of ham and mustard or cheese and pickle sandwiches, soup and a roll, ploughman's, cakes etc. Amused, she noted that there wasn't a panini in sight. She settled on afternoon tea and took up a position at a table by the window where she could watch the world go by.

As she piled jam and clotted cream onto a large moist scone and watched the steam rise from the china cup in front of her, she thought back to the night of the snow. So, there had been a power cut. That explained why she hadn't been aware of any other houses round about. Probably Angelica did have electricity and her apparent eccentricity was just a practical necessity. Angelica, had she really died whilst Emily was in the house? Was there anything she could have done to save her? She seemed so fit and well, even though she was 100. Wow, 100! What must it be like to live so long? All the changes she must have experienced. She had lived through two world wars, the advent of plane travel, man landing on the moon, television, movies, all the different fashion changes, jazz, swing, rock and roll, pop etc. What jobs had she had? Had she been married, had children? If Emily lived to be a hundred what would her life be like looking back? Would she be as pleased with her memories as Angelica? Emily was 28, had a history degree, a 12 year old car and not much else. No house, no husband, no children, not even a place to call her own. Just then a Sunshine minibus drove slowly past the café. Several happy faces looked eagerly out of its windows and Emily let out a deep sigh. She should count her blessings.

Yes, she should count her blessings! A picture of Angelica counting her birthday cards and contentedly tossing them into the flames leapt to mind. 100 cards! Had Emily received even 28 for her last birthday? She doubted it. Suddenly she envied the old lady and her apparent satisfaction and contentment with such simple delights. Had she spent all her life in this village?

As the waitress cleared the adjacent table Emily asked her what the village was called. The young waitress tucked a strand of orange hair behind her left ear, revealing a series of studs and a large lightning shaped earring, and looked at Emily as if she were stupid, "Greater Blessing, of course!"

'Greater Blessing, wonderful!' thought Emily. "Is there a Lesser Blessing?"

"No!" replied the waitress without a hint of comprehension, "There's a Li'ul Blessin' if that's what ye mean!" Emily just smiled and took a sip of her tea. Through the window she watched as a mixture of locals and the odd tourist wandered by. For a Saturday afternoon it wasn't very busy. Maybe later on in the year it would attract more tourists. It was a pretty village, and she was surprised that she had never heard of it. She wiped the last of the cream from the edge of her plate and sucked her finger clean. Pushing the empty plate away she let out a despondent sigh. The orange haired waitress materialised silently at her shoulder, plonked the cup and saucer on the plate and picked them all up. Rotating the cup slightly and glancing at the leaves stuck to its bottom she said, "Huh! Don't know what you've got to be so miserable about!" and flounced off into the back of the shop.

Outside Emily shook her head. Wasn't there anyone normal in this delightful little village! She continued down the main street looking in the shop windows until she found herself outside an estate agents staring at the details of Wishing Well Cottage. Angelica's house had four bedrooms, a farmhouse kitchen with range, 2 reception rooms, utility, cellar and a couple of outhouses. It stood in 2.3 acres of land consisting of lawn, flowerbeds, herb garden, fruit trees, vegetable patch and working well. It also had access to an adjacent wood and was 'in need of some modernisation'. As Emily read, she became aware of two eyes looking at her over the top of the advert. A middle aged smartly dressed gentleman was encouraging her to enter. She smiled and shook her head, then turned to walk past the shop. As she drew level with the door it opened. He stepped out in front of her, his arms spread wide, leaving her no where to go to avoid him but inside. "I see that you are interested in Wishing Well Cottage. It is a delightful property and just right for a young family. Are you married? Single?"

Emily explained that she was only interested in the property because she had known the owner, at which he offered to show her round it. No that wouldn't be necessary as she had no intention of buying it and she couldn't afford it anyway. He then proceeded to present her with details of other cheaper properties in the area. She told him that she needed to be near her work, so he asked where she was currently living. She found herself explaining that she wasn't currently living anywhere which only encouraged him to tell her all the benefits of living in or around Greater Blessing. She was finding that he was very adept at dragging information from her and invading her personal space. She had stepped back and stepped back until she was squashed against a filing cabinet. Studying the man at close quarters she couldn't decide what it was about him that revolted her. He was actually a good-looking man and his clothes would have put her power dressing Grant in the shade. Maybe it was his deferential posture at odds with his assertive sales pitch that was raising her defences. He wasn't exactly menacing, just a little odd, intense maybe. That was it. It was as if he was struggling to suppress emotions that he was aware were inappropriate for the conversation. She just wanted to get away from him. Being a naturally polite person Emily found it hard to be rude, so she agreed to take the Wishing Well Cottage details and get back to him if she changed her mind.

Having done a circuit of the village green

she arrived at the gates of the church. 'All Saints Parish Church' announced a blue and white board with gold lettering. Emily decided to take a walk around. Maybe Angelica was buried there. Rounding the back of the church she followed the little path as it wound its way through ancient yew trees. At some time, someone had very carefully sculpted them into a variety of geometric shapes which were still apparent but no longer as crisply defined. The trees were still being clipped but nature was asserting herself and slowly adding personality to the cubes and spheres. At their bases large roots surreptitiously tilted and cracked the carved granite headstones, whilst moss and lichen added camouflage so that no one would notice as the earth slowly swallowed them. Oblivious, birds hopped about helping themselves to insects that crawled amongst the snowdrops which were scattered in clumps between the graves. Emily didn't think that she had actually walked round a graveyard before. She had imagined them to be dark, depressing, scary places. Now she was surprised to find that she was enjoying herself. It was a beautiful tranquil place and not at all scary or supernatural. In fact, it was all perfectly natural. We live. We die. The circle of life is complete and continuous. She shuddered. That sounded like something Angelica would have said.

Walking on she saw an elderly gentleman

standing silently by a grave, a small bunch of flowers betraying the slight trembling of his hands. Emily watched as he bent and removed a faded bunch from a small flower holder, and replaced them, carefully arranging the new bunch. Standing, he straightened his sharply pressed trousers revealing highly polished brown shoes beneath. Removing his tweed trilby from his head he smoothed his wispy grey hair. Then, clutching his trilby to his chest he stood for a moment, head bowed between sagging shoulders and spoke in a voice Emily couldn't hear. Embarrassed at her eavesdropping she scuffed her feet on the gravel alerting him to her presence. He looked up apologetically and with shiny eyes said, "I miss her so!" Then he walked off down the path. Saddened, Emily read the headstone.

Sarah Anne Hartley
beloved wife of John,
mother of Jack, Michael and Emma.
born 24th July 1937
died 14th May 2008

Emily was stunned. All these years later he was still talking to her and putting flowers on her grave. She couldn't help feeling a little envious of their relationship but scared that it should have such a lasting effect that he couldn't move on. Would she ever love someone that much or have some one love her?

As she approached the rear of the grave-yard, she noticed that the graves looked newer. Working her way down the rows she read the headstones, looking for Angelica Wells. Reaching the end without success she wondered whether Angelica had been cremated, or maybe buried elsewhere. Then, set apart from the others in a large plot under a hawthorn tree, which stood against the wall backing on to Wishing Well Cottage, she spotted a simple limestone block sticking out of the ground. Unlike the other headstones this consisted of a large, undressed block of stone. The face of it had been carved smooth to provide a surface for engraving but otherwise it was in its natural state.

Angelica Susannah Wells
born 29th December 1913
died 29th December 2013
much loved sister of this grateful parish

Emily wondered what that meant, although if Angelica had spent the last century being as helpful to the people of Greater Blessing as she had been to her, then it was no surprise. Thinking back to the words of the shopkeeper though, it seemed that not everyone in the village 'approved'! Didn't approve of what?

A slight rustle of leaves and the merest hint of movement drew her attention to the mound of earth in front of the headstone. Standing stock still, her breath caught in her throat, she stared until her brain registered the curled shape of a cat, its tabby fur camouflaged amongst the earth and leaves. "Kevin? Is that you?" The ball uncurled, stretched and, nearly turning his head inside out, yawned, before strolling up to Emily and greeting her with a welcoming meow. "Kevin, it is you. What are you doing sleeping on Angelica's grave? How much time do you spend here? Oh, Kevin!" Emily felt quite sad; first the old man, and now Kevin. She bent down and stroked him. "Well, someone is obviously feeding you, although I doubt that you would have much trouble catching your own meals. You are certainly fit enough."

Just then the church clock struck five reminding her that she ought to be on her way. Lou and Mike would wonder where she was. She set off down the path, deep in a one-sided conversation with Kevin as he rubbed round her ankles making it difficult to walk. As they approached Wishing Well Cottage Emily realised that they weren't alone. A woman in jeans and a T-shirt, her long brown hair tied up in a scrunchy, was standing in the gateway. Curiously, she appeared to be studying Emily.

"Hi. You two seem to be getting along well. Kevin doesn't approve of many people." The woman bent down and stroked Kevin, and with a nod at Emily's hand smiled up at her. "I see you have the house details. You interested in buying?"

Emily smiled and said that she would love to buy the house, but it was a bit too far to commute even if she could afford it. She explained about Angelica giving her a room for the night and about being shocked by her death, and about the pushy estate agent. The woman gave an understanding laugh. "Ah, Gerald! Would you like to look round anyway? I'm Anna, by the way and I would hazard a guess that you are Emily. Yes, thought so. I've been looking after the place, and Kevin. I am actually the vicar's housekeeper." At this she nodded towards the large building hidden behind the yew hedge at the other side of Wishing Well cottage. "Come on, it's no bother. I'm going in anyway to get Kevin his tea."

Anna let the three of them in through the red front door and switched on the hall light. So, there was electricity after all! She led the way down the hall, past the bottom of the stairs and into the large kitchen with its open fire, bereft of heat, reflecting the coldness of the empty house. What a contrast to the night of the snow! How warm and welcoming this house was then. Now, it was as if the house itself was in mourning.

"Go on," said Anna. "You have a wander round whilst I feed Kevin. I'll come and find you when I'm done."

Emily, feeling a little uncomfortable,

wandered back into the hall and down the passage to the front room. It was a large room, and the two long low windows gave it a light and airy feel. One of them looked out onto the cottage garden at the front of the house and the other looked across the lawn towards the church. On the back wall was a large stone fireplace. Sitting in front of it were some comfy looking floral armchairs sporting lace antimacassars and velvet cushions. Various other pieces of solid oak furniture dotted the room. Several strange faces stared at her from photographs, placed here and there, confronting her intrusion. She backed out into the hall and headed for the back room that led to the outhouse and the long drop toilet. In daylight she realised that it was quite a pretty room. Angelica had done her best to make it welcoming with floral curtains, a little rug and some pale blue china accessories. Back in the passage again the next door she opened led down to the cellar. She closed it and moved on. At the left of the front door was another large room, again with a stone fireplace but this time decorated with a wooden surround. The main wall was covered in shelves filled with glass bottles and stone jars with either cork stoppers or muslin covers. Wicker baskets stood on the floor containing a variety of twigs and dried herbs. Piles of books, printed and handwritten, leaned against the other wall and in the centre of the room stood a table with a set of scales, ladles, knives and a variety of other tools, scissors, string, candles etc. Emily was fascinated. What was this room? What did Angelica do with all this? Picking up one of the books she leafed through the pages; pictures of herbs and explanations of their uses, with a little folklore, flipped by. Emily read a little, turning back and forth through the book. The word Angelica caught her eye and she stopped and turned a leaf or two until she found the page again. Angelica (Umbelliferae), renowned throughout Europe as a panacea for all ills and with protective powers against evil. 'Yes,' thought Emily, 'that suits her perfectly'.

Next, she headed upstairs and into the room in which she had spent the night. It felt much larger, or maybe it was just the sunlight bouncing off the cream walls. What a long time ago it seemed since that night. Such a lot had happened since then, yet it was only a month. She quickly popped her head into the other three rooms. Two were set up as bedrooms, the larger one she guessed to have been Angelica's. Was this where they found her? Died peacefully in her sleep her sister had said.

The fourth room had various boxes in it, chairs, a table or two and other odds and ends. There was a small box room on the landing with stairs above leading up to the attic. In the eaves were two low rooms with windows poking out of the roof. From here she had a good view of the church and the village green and all the shops. The two rooms didn't look as if they had been visited for some time. Dust and cobwebs adorned the rafters and coated the dustsheets shrouding a variety of intriguing objects. Having inspected the views from the windows she slipped quietly back downstairs.

Anna wasn't in the kitchen. A quick re-tour of the ground floor found Anna in the lean-to at the other side of the outhouse. With a mimed "Shhhhhhh!" she beckoned Emily to come forward quietly and slowly. Tiptoeing carefully and listening intently Emily went to stand beside her. At first she heard nothing and then, in the corner of the lean-to, from behind a pile of old newspapers she heard a rustling. Then again, from the other side of the room she heard it again. Something small was moving about. Well, more than one it seemed. Anna, barely suppressing her excitement, quietly took hold of Emily's arm and gestured silently towards the corner of the room. A tiny snout was working its way out of the pages of newspaper, bright eyes blinking and spines bristling. Together they watched as one and then two hedgehogs emerged.

"I thought it was about time, what with the weather being so mild. Every day I come in here and check. These are the first two. I am not sure how many there are altogether. They have been hibernating here for years." She then went on to explain that the hedgehogs came in through Kevin's old cat flap and that Kevin didn't seem to mind. They even shared his cat food, although not his dish. That would never do!

Whilst Anna went to get some cat food Emily stood statue-like in the centre of the lean-to feeling quite elated. They were so cute. Tiny little clawed paws made scratching noises on the stone floor as twitchy brown noses inspected the ground. Their rolling waddling motion caused their spines to ripple with each step, revealing shades of copper glinting amongst the cream and brown. Anna returned and placed an old tray on the floor with a heap of cat food in its centre. She took Emily by the arm and guided her back to the doorway where the pair of them watched as the two hedgehogs sniffed out the food and tucked in. They watched for a while and then Anna suggested that they leave the hedgehogs to it and quietly shut the door.

Emily thanked Anna for allowing her to look round the house and expressed her delight at having seen the hedgehogs. Anna smiled, satisfied, and wished her well.

CHAPTER THREE

L ouise had been quite concerned when her friend had insisted on going off on her own on the Saturday. Emily had seemed so lost and inconsolable all week that Lou had been reluctant to let her go, and yet she understood that being stuck in a house with her and Mike, no matter how welcome they made her feel, would be hard. So, when Emily came back bursting with news of her day, barely able to contain herself, Lou was amazed and delighted.

Mike, however, felt rather uncomfortable. Having been angered by the fact that Grant had just thrown Emily out, and not a little annoyed that as a result he was now sharing his house with an unexpected weepy guest for an indeterminate period, he had been to see Grant. What he hadn't been expecting was to find that Grant was as miserable as Emily. Both it seemed had said way too much and although each missed the other, the hurt ran too deep for either of them to make the first move. What they needed was an intermediary and Mike was just the man for the job. After all, if Novaglaze's top regional salesman couldn't persuade Grant that he and Emily were meant to be together then he wasn't worth his quarterly bonus let alone his annual one. It had taken him most of the afternoon to get Grant to talk and then to calm down. Once he had prised open the dam gates, 'damn' wasn't the only word Grant had used in his colourful description of Emily's behaviour. Before he had exhausted his vocabulary Mike was so riled that he started shouting back, surprised by his own need to defend her. Then just as suddenly Grant had caved-in saying that he missed her and wanted her back but had no idea how to go about it as he was scared she would say no. Mike had been delighted. He could fix that. With any luck he'd be back to decorating the nursery by the following afternoon and Sunday lunch would be something to look forward to unlike the 'wakes' that had replaced the rest of the week's meals.

Now, this bouncy enthusiastic Emily was a shock. He tried to be pleased for her but couldn't help worrying that this somehow put the proverbial spanner in his working plan. What if she didn't want to go back to Grant? What if this split wasn't temporary? How long would it take her to find somewhere else to live? He decided to wait and choose his moment to mention his visit to Grant.

Emily talked non-stop. They got a full description of the house and the village, of Emily's shock at Angelica's death and of meeting her sister, of all the odd characters in Greater Blessing and of Kevin and the hedgehogs. She showed them the sales details for Wishing Well Cottage and told them how peaceful and fascinating it was. There seemed to be something to delight in every corner of it. Someday, she would love to live somewhere like that. She would love to grow her own vegetables and have an herb garden and know all their different uses.

Mike laughed, "You, live in the country! You, get your hands dirty! Tell me, does Greater Blessing have an emergency room for nail extension repairs? Do they sell Louis Vuitton handbags and Jimmy Choo shoes? Does the local spa do 'wraps'? Does it even have a spa?"

"Okay, laugh all you want. Its just a different way of life, a much less frantic one, one where you get to see...," Emily paused, thinking, "One where you get to realise what is really important in life and how...and now you really are going to laugh...how just seeing a snow drop can make you smile!"

"You didn't help yourself to any of those herbs whilst you were there did you?" said Lou, one eyebrow raised.

* * *

On Sunday Mike decided to mention

Grant and see what reaction he got. "So, have you spoken to Grant yet?"

Emily looked at him and let out a deep sigh. "Why would I want to speak to Grant? I'll never forgive him for what he did. At first, I hated him. I was so angry and upset I couldn't even see straight. After all those years together, he just turfed me out on the doorstep. You wouldn't do that to a dog."

"He did book you into an hotel."

"For three nights! How is anyone supposed to find rental accommodation in three days?!"

"Well, I suppose he knew that Lou wouldn't see you out on the street, and me, of course"

"He's just a selfish inconsiderate...why didn't I see it before? Why have I put up with him all these years? The relationship was going nowhere. He doesn't want to get married. He doesn't want to have children...and I ...I do...I really want to have children...! No, there really is no point in talking to Grant. I need to move on, and Greater Blessing has let me see that there is more to life than being stuck in a flat with a man who is only interested in his flashy cars and manipulating money. Greater Blessing has let me see that I can be just fine on my own. I don't need Grant. I just need me. I just need to be able to stand on my own two feet and decide what I want to do with my life. In fact Mike, I was thinking, have you considered a live in nanny for your firstborn? Have a chat with Lou. You needn't to let me know now." With that she turned away, leaving Mike uncertain as to whether she was serious or not, and disappeared into her room.

* * *

On Monday she went back to work and found that just like last week she was having difficulty concentrating except this week her mind was on Greater Blessing and Wishing Well Cottage. Every time she thought of the hedgehogs she smiled. Then she wondered whether Kevin was lying curled up on Angelica's grave again. Cats! She had never had a cat. She had never had any pet come to think of it. Well, not unless you counted Mr Chips the goldfish, and he was hardly the same as a cat or a dog. Having a mother who was allergic to cat fur and extremely house proud had put paid to anything that wasn't neatly controllable and hygienic. In fact, Emily always suspected that it was her mother's liberal use of disinfectant that was responsible for Mr Chips' goodbye. Emily had kept Mr Chips in a margarine tub for five days waiting for it to stop raining so that he could have a proper burial, and in all that time the fish had only ever smelt faintly of pine.

She did manage to get a reasonable amount of work done and what she didn't achieve she was content to let Jennifer think was due to her distress over Grant. On her way home from work she picked up a copy of the local evening paper and flicked through it on the train. The council were planning to re-vamp one of the local shopping centres to encourage more people to use public transport. This had prompted a flood of letters and details were given as to where to sign a petition. Two local youths had rolled a car and wedged it between some trees on a roundabout. The passenger was dead, and the driver was in hospital. Police were waiting for him to regain consciousness so that they could interview him. More man-hole covers had been stolen from The Mari-golds housing estate and new CCTV was being installed by neighbourhood watch. An elderly gentleman was calling for the death penalty to be brought back. A Mrs Parker was complaining that there was nothing for the young people to do since the council had chained up the gates of the skateboard park whilst the graffiti was replaced with specially treated surfaces that re-pelled paint. A hundred-year-old lady had died from shock when her lottery numbers came up. A large black cat had been seen on the moors... What! Emily's eyes honed back to the previous article 'Lottery win kills 100 yr old.' Emily stared at the short paragraph. No. It couldn't be! 'Ruby Wells, aged 100, was found dead on Sunday morning sitting in front of her television set holding her winning lottery ticket. It seems the shock of winning £1.2million was too much for Ruby.' Emily couldn't take in the rest of the article. Not Ruby too. She had only spoken to her that afternoon. The article went on to say that the funeral would be held on Friday at All Saints Church Greater Blessing, family and friends welcome. Emily spent the rest of the journey home in a trance. She didn't notice the police car by the kerb.

She let herself in and was met by Louise who was trying hard to control her amusement. "There are two policemen here to see you. You didn't tell me you were going to need an alibi. These things need to be planned, Em!"

Emily went warily into the living room. The two officers stood and introduced themselves and ascertained that Emily was the Emily Hope that they were looking for. "We'd like you to tell us your movements this last Saturday."

'Oh! No!' thought Emily, they think I killed Ruby! Her bag strap slipped off her shoulder and trying to control it she dropped the newspaper at the policemen's feet. 'Lottery win kills 100yr old' shouted up from the floor and flashed black and white as Emily blinked at it in horror.

"I didn't kill her. I only helped her fill out her lottery ticket. I swear! Ask the shopkeeper."

"Just tell us what you did and where you went that day."

Emily detailed her day; giving approximate times as she remembered them whilst one of the policemen made notes.

"So, you left Greater Blessing at about 5:40 and came straight here?"

"Yes, well apart from stopping for petrol and going through the car wash."

"Ah, so you will have a receipt?"

Emily pulled her purse out of her bag and removed various bits of paper. She straightened them out one by one but none of them was the garage receipt. She rummaged through her bag and extracted more crumpled bits of paper and nervously flattened them on the coffee table. Why was she so worried? She hadn't done anything wrong. She certainly hadn't killed anyone. How could they even suspect her? Did they suspect her? They hadn't said so but then why else would they be here! With only two receipts to go she found the petrol one and triumphantly presented it for inspection.

"Thank you. Just following up our enquiries. No need to bother you further." And with that they left. Emily breathed a sigh of relief.

"I can't wait for Mike to get home," said Louise, "he'll love this, your face was a picture!"

"It's not funny, you never met them. Two lovely old ladies and they are both dead and it seems that I was the last person to speak to both of them. Have you any idea how scary that is?"

"Em! I'm sorry," but the apology lacked all sincerity as Lou snorted through her chagrin.

"How on earth did they find me? How did they know who I am? The only people who knew I had spoken to her were the shopkeeper and the vicar's housekeeper, but they have no idea where I used to live let alone that I'm staying here. Ahhh! Gerald! It's got to be Gerald, that creepy est,ate agent! Question after question! He just never shut up. Heaven knows what I told him!" Emily shuddered.

"You're way too polite. You should have just told him where to go and walked out."

She knew Lou was right but she just never knew what to say. She could never find the words to say 'no' without it sounding rude and she just didn't seem to have it in her to be rude. Yet she would spend hours mulling over what she could or should have said, composing witty put downs that she never had the opportunity to use. Why couldn't she say what she felt? Except, when she let rip at Grant! She'd loosed both barrels at Grant and it had felt good. Really good! At the time! Later however, she had gone over and over what she had said, wishing she could take most of it back, agonising over the vicious things she'd accused him of. At the time she wanted to hurt him, punish him for what he had done, make him feel as bad as she did but later, alone, she had just wanted to curl up and disappear, cringe herself into oblivion. Waves of rising panic would wash over her, making her shudder, desperate to run away but unable to escape from herself. She badly wanted to apologise, to make it all right, but she was equally as bad at apologies as she was at being rude. Maybe apologising would be easier if she was rude more often. Maybe the two went together. Now, days later, she didn't feel as bad, just angry. She couldn't bring herself to apologise. She couldn't even bring herself to speak to him. She wasn't the only one who needed to apologise, and even if he did, she wasn't sure she could accept it. Nothing could ever be the same again.

Work dragged. Now, answering the queries that arrived daily from Delhi seemed tedious. Since her break-up with Grant her attitude had changed radically. She used to love her work and take pride in it. Now, providing a 'helpline' to those she had trained was annoying. Virtually every query could have been answered by just reading the training manuals she had left them. She plodded through them resisting the urge to practise being rude as Lou had suggested. It was an art and needed to be practised. Lou liked to use door-to-door salesmen. She took great delight in volleying their sales pitch with obscure questions and then when they got round to suggesting making an appointment, she would say that it wasn't up to her as she was just the baby-sitter, but it had been nice chatting. She had graduated from cold calls, although they were a good back-up during the winter when it was nippy standing with the front door open. She was also adept at fending off town centre researchers. They were usually easy to spot, clutching their clipboards with pen drawn like nervous gladiators. Lou only needed to look at them and they would back from her path. It was all about attitude and body language. Emily envied Lou but couldn't help feeling sorry for the victims, they were only doing their job, just as she was, and she hated people being rude to her. Lou didn't seem to care what people thought, whereas Emily wanted everyone to be happy.

The journey back and forth to work was driving her nuts. All sorts of little things were starting to irritate her, things that she hadn't even noticed before. The train carriage was either too hot or too cold and if she managed to get a seat then inevitably it would be next to someone either lacking tissues or deodorant or both. She wasn't sure which was worse. Bits of graffiti leapt out at her and litter swirled round her feet as she walked the five minutes from the station to her office. Her despair turned to mild hysteria when she witnessed a street cleaner in one of the arcades stop, lean his broom and long handled dustpan against his hip, pop a sweet in his mouth, throw the wrapper on the floor, and then continue sweeping leaving the litter behind him. Unbelievable! People just had no respect for their surroundings. It wasn't like that in Greater Blessing. She didn't remember seeing any litter there, or was it just that she had had other things demanding her attention. It was so peaceful and relaxing. Perhaps she should go back. Would it be all right for her to go to Ruby Well's funeral? She wasn't a relative. She wasn't even a friend. She had only talked to her once, briefly. Would it look odd, especially after the visit from the Police?

When she got home that evening, she phoned directory enquires. Well, that is, after a bit of research to find a number for directory enquires. It used to be so simple, 192, but not anymore. Why had life got so complicated? Having obtained a number for the vicarage at Greater Blessing she rang and was told that the funeral was to take place at All Saints Church at 2:30pm on Friday.

CHAPTER FOUR

U sing her 'flexi-hours' Emily took the day off work for the funeral. She had hoped that Lou would accompany her but as she had an antenatal appointment Emily reluctantly had to go on her own. She had never been to a funeral before and didn't know what to expect. She hoped that there would be no filing past the coffin. She didn't know if that was universal, a Catholic thing, or just for VIPs so that everyone could see that the deceased actually was – deceased!

This time she drove into the village via Little Blessing, and she could see why not many tourists made it as far as Greater Blessing. Little Blessing wasn't very inspiring. It consisted of a crossroads, a bus stop, what could have been an off-licence, a scattering of run-down houses and a disused petrol station. Driving on for another two miles she entered Greater Blessing. Parking in the deserted high street she made her way to the church where it appeared that the entire population of the village had congregated. She found herself a place at the back under an oak tree. The ground there was a little higher giving her a view of the heads of the people gathered round the grave. She could just about see one end of the coffin. To her relief the lid, it seemed, was firmly screwed down, brass fittings glinting in the sunlight.

Emily listened, only able to catch bits of what the vicar said as he spoke with obvious affection for Ruby. She had been a very popular and well-loved character in the village. He spoke at length of her unorthodox views on life, some-times at odds with the teachings of the church but said that he was sure God understood. It seemed that the Wells sisters had always been at the centre of whatever good had befallen Greater Blessing.

The coffin was lowered into the grave, a prayer was said and then the vicar led the mourners away down the path towards the church gate and Emily. As they approached, Emily's eyes zeroed in on a sight that made her stomach flip and her cheeks flush. He was gor-geous. She was completely taken aback that an undertaker could have that effect on her. She never once dreamed that an undertaker could look like that. Actually, undertakers had never featured in any of her dreams. He was a tall man, but the top hat really made him something to behold! If only! His solemn expression and the tender concern with which he guided the small elderly figure at his side made her knees weak. Then Emily stared at the small figure. No! No! Emily was aghast! The small figure at his side was identical to Ruby, and Angelica! Either the figure was a ghost, or ...

Before Emily could recover, a large hand slapped her on the back, "So, couldn't keep away then. Still, lots to be grateful for, eh?"

It was Gerald, the estate agent. "Who's that?" hissed Emily pointing at the 'ghost'.

"Ha! That's Myrtle."

"Who... is Myrtle?"

"The sister!"

"There's another of them!" Emily shrank back behind the tree to avoid Myrtle as she passed. Gerald wrapped an arm round the trunk and swung round to join her.

"Ha! Didn't you know, they were triplets!"

"Triplets! 100 year old triplets?" Emily was stunned. Incredible!

"Yes. Amazing ladies, just like you. And an amazing person needs an amazing house. How about I show you round Wishing Well Cottage. It really is an amazing place, even older than the Wells sisters. Parts of it are over four hundred years old with a beautiful working well in the grounds. The front aspect looks out over the village green......."

"Gerald! Leave the lass alone." Anna had

stepped out of the procession as it headed towards the gate. "You should be ashamed of yourself. This is a funeral not a sales event. Now be off with you. If she wants to buy Wishing Well Cottage she knows where to find you. Show some respect."

Alone, Emily thanked Anna for rescuing her and told her how nice it was to see a friendly face. She explained that she wasn't sure she should have come but Anna reassured her and suggested a brew back at her house. So, together they followed the remains of the mourners out of the church gate.

Unseen by Emily and Anna, a lone figure stepped out from behind a large, twisted yew and watched as the two women headed across the village green. She ceased fingering the large red stone that hung round her neck and straightened her pale blue cardigan. 'So, it was working!' Irritation stoking her resolve, she headed purposefully home.

Behind her, another, much smaller figure, leapt silently down from a nearby tomb and watched through amber eyes, their vertical slits narrowing.

* * *

Anna handed Emily a mug of coffee, "So then, what are your thoughts on Wishing Well Cottage, now that you have 'the means'?"

Emily was baffled. It took Anna a while to get her to understand that she could now afford

Wishing Well Cottage if she wanted to. So much had happened that it hadn't occurred to Emily to get her lottery ticket checked and she hadn't realised that Ruby had put the same numbers on both their tickets.

"Emily, you are now a millionaire! You won £1.2 million. That is...you have still got your ticket, haven't you?"

Emily had no idea. She couldn't think. She had no idea what she had done with it. She tried thinking back to Ruby handing it to her, of her conversation with the shopkeeper. She would have put it in her purse, but it wasn't there when she emptied it for the Police for the petrol receipt. At least she didn't remember it being. She couldn't possibly have lost it, not £1.2 million. Think! What was she wearing at the time? Her jeans, she was wearing her jeans. Maybe she had put it in a pocket. Had she washed them? Had she laundered £1.2 million? No, she hadn't done any washing. She really ought to. Lou had been very good about lending her clothes for work, but it was about time she got her own stuff out of storage. She just didn't have anywhere to put anything if she did. Emily racked her brains and wrung her hands agitatedly in her lap.

"It's all right. All will be well." Anna placed her hand on the back of Emily's and smiled. "Ruby didn't give it you to lose."

Emily relaxed and with a small feeling of hope she slipped her left hand inside her jacket pocket and felt a rather dog-eared bit of paper. Pulling it out she stared at it. How could £1.2 million look so tatty!

* * *

Grant hunted round his living room. He lifted newspapers, flung cushions, stepped over the odd plate but the remote was nowhere to be found. Crossing the room, he switched on the TV, flipped down the control panel and stared at the buttons. Getting down on his hands and knees he tilted his head to one side so that he was no longer blocking the light from the ceiling lamp and located the channel up/down buttons. Selecting the sports channels, he found the 'Six Nations' England 'v' Wales. Five minutes into the match he got up and headed for the fridge, then the cupboard next to the sink. He fished out half a dozen 'stubbies' and put five of them in the freezer. Grabbing the bottle opener from the cutlery drawer he prized the top off the remaining bottle and took a glug. "Ugh! Warm beer!" Emily would have restocked the fridge. She would have thought to do that.

* * *

Emily was checking her lottery ticket and getting it verified. Emily was arranging to have her £1,226,455 paid into a high interest account and arranging an appointment with a financial advisor. It turned out that money could get quite a lot done on a Saturday afternoon.

As soon as her win was confirmed she phoned her parents. "Mum, mum, you'll never guess what! I still don't believe it myself. I won one million two hundred and twenty six thousand four hundred and fifty five pounds on the lottery. There was this 100 year old lady who took me in when it snowed on the way to the airport and when I went back to thank her she'd died and her sister gave me a lottery ticket as a thank you for showing her how to fill them in, she'd never done it before and she liked to do something new every year, and well, the win killed her and the police thought I did it until I showed them the petrol receipt and then when I went to the funeral I was told that I had the same lottery numbers and now I'm a millionaire!"

"How was India?"

"Mum it was fine. Great! I've just told you that I'm a millionaire. Didn't you hear me?"

"So that's why we haven't heard from you since Christmas, is it? Grant said you were busy."

"Mum! I'm sorry. A lot has happened!" Then, "You've spoken to Grant? What did he say?"

"Nothing. Why?"

"He didn't tell you that we'd split up?"

"Split up? Oh, Love! No! I am sorry. Why, what happened? Why didn't you call?"

So, reluctantly Emily explained, her elation of a moment ago gone, her guilt at not having confided in her mother very real. Why was it easier to confide in a friend when things went wrong? Why had it been so difficult to call her family? She had thought about calling, wanted to even, but had had a list of ready excuses not to. Now, conversely, she had automatically called home to tell them her good news. She guessed that it all boiled down to wanting to please them, wanting them to be proud of her success and not disappointed by her failure, to her wanting them to approve of her choices. She knew that they, well her mother really, didn't approve of her and Grant living together. She had never actually said, but Emily had always felt just that little bit uncomfortable. Now she and Grant had split up and she half expected her mother to say 'told you so' even though splitting up would have been a whole lot worse had they been married. She didn't want to admit to her parents that she had made a bad choice, but then had she? She and Grant wanted different things but that didn't necessarily mean that they didn't love each other. It just meant that they couldn't live together and if that was the case then he wasn't the right man for her. Her parents though, were her parents, and nothing could change that. That was a constant. She could only change herself to measure up. If necessary, she could find new friends, she could find a new partner, but her parents were irreplaceable.

On Sunday, she took Lou and Mike out for Sunday lunch. She ordered a taxi, so that no one, not even the temporarily teetotal Louise, needed to drive. She had tried to get them a table at the Three Wells in Greater Blessing as it somehow seemed appropriate but unfortunately it had been booked for a private party. Instead, she phoned the most expensive place she knew of and booked them in there. She told them to order whatever they wanted and, just because she could, asked the waiter for the hotel's most expensive bottle of champagne + another unopened one for Lou to take home to drink when she was no longer pregnant.

"So, what does Ms Nouveau Riche plan on doing next?" asked Mike.

"Absolutely nothing until I've had time to think about it. I plan to go to work on Monday as if nothing has happened, see my financial advisor and decide from there. I do not plan on blowing it all on fast cars, wild parties and expensive holidays. After all, one million two hundred and twenty six thousand four hundred and fifty five pounds may make me a millionaire but it is only 4-5 reasonably priced houses. You can only just get a decent sized mansion for that these days. If you want to stable the racehorses as well, forget it! Anyway, talking of houses, I just want to say, thank you both very much for putting up with me these past few days and I promise to find myself somewhere to live by the end of the week, even if it means moving into an hotel."

"Oh, don't be silly. We wouldn't hear of it!" said Louise, deliberately not looking at Mike. "You stay as long as you need."

"No. You two need your own space and I'm fine now. Thank you. I won't forget it." With that she raised her glass, "Here's to a new life," and took a very enjoyable swig.

* * *

Grant wasn't having a good time. The beers he had put in the freezer for a quick chill and forgotten about had frozen over night and popped their caps. He had put the leaking bottles in the sink whilst he tried to scrape the frothy brown ice off the bottom of the freezer. The whole flat now smelled of stale ale. The Scotland v France match was about to start, and he was pinning his hopes on Scotland to brighten his weekend as England had lost badly yesterday. The flat was a mess, he had nothing to drink, and he was thoroughly fed up. Using the 'pause live TV' facility to record the match he put on his jacket and headed down the street to the supermarket.

* * *

"There is one little extravagance I am going to allow myself," said Emily. "I am going to buy a decent chain for this," and she pulled the periapt out of the top of her jumper to reveal a piece of yellow plastic string fastening it round her neck. "I think it deserves better."

"Well, I am surprised. I never thought I

would see Emily Hope with a piece of string round her neck. That little gem must mean a lot to you," marvelled Louise.

"It does, and I don't really know why. It's strange but I am getting quite attached to it. "

"So that's why you keep clutching your chest," said Mike, "It's quite distracting."

"Sorry. The knot tends to work its way down and it itches. Once I get a chain, I can wear it on the outside and then you can occupy your brain with something else."

"Oh, don't worry on my account."

"Excuse me, pregnant wife here. If you want to be unfaithful at least have the decency to do it behind my back."

"Sorry, my love," said Mike. "I was just trying to cheer up your friend. I understand it can be very lonely being a millionairess. Money can't buy everything."

"No, but it can get you a decent solicitor!" quipped Lou.

"Anyway," said Emily raising her glass again, "Here's to my new life and here's to the new life you two are about to bring into this world. Have you thought of a name yet? And when are you going to tell me what sex it is so that I can go shopping."

Lou looked at Mike who nodded. "It's a boy, but we haven't decided on a name yet."

"No, but we have a probable spelling," joked Mike.

"Huh?" said Emily.

"D.i.v.o.r.c.e. We just can't agree."

"No. What I like he hates and vice versa," said Lou.

"Well, if I was going to choose a name for a boy, I would pick a sensible, everyday name that his mates can abbreviate without taking the Mick. Something like Peter or Michael or Steven. Then give him a middle name that is a bit more unusual or romantic that he can choose to use instead if he wants. Something like Clint or Kyle or Bradley. You need to weigh the sound of the whole name. Does it roll nicely off the tongue? Does it make him sound like a wimp or a pompous idiot or does it make him sound like someone trustworthy and dependable. You know, someone you'd trust your life or your life savings to? Then check that the initials don't spell anything obscene, and your child won't hate you forever more. Simple."

"You'd think. And that would work well if we could agree which names were the solid everyday ones and which were the romantic, unusual ones," said Louise.

* * *

Grant returned from the shop. "Ugh! Shit!" The place really did stink! He ran the kitchen tap to rinse away the melted beer. Then for good measure threw some bleach down the sink before closing the door. Sitting in front of the telly with a cold beer he plonked his feet on the coffee table and pressed 'play', satisfied that at last he had everything he needed, rugby match, cold beer and somewhere to rest his feet. Then slowly, tiny distraction by tiny distraction he realised he was wrong. He couldn't concentrate on the match. Something wasn't right. Emily wasn't there and it was no fun watching the rugby without Emily. No one was yelling at the screen. No one was crushing his hand and dragging it bit by bit, play by play, towards the opposition try line.

* * *

"How about Edward Sheridan Parker?"

"I knew this would happen. We are now going to be deluged by names and none of them sensible," said Mike.

"It could give your boy a nedge. That little bit of help in life."

"Yeh! Yeh! Yeh! We get it. E.S.P! And before you start, we have done all the nosy Parker ones," said Mike.

"Or Charles Richard Archibald Parker."

"I just love being sober when no one else is!" said Lou.

Just then muffled music drew everyone's attention to the back of Emily's chair. As she released her phone from the depths of her bag the notes arranged themselves into the theme tune from 'Who Wants to be a Millionaire'. Emily silenced it, instantly sobered by the name on the screen. Grant. She switched it off and quickly stuffed it back in her bag.

CHAPTER FIVE

On Monday morning as Emily walked to the station she switched on her phone and listened to Grant's message. "Em. Hi. It's Grant. Er, can we, er, talk? Give us a call." That was it and he sounded as if he had had trouble saying that much. Emily wasn't impressed and she certainly had no intention of calling him back.

At work, as she logged on to her terminal, she wondered why she was doing so. She didn't actually need to anymore. As she waited for the system to start up, she looked around at her colleagues. What would they think if she announced that she really couldn't be bothered to do any work today? How would they react if she got up, announced that she was a millionaire, and walked out? Jamie, the 25-year-old systems analyst, sat reclined in his usual position. His black ergonomic chair was tipped back as far as it would go and his feet, ankles crossed, were resting on the corner of the desk whilst he typed earnestly on the keyboard on his lap. Oblivious to all around him his head nodded rhythmically in time with whatever was being piped into his ears. Across from him Lisa, one of the sales managers, was trying to get into a packet of coffee and berating everyone within earshot for not washing the percolator on Friday as there was now a green tinge to the surface of its remnants. In the corner by the window sat Jennifer, scribbling and frowning as she played her answerphone messages.

It was strange how different it seemed. She felt oddly removed as if she was watching a scene from a movie. Her screen finished initialising and she clicked on 'Outlook'. She had 72 e-mails, 5 of them appointments and one of them from a friend who worked in the county council transport department suggesting lunch on Wednesday. She scanned down them all and then went over to where Lisa was cursing and struggling to fit the appropriate tea and coffee making items onto a tray. Emily unhooked her mug from the mug tree and held the door open whilst Lisa carried the tray through.

"Good weekend?" asked Emily.

"Just brilliant! The car broke down with a boot full of tiles for the kitchen and the mother-in-law broke her hip. So, what with trying to get the tiles home from the garage so that the tiler would have them this morning, then trying to get to the hospital to visit Joan and finding someone to replace her to house sit the tiler, it's been great fun. Bill has taken today off to be there instead. I'm glad to be back at work."

"Well, if you need any help, you know, like a lift to the hospital or whatever..."

"Thanks, but we should be getting the car back this evening. Did you have a good weekend?"

"Oh, not bad. I went out for a meal with Lou and Mike."

"Oh, nice, it's good to eat out once in a while."

As they carried the drinks back into the office and handed them round Emily felt guilty at keeping her secret to herself but didn't know how to tell them. She wanted to share her good fortune, shout it from the rooftops but didn't know how they would react. Would they be pleased for her or jealous? Would they treat her differently? She would like to take them all out to celebrate, maybe for drinks or a meal. Would that be appreciated or seem too small a gesture? Would it look like she was flaunting her wealth and rubbing it in? She didn't know. Having told herself, and Louise and Mike, that she wasn't going to make any changes to her life until she had had time to think about it she still couldn't stop herself from day dreaming. So, she could now afford to buy a house, but what and where? Did she want to live in town to be near work? Did she want to work? She didn't really have to, but what would she do with herself all day if she didn't?

"Emily, have you got those quarterly training 'stats' I asked you for last week?" Jennifer was standing at her shoulder.

No, she hadn't. She had had other things on her mind last week. "Sorry, would an hour be alright?"

"I need them for 10:30, for the OTP meeting! I've got to see John before that," said Jennifer agitatedly. "Find me as soon as they are done."

Bringing up the spreadsheet and the various training lists she set about collating the sets of data. After about 15 minutes a message notification popped up and she clicked on 'Outlook' to read it. The message was suggesting a venue for lunch on Wednesday, so she composed a quick reply and hit 'send'. The cursor 'hung' and she sat staring at the egg-timer icon. Sipping her coffee and fuming she pressed 'control alt. delete' and brought up the 'task manager'. When she finally returned to the spreadsheet, she had to work through the data again as she no longer knew what she had added and what she hadn't. With just five minutes to spare she printed a copy and went in search of Jennifer who was relieved but not pleased with the intervening uncertainty.

As she returned to her desk, dissatisfied with herself for stressing her boss, she tried to concentrate on working through her e-mails and prioritising them against the rest of her work. Before long she found that she had also factored in a ranking for 'want to do' 'don't want to do'.

Tuesday dragged and by the time the 13:00 team-building workshop arrived her colleagues were commenting on her flippant derogatory responses and asking her what was wrong. She couldn't tell them that it all seemed so meaningless. She really couldn't care less whether the shark repellent would be more useful than the sextant if they were adrift at sea in a life raft. As for whether the decision-making process would be more effective if left to a loud-mouthed know-it-all or through discussion consensus, she didn't see the relevance. If she went to sea in a small boat, she would expect it to be crewed by experienced sailors not a management team and the facilitator would certainly be overboard before the quart of rum.

Back at her desk she found that she was achieving very little and so, feeling restless, she left work early. The string of the periapt had been irritating her all day and she felt that at least if she bought it a chain, she would feel that she had achieved something constructive.

She peered into a number of jeweller's windows, but nothing took her fancy, regardless of price. The chain needed to be something substantial to take the weight of the two carved rings, but all the larger chains smacked of 'bling' and that wasn't her style at all. It needed to be something ornate and unusual but without detracting from the periapt itself. Following the window display round the side of the third jewellers her attention was drawn to several items sitting on the pavement further up the side street. Walking on she spotted a couple of stacked chairs and a tin bathtub. Nearer, she saw a hand cranked gramophone complete with needles (apparently), a wicker basket full of packs of playing cards, a small folding table with tea ring stains on its surface, a wooden box full of rusty carpentry tools, a child's bicycle and sundry other items all huddled neatly round a shop doorway. Pushing open the door with its bull glass panes she stepped inside and stopped dead, taken aback by the pungent aroma of bees' wax and Brasso. Resigned to this assault on her senses she wandered round. Balloon and shield back chairs hung from the ceiling, inlaid marketry wardrobes stood, doors open to reveal stacks of eiderdowns and embroidered cotton nightgowns. Books and ornaments covered practically every surface and framed pictures hid every bit of spare wall. To reach the glass display case at the back of the shop she had to plot a route and then twist and step sideways to reach her goal.

Behind the counter a tiny man was busy polishing some brass items. He looked up and smiled and then continued to buff a brass plant holder. Emily looked through the glass display pane, her eyes travelling rapidly over the selection of jewellery, cutlery and watches etc.

"Are you looking for anything special?" asked the man, standing and wiping his hands on his white canvas apron.

"Well, I was trying to find an appropriate chain for this," and she pulled out the periapt.

Taking it from her and putting on the glasses that hung on a chain round his neck, he inspected it closely. Turning it round and holding it up to the light he studied its milky smooth translucency and gently caressed its curves. A sweet smile lit his face "You wouldn't like to sell it would you? I'd give you a good price." Before Emily could respond the hint of a shadow soured his features, an instinctive reaction to nothing apparent. "Maybe not." He placed it cautiously on the counter and slid it warily towards Emily. "I can tell it means a lot to you. A chain you say."

Pulling a couple of shallow wooden drawers from the bottom of the counter he placed them in front of Emily. The left contained a variety of white metal chains and the right one yellow metal ones. Emily sifted through them and inspected one or two but none of them seemed right. Seeing her disappointment, he racked his brain, mentally running through his stock. With a little hiccup of delight and an instruction for Emily to 'Wait there!' he scurried off into the back of the shop and returned a few minutes later laden with an old brown leather suitcase. Heaving it onto the counter and balancing it precariously on top of the two drawers, he slid the two rusty catches sideways so that they flipped up allowing him to raise the lid. Several dusty cigar boxes sat inside tied with string. Each had a luggage label attached identifying their contents. Finding the one he wanted he untied the string and opened the box. Pulling out a wad of crumpled yellow tissue paper that smelled strongly of ancient tobacco, he revealed a gold chain.

Emily picked it up. The links were strong but elegant and the clasp simple but secure without being bulky. The best thing of all though, was that every two inches along the length of the chain sat a pearl shouldered by decorative gold filigree work, and the pearls echoed the colour and texture of the periapt perfectly. Emily loved it.

"Oh, will it.........the pearls?"

Reading her mind, he smiled, "I can open the clasp on your pendant and re-solder it to fit round the chain in between the pearls."

"I'll take it," said Emily not even bothering to ask how much. She didn't care.

* * *

On her way to work the next day she detoured through the farmer's market which set its stalls out every Wednesday in the old square in front of the town hall. Wandering around she passed a stall selling daffodils and small pots of snowdrops. She smiled wistfully, reminded of the churchyard at Greater Blessing. What a lovely place that was! Looking round at the throng of people, the miserable resigned faces all drifting purposefully through their day, she wondered who she was kidding. When she told Lou and Mike that she was going to carry on as normal, that her win wasn't going to change her life, she had been plain stupid. Just look at her. It had already changed her life. She was already looking at the world in a different light. Mentally she had set herself apart from it. None of this was relevant to her anymore. Her subconscious was weighing and judging, dismissing the unnecessary. To illustrate her point the town hall clock struck nine. She realised that she was late. Desire was winning out over routine discipline. She was kidding herself if she thought she could carry on going to work. It wasn't fair to her colleagues. They needed someone dedicated, someone who pulled her weight. She had never been late before without good reason, certainly not because she fancied wandering round a market. The truth was that work didn't matter to her anymore.

She bought the snowdrops and hurried to the office apologising to Jennifer but offering no explanation. She tried to concentrate but her mind kept wandering and by mid morning she had come to a decision. A quick search on the internet found her the estate agents at Greater

Blessing and a phone number. Gritting her teeth, she called Gerald. There was no answer. He must be at lunch. Partly relieved, partly annoyed and disappointed she left the office and headed off for her lunch date. She needed someone to talk to, someone who could give her advice. She had never bought a house before and had no idea how to go about it. Putting Gerald in the driving seat would probably drive her insane.

Her friend Karen was waiting outside the café. They went in and found a table. They hadn't seen each other since well before Christmas and Karen was bursting to tell Emily all about her holiday in Peru. She had had a fantastic time. She described Cuzco and its churches and markets, the fascinating train ride to Macchu Pichu and the climb to the Sun Gate with its breathtaking views from the top. She told her all about the cold early morning ride over the Altiplano to Colca Canyon to watch the condors flying and about bathing in hot springs on the way back. Then she described all the wonderful people with whom she had shared the holiday. Emily listened politely, thrilled by her friend's enthusiasm and delight. Finally, Karen came to a halt. "So, what have you been up to lately? How was India?"

"India was great, but there is something else I want to tell you about and I need your advice." So, she explained about splitting up with Grant and about the old ladies and then about winning the lottery and needing advice on how to go about buying a house.

Karen was amazed and delighted at Emily's good fortune. She couldn't believe that Emily had sat there whilst she had rambled on about Peru and she couldn't believe that Emily hadn't shouted her win from the roof tops. When she eventually responded to Emily's 'shushing' and the rest of the diners had gone back to minding their own business, she was eager to help. Having moved house a number of times with her parents and then a couple of times with her husband she had lots of advice. Emily was soon bemused by the list of 'do's' and 'don'ts' and had to get Karen to back-track and concentrate on the first step, i.e. putting in an offer. "Well, if you are adamant that you want the property regardless, and you don't need a mortgage, I guess you can skip the structural survey, but you don't want to find, for example, that the land is contaminated in some way."

"Well, if I am going to have my life span shortened to only 100 years, I think I can live with that."

"Well, phone the estate agents and put in an offer. I would go for 10% less than the asking price as a first shot. Then wait and see what the response is. You can then raise your offer accordingly. Is anyone else interested do you know?"

Emily's heart sank. She hadn't thought of that. What if it had already been sold! She would be devastated.

With Karen's urging she rang Gerald. The phone rang, and continued ringing. How long a lunch break did he need! She let it ring. When he answered it was a surprise, but she managed to stammer, "Hi, Gerald, remember me, Emily Hope? You were trying to sell me Wishing Well Cottage. Is it still for sale? I'd like to put in an offer."

"Emily," gushed Gerald, instantly enveloping her with his seductive smarm! She felt like she was being devoured, like she had crawled into a Venus flytrap. Even the mobile in her hand felt slightly sticky at the sound of his voice. All he had said was her name and yet her skin crawled at the sound of it. "So, when would you like me to show you round?"

Annoyed and repulsed, Emily, to her surprise, managed to assert herself "I don't need showing round. I just want to put in an offer, and have you call me back when you have an answer from your clients. Can you do that?"

Within ten minutes her phone rang. Nervously she answered it and as Karen looked on excitedly, she said, "Thanks. Great, I'll be in touch with my solicitor. Bye." Hands shaking, she put down her phone, stunned. "They accepted, just like that. I can't believe it. I'm buying a house. I'm buying Wishing Well Cottage. Help! What do I do?"

* * *

Mike couldn't believe it. "They accepted, just like that, when Gerald and probably the entire village knows that you won the lottery! Someone must really want you to have that house! Don't you find all this just that little bit weird?"

"I know, but I really want that house." Unconsciously playing with the periapt Emily added, "It is so beautiful and peaceful there. It's like, that's where I belong, as if it is all just meant to be..."

The tinny version of 'Who Wants to be a Millionaire' trilled from her pocket. It was a text message from Grant. 'Please call I miss U.' "Yeah, me and one million two hundred and twenty six thousand four hundred and fifty five pounds!"

CHAPTER SIX

Having found herself a solicitor and visited the bank Emily was now impatient to move into the cottage. Having been told that these things take weeks and warned of all the things that could go wrong and that nothing was final until contracts had been exchanged Emily tried not to let herself get too carried away with colour schemes and curtains. Mentally, however, she had already moved in.

Texts and answerphone messages from Grant increased in frequency and Lou tried to get her to answer them but Emily wanted nothing to do with the 'money-grabbing monster' as she called him. Every time she switched on her phone there was another message. Finally, she decided enough was enough and bought a new phone. It was a bit of a pain telling everyone her new number and humiliating asking them not to give it to Grant, but it had to be done. She did wonder whether he would turn up on Lou's doorstep once he couldn't reach her by phone. So, she moved into an hotel, as she had told Lou and Mike she would.

On the Monday she handed in her notice at work and explained about her lottery win, to mixed reactions. Some were pleased, some weren't. Whether they were sorry or glad that she was leaving, or pleased or jealous of her win, she wasn't certain. She no longer felt to be one of them and she couldn't help feeling that they felt it too. Jennifer worked out Emily's leaving date, after subtracting the annual leave she was owed, as 26th February. Eleven whole days! Emily didn't know how she was going to get through them. She knew that if she just walked out there was nothing much they could do. It wasn't as if she cared about references or her pay, but she did care about what they thought of her. She didn't want them to think that she no longer cared about them, that she thought that she was above that kind of thing. So, she arranged a leaving 'do' and told them all that she would pay, her treat. That seemed to go down well and so she booked them all into The Crown Hotel for the Friday after her last working day. Her next dilemma was what to wear. All her belongings were still in storage, so it made sense to go shopping. She could afford whatever took her fancy but now the thought of turning up for her leaving 'do' in an 'in-your-face' designer outfit made her feel uncomfortable. Yet she couldn't help feeling that dressing down would be insulting. Saving up and splashing out on expensive outfits, as she had done in the past, was somehow all right. Now, when money was no object, she felt uncomfortable. When she finally broached the subject with Lou, Lou raised her eyebrows and took a deep breath.

"So, that's what's been weighing heavily on your mind all week is it? Primart or Prada! There was me thinking that erratic weather patterns, drowning polar bears and dehydrating antelope were getting you down. Look, Emily, just find something that you like. If it suits you and it fits, buy it. Just make sure that your tiara matches your earrings, diamonds go with most things, and be yourself!"

"I know that in the great scheme of things this is a pretty minor problem, but I don't want to upset them."

"Em, they're getting a free meal! Those who are genuinely pleased for you won't care what you wear and those who are jealous will always find something to complain about. So, you wear what you feel comfortable in. Bathrobe and flip flops if you like. After all, the eccentric millionaire look is always acceptable."

* * *

When Mike picked up the post from the doormat on the Thursday morning there was a big red Valentine's envelope addressed to Emily. He showed it to Lou. "She won't be pleased but

I guess we've got to give it to her anyway! You know," said Mike, "I think he genuinely wants her back. I don't think it has anything to do with her money. I don't think he even knows about it."

"Try telling that to Emily!"

* * *

Grant had spent ages composing the letter in the Valentine's card. As the days had gone by, he had found it harder and harder not having Emily there. His anger had gradually faded and been replaced by an emptiness that echoed round his empty flat. He missed her desperately. Every answerphone message was a disappointment, every knock at the door a dashed hope. During the day, in unguarded moments, he thought to tell her little things that had happened that might interest or amuse her, only to be slapped by the reality of her absence. At night he reached out to empty sheets.

Dear Emily,

I miss you so. I've been such a fool. Please forgive me. The last few days I have come to realise that I just can't live without you. I keep hearing your voice, seeing you out of the corner of my eye, thinking that I feel you lying next to me in bed, but you're not there and it's breaking my heart.

Today is Valentine's Day. I would like to take you out and for us to start over again. I have booked a table for two at The Single Rose. If you can even start to forgive me, please be ready for 7:30. A car will pick you up.

All my love,

Grant

* * *

Emily made it to work on time for the first time that week, determined not to let her colleagues down. She made the effort to ensure that all her work was up to date. It was actually getting easier because no one was giving her new tasks to take on and she was finding a certain satisfaction in completing work in the knowledge that she wouldn't have to tackle it again. Surreptitiously she marked off the days on the calendar hidden in her desk drawer.

Slowly it dawned on her that it was Valentine's Day, and she couldn't help feeling a little left out hearing the others tell of their cards and gifts. Briefly she thought of Grant and their last Valentine's Day. There would be no large bunch of roses this year.

Mid-morning, several exclamations made her look up from her screen. A large bouquet bobbed its way through the doorway, waved aloft by one of the reception staff. Her heart skipped a beat. From across the room there appeared to be a dozen red roses floating in a mass of green leaves and cellophane. The receptionist scanned the room briefly until her gaze alighted on Lisa. There was a screech of delight as Lisa got to her feet to receive her flowers and Emily, deflated, returned her eyes to her screen. Stupid! Stupid! Why did she think they might be for her? Did she want them to be for her? No! No, of course she didn't!

* * *

On her way home from work Emily bought herself a bottle of red wine and a box of chocolates. She planned on spending Valentine's night curled up in front of the TV. She ordered room service so that she didn't have to eat surrounded by a lot of cooing couples in the restaurant, happy to be just by herself for once. She was quite enjoying doing just what she wanted, when she wanted, without having to consider anybody else.

* * *

Lou and Mike were going out for the evening, determined to make the most of their diminishing opportunities to eat out before the baby arrived. As they left the house they spotted a white limousine turn into their road. "Ooh, someone's in for an expensive evening." commented Mike. "Who do you reckon that's for then?"

On the way to the restaurant, they stopped off at Emily's hotel and dropped off her mail at the reception desk.

* * *

Grant waited at the restaurant, nervously sitting at the bar with a tonic water, resisting the temptation to consume any alcohol. There would be time for that when Emily arrived. If she arrived!

* **

There was a knock at the door and Emily opened it. The waiter wheeled in a trolley and placed her meal on the table. She had ordered a starter of goat's cheese and cranberries followed by steak with a slice of cheesecake to follow. The waiter plugged in the hotplate on which sat the covered steak and then arranged her cutlery and napkin, before serving her starter. As he wheeled the trolley to the door he stopped and pulled a small stack of envelopes from under the trolley. "These were handed in at reception for you."

Emily took them and flicked through them. Picking out the red envelope she stared at the handwriting.

* **

Grant's hopes were rising. The car should have picked her up by now. If things hadn't gone to plan, then the driver should have phoned. A quick look at his watch told him that it was 7:45. She should be arriving any minute. He ordered another tonic water and waited. At 7:50 he was still waiting. At 8pm she still hadn't appeared. He pulled out his phone and was horrified to see that there was no signal. Using the phone on the bar he called the taxi firm and asked them to get in touch with the driver. Again he waited, praying that she would come.

* * *

Emily stared at the envelope. Half annoyed, half pleased, she ran her fingers over the familiar writing. Why was she sitting alone in a hotel room eating by herself, her only companion a television set? What was the point of all that money if there was no one to share it with? He was obviously trying to make amends. Maybe it was her that he wanted and not just her money. She thought of Lou and Mike and their soon-to-be baby. That could be her. That should be her! It wasn't going to be though, not with Grant. Annoyed with herself for even contemplating going back to him, she threw the card in the bin.

CHAPTER SEVEN

When the weekend came, she drove to Greater Blessing. She would dearly have loved to make an appointment to view the house again but there was no way that she was risking being alone with Gerald. Instead, she called at Anna's in the hope of being let in by her. Anna appeared to be out. So, Emily had to content herself with walking round the garden and peering through the windows. She was going to have to do something about a parking space. The cottage had plenty of land, but it was all garden. She was going to have to clear some of it and make some hard standing for at least one vehicle, preferably two. Mentally she plotted out a driveway. At the side of the house, she visualised two parking spaces and a turning area so that she didn't have to reverse all the way down the drive. She tried to think of how it would look, and the different practicalities involved. As it started to rain it occurred to her that having the parking spaces near a door would be a good idea and revised her initial plan. Using her phone, she photographed the different sections of garden so that she could think about it later. She needed to find a landscape gardener. As the rain increased, she decided to head back to the hotel, to some paper and her laptop.

* * *

On the Sunday she found herself wandering round garden centres and DIY stores and to her surprise finding them interesting. She had no idea that there was so much choice. All the different flags and bricks and chippings were a revelation. Deciding what would look best was going to be harder than she thought. Employing a landscape gardener and telling him to 'put a drive there' wasn't going to be as simple as she thought. Looking on-line she found plenty of examples and gradually she got some idea of what she wanted.

* * *

At work she made a few phone calls and arranged to meet three landscape gardeners at Wishing Well Cottage on the following Saturday. She felt a little guilty about doing so but work-wise she didn't have much to do now. She made herself busy by making coffee for the rest of them and answering the phone.

Back in her hotel room she was surprised when the hotel manager knocked on her door. He had come to apologise because they had found an unopened envelope addressed to her in the rubbish. It may be that she had deliberately thrown it away, but they couldn't assume so and if that was the case then he was profusely sorry. Emily assured him that the hotel wasn't to blame but took the envelope anyway. With a deep sigh she sat on the bed and opened it. Scanning the letter her heart wept. She read it three times. Then she phoned Lou. "Lou, I need to talk. Can I come round?"

Lou let her in and Emily showed her the note. "Oh, wow! That was for you. Em, it was a huge white limo. It must have cost him a fortune. He must really want you back."

"Either that or he thinks that the way to accumulate is to speculate!"

"Oh, Em!"

"When I first read the note, it upset me. The thought of him sitting there alone in the restaurant waiting for me to turn up, cut me to the quick, but the truth of it is that I don't want him back. I want someone who wants what I want. Grant wants his fast cars and flash clothes and I want a home and a family. It's over Lou."

* * *

On Thursday evening Grant called to see Emily, desperate to talk to her but not knowing that she was no longer staying with Lou and Mike. Mike invited him in and explained that she had moved out. Surprised, Grant told them all about the Valentine's meal. He had wanted to make a grand gesture to impress Emily, to 'go out on a limb' and do something special to show her how much she meant to him, in the hope that she would come back. When they told him that she had bought a house he couldn't believe it. It was obvious to both of them, he had no idea that Emily had won the lottery.

They told him how sorry they were, but Emily was adamant that she didn't want to see him. They felt really awful, refusing to give him her address, but promised to tell her how he felt.

* * *

With her parents for back-up and three landscape gardeners booked at half-hour intervals Emily arranged to meet Gerald at Wishing Well Cottage. The day was a little overcast and rather windy. Emily was disappointed. She wanted her parents' initial impression of Wishing Well Cottage and Greater Blessing to be perfect. She had told them all about it and was keen for them to love it as much as she did.

When they arrived, Gerald was waiting eagerly at the gate. They got out of the car and Emily introduced them all. Gerald had had a haircut. Nothing dramatic, but just a wee bit too short in places making him look slightly thuggish. He had obviously shaved too, judging by the haze of aftershave. Hopefully, the wind would pick up. Emily kept trying to look away but there was something about him that kept drawing her eyes back to his face. Gerald seemed to be revelling in the attention. She noticed that her parents kept giving him surreptitious glances too. Then it dawned on her. He had had his eyebrows waxed and his eyes were now a startling blue. He was wearing coloured contact lenses. 'Shooting' the cuffs of his well tailored suit to reveal large gold cufflinks he opened the gate and held it open so that they could all walk through forcing Emily to pass him at close quarters. She held her breath, literally and metaphorically.

Gerald gave them the grand tour and managed to use every doorway as an excuse to manhandle Emily in some way, either by guiding her through or taking her hand for the odd step up or down. Her parents appeared to be amused and were no help at all.

A knock on the door announced the arrival of the first landscape gardener. So, as they had seen the house Emily told Gerald that he could 'lock up and thank you', but they didn't need him anymore. He protested saying it was no trouble for him to stay. So, exasperated, she borrowed one of Lou's looks and stared at him, one eyebrow raised. To her surprise he mumbled his goodbyes and backed off down the path. Well, it wasn't that difficult after all. Pleased with herself she turned her attention to the first landscaper.

At the end of the morning, she had a good idea what she wanted. Now all she had to do was wait for their quotes and decide from there.

She and her parents had a wander round the village and then stepped into The Three Wells pub for lunch. A stone floor, similar to that in Wishing Well Cottage, graced the entrance and the area in front of the bar. A thick, almost new, terracotta carpet marked out the seating area which was covered in sturdy oak tables and chairs. Traditional brass ornaments hung from the huge old beams that supported the ceiling, and guilt framed prints and oils of local scenes festooned the walls. As their eyes adjusted to the interior, Emily and her mother settled themselves at a table in the corner whilst her father got them all drinks.

"So, what do you think?" Emily asked her mother.

"I think it's wonderful. A lovely house! But are you going to be all right here all on your own? It's such a big house. Won't you be lonely?"

"I'm sure I will have enough people wanting to visit once they find out where I am and I have already made a friend, Anna. She's the vicar's housekeeper and she's been feeding Kevin. Kevin! I wonder if Kevin is staying? Mum, you didn't start sneezing. Maybe you aren't allergic to him."

"No, I didn't."

"Didn't what?" said her father as he set the drinks on the table and handed round the menus, that he'd been carrying under his arm.

"Mum didn't appear to be allergic to Kevin, the cat I told you about. She went all through the house and not a sniffle. That's great. I so hope he is staying with the house."

Later when her mother disappeared to the ladies her father said, "I don't think she's ever been allergic to cats, just mess. You know how house proud she is, and she's scared of dogs, animals in general really. It took a lot of persuading for me to get you that goldfish you had as a kid. I'm sure she'll get used to this Kevin if she has to. Kevin! Who'd name a cat Kevin?"

"Dad, don't ever say that to his face."

* * *

Tuesday was her last day at work and now it had arrived she didn't want it to end. Despite having virtually nothing to do but pack up her belongings the time just whizzed by. She logged off for the last time and handed Jennifer her drawer key. Jennifer coughed loudly to draw everyone's attention and then set about embarrassing Emily by telling them all what a good job she had done and that she would be missed etc. Emily looked round at them all, blinking madly to keep the tears at bay. As she fumbled with the wrapping of the present they had given her, clapping erupted, followed by the chant "Speech, speech!"

Emily didn't know what to say. She mumbled her thanks and said she'd miss them all and that she hoped to see all of them at her leaving 'do' on Friday. Jennifer said that she was looking forward to it and assured Emily that should she ever need a job, if she was stupid enough to throw away £1.2 million, then she would be welcome to pop in and give them all a laugh! With a last look round, she walked out the door clutching a black tee-shirt with 'Filthy Rich' in gold letters on the front, and a plastic tiara.

* * *

Grant couldn't get Emily out of his head. If he could just talk to her, maybe he could change her mind. He had tried phoning and writing and e-mailing but she wouldn't reply, and no-one would tell him where she was. Somehow, he had to get to see her.

* * *

Friday came and the dilemma of what to wear was solved. She would wear the 'Filthy Rich' tee-shirt, jeans and plastic tiara. After all her worry her work mates had solved the problem for her. She didn't even need a coat as all she had to do was to walk downstairs to the bar to meet her guests. For the first time since winning the lottery she felt like a millionaire. Strolling down the hotel stairs and welcoming her guests as they arrived, whilst waiting for dinner to be served, was like owning her own stately home full of servants. The staff all knew her, and she had reserved a private room for the evening with an open bar. The latter was made good use of by her old work mates, and she had to personally put two of them in a taxi at the end of the evening. They appeared to have enjoyed themselves, and Emily went to bed satisfied that she had got it 'just right'.

* * *

As the days went by Grant pondered the problem of how to track down Emily. He continued to write letters and send them to her at Louise's in the hope that Emily would get them and read them, but he heard nothing from her.

CHAPTER EIGHT

F inally, the great day arrived. Contracts had been exchanged, money had been transferred and Emily had survived the necessary encounter with Gerald, escaping triumphant with the keys to Wishing Well Cottage and no pending lawsuit.

Parking beside the green, she stood and looked at her new home. She didn't think that she had ever been happier. Grabbing a couple of the bags from the back seat of the car she crossed the street and entered her front gate. Unlocking the front door, she headed down the hall and into the kitchen where she deposited the bags. Doing a tour of the house she was surprised to find that all Angelica's belongings were still there. She had been expecting the furniture but not all Angelica's personal items. She phoned the solicitor who assured her that Angelica's relatives wanted her to have everything but that she was at liberty to throw out whatever she didn't want. Stunned and a little unnerved she went and got the remainder of her own things from the car.

* * *

From the other side of the green, at a window above the store, net curtains twitched with irritation.

* * *

Returning to the kitchen Emily found a vase of fresh flowers and an envelope with her name on it on the kitchen table. It was from Anna, welcoming her to Wishing Well Cottage and giving her brief instructions on how to keep the range lit and use the kettle. Anna it seemed had lit the stove and put water in the kettle. All Emily had to do was put the kettle on top of the range and wait. Anna had even stocked the fridge with milk and margarine and left a loaf of bread, a tin of baked beans, tea bags and a plate of biscuits for her. As she waited for the kettle to boil, she suddenly got the feeling that she wasn't alone. Something was behind her. Turning slowly, she found that Kevin was sitting in the middle of the floor staring at her. As their eyes met, he stood with a "perrrrup" and trotted towards her.

"Kevin. I'm so glad you're here!" and she got down and held his furry face between her two hands then stroked his back. He rolled over and let her stroke his stomach luxuriating in her touch. Just when Emily's knees started to protest, he got up and headed over to the corner of the room looking back twice to ensure she was following. On the floor at his feet was an empty dish and a water bowl.

"Ah. I see." So, Emily had a brief look round for cat food and then fed him. As she watched him eat, the kettle began to whistle so she made herself a cup of tea. Then she sat in her new kitchen in her new house and planned what to do next. She needed to decide which bedroom she was going to sleep in and clear some space for her belongings. The van from the Storage Company would be arriving in the morning with the rest of her possessions.

Carrying her bags upstairs she settled on the bedroom she had slept in the night of the snow. It wasn't the largest room but apart from feeling that it wasn't quite right to use Angelica's room she also knew that it was the one room that Angelica hadn't died in. She knew it was silly, but she also knew that alone in the house at night her mind was likely to play tricks on her. She decided to clear some space by emptying out the wardrobe and chest of drawers. Opening the wardrobe door, she was presented with a selection of dresses and coats dating back decades. There were elegant suits from the 40's and 50's, mini and maxi dresses and skirts and a see-through plastic coat from the 60's and 70's and even a fringed flapper dress from the 1920's. Holding the flapper dress in front of her she looked in the full-length mirror inside the wardrobe door. All she needed was a feather boa, a cloche hat and a cropped hair 'do'. She would need to lose the trainers of course and the jeans. She was just considering trying on the dress when the doorbell rang.

Bounding down the stairs she raced to the front door. It was Anna inviting her for dinner that evening to give her a chance to settle in before having to get to grips with cooking on the range. Emily invited her in and thanked her for the flowers and the supplies. She also took the opportunity to ascertain whether Kevin was staying, or just visiting. As they entered the kitchen it was patently obvious. Kevin was lying curled up on a chair by the fire. He opened one eye briefly, inspected a claw, and settled back expansively into the leather seat. Kevin was going nowhere.

"So, I've got a cat. Excellent!" grinned Emily.

"I think probably ...the reality is ...that Kevin has got a new human!"

"Ah, I see! Do you know how old he is?"

"No. I believe he just turned up one day. I know it wasn't long after Angelica's husband died. That would be about 10-12 years ago now. He was called Kevin too. Makes you wonder."

"Oh, she was married then?"

"Yes, he was an artist. Well, he owned a bookstore, but he was better known for his paintings and sketches: mainly local landscapes. That's one of his there." Anna pointed to a painting on the back wall.

"Oh, isn't that one of Kevin Dewhurst's?"

"Yes, that's him. Angelica reverted to her maiden name when he died. All the Wells sisters have done. I say reverted, they only really changed them for legal purposes. Everybody knew and referred to them as the Wells sisters. The Wells sisters are, were, Greater Blessing. The Three Wells pub was originally owned by the Wells family, as far back as 1780. They owned quite a bit of land back then. Now, most of them are scattered far and wide."

"So, there is family then. I was beginning to think that there was just Myrtle Wells which was why she didn't want any of this." Emily waved her arm to indicate the house and contents."

"Well, I suspect that Myrtle not only inherited this, but Ruby's estate as well. What'll happen to it all when Myrtle dies who knows, but you can be sure of one thing, whatever it is will have been planned out carefully. The Wells sisters have never done anything without purpose. Luck and chance are not random occurrences in Greater Blessing. Events need to be managed, and the Wells sisters were experts at... shall we say... 'multi-tasking'. Well, it is time I was going. So, I'll see you about 6:30 then?"

Emily nodded.

"You can be certain of one thing Emily Hope. You are not here by accident." Chuckling to herself, Anna stroked Kevin's head and left, leaving a somewhat disturbed Emily staring after her, unknowingly fingering the periapt.

CHAPTER NINE

T he storage van arrived just after 11:00 the next day and within half an hour all her worldly possessions were safely inside Wishing Well Cottage. She set up her CD player in the kitchen and soon had Katie Tunstall energising her cleaning as she set about sorting the cupboards. She wanted to make sure that she had some mugs ready to make drinks for the landscapers when they arrived the following morning. Yes, there were mugs. So that was that sorted. Next, she set about clearing all Angelica's old tins and jars and packets and sorting them into piles of 'usable' and those that had passed their sell by dates. Once she had been through all the cupboards the kitchen table was full. She emptied all the contents of the expired items into a bowl to take to the compost heap and then washed the jars and tins for re-cycling. Then, popping her jacket on she picked up a wicker basket that she found hanging on a hook by the door and headed off to the store for some supplies.

As she rounded the green a number of people nodded to her and smiled. Some wished her good day, and one elderly gentleman doffed his cap. Obviously word had got round that she was now the new owner of Wishing Well Cottage. Entering the store, she gathered the items she needed and headed to the till.

"So, you've moved in then." said the storekeeper, lips pursed.

"Yes, yesterday."

"Well, what will be, will be. £22.50, if you please." Then with the same fixed smile as before, "Take care of yourself."

Emily had no idea what she had done to upset the storekeeper. It had to be something to do with the Wells sisters but why she should be blamed she had no idea. She must ask Anna. She couldn't help feeling though that Anna wasn't being as forthcoming as she might!

Next, she set about preparing a bedroom for Louise who was coming to stay for a few days whilst Mike was away in Birmingham for a sales conference. She picked one of the bedrooms that looked out at the front of the property, stripped the bed and went in search of some fresh bedding. Finding some in a big chest of drawers in the corridor she held it up to her nose and sniffed. Sadly, it all smelt musty. Could she get it washed and dried in time? Did she have a washing machine? She knew there wasn't one in the kitchen, so she had a look in the outhouse. Yes. It was a bit ancient but there was a washing machine and some powder. Using a combination of common sense and guesswork she managed to get it going and went back upstairs to make Louise's bedroom welcoming.

She emptied a couple of drawers and made some space in the wardrobe, deliberately not sorting through any of the items. If she started looking, she knew that she would get carried away. The house was a veritable time warp. She placed everything in plastic bags and transferred them to the fourth bedroom. Then she dusted round and opened a window to air the room. Next, she went in search of a vase and some scissors so she could get some flowers from the garden whilst the rain had stopped.

Tiptoeing up the garden path to avoid the puddles she decided that she was going to have to get some Wellingtons. In fact, there were quite a few things that she was going to have to buy. She probably ought to start making a list. A decent washing machine and drier for a start, and a plug-in kettle. She picked some snowdrops and a selection of blue and yellow flowers. She was going to have to learn the names of them all. No doubt one of Angelica's books would tell her. Arranging them in the vase with some sprigs of greenery she placed them on the small table at the end of Louise's bed. She was just admiring her handiwork when the doorbell rang.

As she reached the top of the stairs, she was shocked to see a man standing at the bottom wearing a slightly too large overcoat and clutching his flat cap. Cautiously she stepped down towards him as he smiled up at her working his mouth to rearrange his dentures. Swallowing hard he beamed, "Hello Love, I've come for me ointment."

"Pardon?"

"Me ointment!"

"Er, do you live round here?" asked Emily politely. The man was obviously confused. "I think you want the doctor's. That's at the other end of the village, I think."

"No." At that he turned round and headed for the front door but instead of going out he veered left into the room with all Angelica's bottles and jars. When Emily arrived in the doorway he was climbing onto a chair and reaching up to a jar on one of the shelves. Grabbing hold of it he edged it towards him and knocked it off the shelf, catching it as it fell. Then, to Emily's horror, one hand clutching the chair back, he stepped shakily backwards down onto the floor. Holding the jar in both hands he rotated it until the label was facing Emily, and thrust it towards her.

"Me ointment!"

As Emily watched he placed it on the table and took a small jam jar out of his pocket. Unscrewing both jars he picked up a spatula from amongst the items on the table and scooped ointment from Angelica's jar into his own. When it was full, he screwed the tops back. Pushing the big jar into Emily's hands he said, "You're gonna 'ave to make some more o' that. There's not much left." Then sucking in his dentures again he rummaged in his coat pocket and, after several attempts, managed to tug out a large bundle of bubble wrap. Carefully unwrapping it he gently extricated its contents and offered them to Emily. Warily she held out her hand and received two eggs.

"They're duck, Love. Thanks. Bye." At which he picked up his jar, flipped his cap back on his head, nodded and let himself out.

Carefully placing the eggs on the table Emily unscrewed the jar. Taking a sniff at the contents she wondered just what other surprises Wishing Well Cottage and the inhabitants of Greater Blessing had in store for her. So, this is what Angelica did with this room. How many other 'patients' did she have, and would they all expect normal service to be resumed now that Wishing Well Cottage was occupied again? Replacing the lid on 'Ointment No. 23' she wondered if she would be expected to concoct ointments 1 – 22 and how ever many others there were. What was it for, and was it even legal? Was she going to find that the angelic Angelica was growing cannabis in the greenhouse? The police would love that. Taking over the drug factory would give them a motive for her bumping off Angelica and Ruby.

Movement by the door caught her eye. Kevin had arrived. She asked him what he knew about it all, but Kevin was no stool pigeon. He told her nothing. She decided to feed them both and then have a play with the range in the hope of figuring out how to cook on it before Lou arrived. She wanted to be able to impress Louise with her culinary skills and ultimately not poison her.

She had let the fire go out, so she had to start by clearing out the ash and then building a little bonfire in the base. After several matches had been spent and the pile rearranged several times, she managed to get it lit and sat for a while feeding it with bits of firewood from the collection on the hearth. She shut the door and put the kettle on one of the plates and waited to see how long it would take to heat up. Whilst she waited, she busied herself tidying and arranging the kitchen. She also started the list of things to buy.

* * *

The landscapers arrived early the next morning and whilst she waited impatiently for the kettle to boil, they set about removing the fencing along the front of Wishing Well Cottage. By the time the tea was ready they had unloaded a small digger and started clearing the shrubs. Dave the boss wanted to know what she wanted them to do with the peony bush. Seeing Emily's blank expression, he pointed it out and explained that it was obviously an old, well established plant and would be quite spectacular when it flowered. He suggested moving it to a spot under the front window where it would be visible from inside and also provide a nice display from the drive. She agreed and gave him 'free rein' to move the plants as he thought best.

Leaving them to get on with it she went back inside to iron Louise's bedding, mainly in the hope of getting it dry before Louise arrived. Having hunted round and only found an ironing board it eventually dawned on Emily that the 'ornaments' that she had admired on the hearth probably weren't ornaments at all but Angelica's irons. Picking up the largest of the three she saw that the handle was well worn and clean and that the base was well polished. It had obviously been recently used. She placed it on one of the hot plates and set up the ironing board. Once she had got the hang of holding it with the padded cloth that she found hanging on a hook next to where the iron had been sitting, she found that it worked very well. There was no flex to contend with or silly base tray to sit it back in each time she put it down. By experimenting she found that she could vary the temperature of the iron by placing it on different areas of the range although it was a bit time consuming waiting for it to heat up repeatedly. Then it occurred to her to use all three irons in rotation. The different sizes meant that she could choose the best size for the job. It was a bit hot standing next to the range and she didn't like the thought of ironing in summer, but the fact that she was ironing without using the national grid pleased her enormously.

Mid-morning, she took more tea out to the landscapers, and inspected the progress. They had stripped to the waist and the tea was greeted with much gratitude. They had cleared half the drive and were marking out the turning area. The garden was a real mess. If Angelica was watching she hoped she didn't mind. What Kevin thought of it she wasn't sure. When she turned to go back inside, she spotted him perched on top of the porch looking inscrutably down at the humans invading his garden.

Just after lunch Louise arrived and Emily went out to help her carry in her bags. Louise stopped in front of the house and had a good look around. Grinning, she said, "Terrific view!"

"Yes, unfortunately they'll have to go once the drive is finished."

"Have you considered having a pool?"

"I don't think they do pools. A big pond maybe?"

Emily showed her to her room and then gave her a cup of tea before embarking on the grand tour. Louise 'oohed' and 'aahed' her approval as they went from room to room, and she volunteered to help Emily sort out some of Angelica's belongings. When Emily showed her the flapper dress she couldn't wait to get started. It was like walking into Aladdin's cave. She was disappointed that she wasn't going to fit into any of the dresses, but she could try on the hats and shoes.

When they came back down and entered the kitchen, they found Kevin curled up on one of the chairs by the fire.

"Lou, let me introduce you to Kevin."

Kevin sat up politely.

"Kevin this is Louise."

"Kevin, pleased to meet you at last. I've heard such a lot about you. You take good care of my friend Emily." She slowly and gently stroked Kevin's head and he leant into her hand appreciatively.

"Excellent!" said Emily. "I'm so glad that you two are going to get along. Kevin doesn't approve of many people." She picked Kevin up so that she could sit in the chair and Kevin settled on her lap whilst Lou sat in the other chair.

They chatted for most of the afternoon, Lou telling all about how her pregnancy was progressing and Emily about the cottage and Greater Blessing. Lou laughed her head off when Emily told her about the old man and his ointment.

"I can just see it now. A dark and stormy night, owls hooting, and you stirring your cauldron brewing up lotions and potions."

"That's likely. I have enough problems brewing tea on that thing," said Emily pointing at the range. "Oh, no! It's gone out again. I'm running out of wood too. Do you think Angelica chopped her own?"

"I would imagine so. There is so much land here with trees, and then you've got the wood at the back. I doubt anyone living here would have been daft enough to buy firewood. I'm sure you can learn. Besides, you can always ask your landscapers to chop up the shrubs they've removed for kindling."

"Lou, you're a genius!"

The doorbell rang. It was the landscapers asking her to inspect their work before they left for the day. Miraculously they had finished clearing and levelling the drive and turning area. Was she happy with the size and layout? Tomorrow they would start laying the edging ready for the limestone chippings. Once that was done, they would commence on the landscaping, fence and gates. Emily wandered up and down and had a good look from various angles. They had created a wonderful sweeping drive with a slight incline to the side of the house where there was a large flat turning area and parking for two cars with room to put a garage if she wanted. Once landscaped it would look quite majestic without detracting from the vernacular style of the cottage. Yes, she was pleased.

Once they had gone, she set about re-lighting the range. It was still a struggle, but she managed it quicker than before. Once the oven had heated up she put in a pizza and prepared some salad. She felt she couldn't go too wrong with pizza. It was fairly easy to tell if a pizza was cooked enough, and opening the door to check wasn't going to ruin it.

By the time it was ready it was dark outside, and Emily drew the curtains. She and Lou sat at the kitchen table and ladled salad and pizza on to their plates. Emily raised her glass of wine and Lou raised her glass of grapefruit squash.

"So, how are you going to occupy your time once you've settled in?"

"Well, sorting the house could take months. Once the drive is finished I plan on updating the bathroom and this kitchen and maybe getting a decent sound system wired in."

"I meant you. Are you planning on being a lady of leisure and holding coffee mornings or do you plan on getting a job?" asked Lou.

"No doubt I'll end up getting a job of some sort but first I want to enjoy all this and get to know the people in the village. Then when I have got the hang of village life I can take up 'good works' of some kind. I may even join the Women's Institute and make jam."

"Yeah, right! After you've mastered alchemy or whatever Angelica did in that front room."

There was a sudden movement and frantic clawing from the chair by the hearth as gravity rudely interrupted Kevin's nap. Hauling himself back to his original spot atop the chair back he settled down with his back to them, balanced precariously in defiance, challenging them not to laugh. It didn't work. Emily, chuckling, went over to him and stroked his ruffled fur drawing attention to his humiliation. With a disgruntled rumbling he jumped down and headed for the door.

"Emily, you should never laugh at a cat. Dignity must be maintained at all times."

"I was only going to see he was alright!"

"It's best to pretend you never even noticed. He'll come back when he thinks you've forgotten or it's food time."

CHAPTER TEN

T he landscapers were hard at work by the time Emily and Lou got up. They had talked late into the night laughing and joking and raking over old times. Grant inevitably featured in their reminiscing and Emily wondered what he was doing. She hoped that he was getting on with his life.

* * *

Grant had a plan. Grant had been shopping and his preparations were complete. On Saturday he would put his plan into action. If it worked, he would soon know where Emily was.

* * *

Emily took Lou for a walk round the village. As it was a sunny day they sat for a while on the benches by the pond and watched as a young mother handed her daughter bits of bread to throw to the ducks. Five mallards noisily fought for the soggy pieces, quacking throatily as they floated about and waddled in and out of the water. The little girl giggled and paddled amongst them, her brightly flowered Wellingtons muddying the water. Emily watched with envious eyes and Lou smugly cuddled her belly. If only Grant had wanted children!

Having done a tour of the high street they popped into the store for some milk. They waited patiently whilst the shop keeper, deep in conversation, served another customer further along at the post office counter. The two of them glanced at Emily and Lou and a whispered confirmation appeared to pass between them. Whilst Lou and Em were contemplating this, a buzzing, beeping sound came from Emily's pocket. Extricating it, she flipped it open, pressed relevant buttons and read the text. Then she snapped it shut and stuffed it back in her pocket. "Grant. Someone must have given him my new number."

"Just talk to him. I'm sure the two of you can sort this out."

"After what he did - no way - the evil money grabbing bastard!"

"Look, Em, Mike and I are both certain that Grant has absolutely no idea about the money. He really just wants you back. He's miserable without you."

The shop keeper came over and took the milk from Emily and proceeded to swipe its bar code.

"Lou, I don't want to see him. I can never

forgive him for what he did. It is over. Grant Dobson is history." She then realised that Lou wasn't looking at her but at the customer from the post office counter who had stopped and was glowering at Emily.

The customer, a short stocky woman with permed and lacquered hair was wearing a wool coat over a pink roll-neck and matching cardigan. She snapped her purse shut and rammed it into the depths of her shopping bag. Having gained Emily's attention she leant forward and hissed, "That peony were o'er 80 year old!" Without waiting for a response, she hurried away.

Emily had never met the woman before. She stared after her as she headed out the door, the bell echoing in the silence that replaced her. Emily looked at Lou. Lou looked at Emily. Then they both burst out laughing.

They paid for the milk in silence and the shopkeeper handed Emily her change whilst maintaining an air of innocent superiority.

"Well," said Lou when they got outside. "That was an experience. I'd say you have an enemy there and it looks like she's set about poisoning the rest of the village against you. What did that woman mean? What was over 80 years old?"

"I think she was talking about one of the bushes. Dave asked me what I wanted to do with it, said it would be lovely when it flowered. He replanted it further up the garden."

"Ah, so it's Dave now is it?"

"It's his name! Would you be happier if I referred to him as Mr Wallace the landscape gardener?"

"No, just thinking. You Know! Decent looking chap, own business. Diet coke moment every time the sun comes out."

"He's married."

"Or will only millionaires do now?"

"Will you stop it?"

They had now reached the church and Emily led the way up the path,
pointing out the different flowers and marvelling at the topiary. They were nearing the back of the graveyard and Angelica and Ruby's graves when Emily froze in her tracks. There with her back to them was a familiar figure, Myrtle. As she turned towards them Emily quickly pushed Louise behind a yew tree. Quickly explaining, she asked Lou to take a peek, and see which way Myrtle was going.

Lou slowly leaned out. "She's not there. She's gone!"

"She can't have. She hasn't had time!"

"I tell you, she's not there!"

Cautiously Emily peered round the thick verdant branches. Myrtle was nowhere to be seen. As Emily scanned the graveyard, warily looking for Myrtle, Kevin strolled out from behind a gravestone and Myrtle stood up from where she had been bending over stroking him.

He came trotting towards the yew tree as Emily shrank from view. Grabbing Louise by the arm she set off through the marble and granite obstacle course, keeping the yew tree between herself and Myrtle. At the church gate she crouched behind the stone wall and ran commando-like towards her own gate. Glancing back over her shoulder, in dread of Myrtle, she tripped and fell full length at Dave's steel-toed boots. When Lou arrived at a dignified stroll Dave was helping an embarrassed Emily to her feet.

"Ah! Sir Galahad," teased Lou. "No dragons to slay today? The fair Emily is safe. The mysterious Myrtle went the other way."

Safely back in the house. Emily breathed a sigh of relief. She couldn't bear the thought of Myrtle dying too. If she could just steer clear of her until the old lady died of natural causes, all would be well. Not that Angelica and Ruby had died of unnatural causes it was just that, well...it was a bit weird that they had both died after she had spoken to them. In fact, there was a lot that was a bit weird. Like, for instance, the hints that her moving into Wishing Well Cottage was part of some great plan. 'Why?' she asked herself! What reason was there in that? What was special about her? Realising that she was biting a finger nail she looked to find that she was a nail short. She must have lost it when she fell. Damn, she'd need to make an appointment. She didn't fancy driving all the way over to her old salon but didn't know of anywhere nearer.

Having got lunch under way she went in search of Lou and found her in the front room with all Angelica's books and jars etc.

"These are fascinating," enthused Lou. "Do you know that you can polish your teeth with a sage leaf? Just rub it over your teeth and gums. And, you can make sunburn oil out of lavender." Flicking a few more pages she added, "You don't have any freshly grated ginger and cinnamon bark, do you? Apparently, it's good for morning sickness."

"Perhaps you could concoct some more ointment 23 for me whilst you're here."

"Ah, I've found the list. The ointments! They are all in this book here." She showed Emily a medium sized hardback book with numbered hand-written pages. Each page was devoted to an ointment and detailed its use and preparation.

Emily glanced at the ingredients. Some of them she had never heard of. Some of them appeared to be in Latin. "I've been concocting in the kitchen if you'd like to come try my latest cure. It works."

"Oh, yeah? You found a cure for the blues?"

"No, hunger. It's beans on toast and it's going cold."

The three landscapers had done a great job and finished cementing the edging round the parking area. At three o'clock the first lorry load of chippings arrived and was tipped onto the layer of weed-suppressant membrane. It was then raked out to within a foot of the edging. They would rake to the edge tomorrow when the cement had had time to dry.

* * *

That afternoon Anna called. Emily introduced her two friends and took them into the living room at the front of the house so that they would all have somewhere to sit. It was the first time that she had used the room and whilst Lou and Anna got acquainted, she mentally redecorated. The old flowery wallpaper would have to go and the patterned curtains but mostly the red carpet with its busy pattern. It looked like a reject from a 70's pub. With plain walls the large old suite would probably look quite good in the room. The settee and two armchairs were just the right size and balanced the fireplace perfectly. If she had seen them in a shop, she wouldn't have looked at them twice. Somehow though, they were just right for the room and the house, and they were comfortable to sit in. Once she got some of her own pictures up, and fitted a new light, this room would be lovely.

"So, we met the storekeeper yesterday." said Lou. "Do you know her?"

"Yes, I know her." said Anna amused. "What you mean is, am I friends with, or related to, that evil minded back-stabbing busybody?"

"Yes, exactly. She's upsetting our friend

and it would be helpful to know why?"

"Well, it isn't Emily's fault. It's this house and its former occupant and siblings that are to blame. Rumour has it that Carla blames the triplets for her bad marriage. Derek started playing away after the birth of their son."

"What did that have to do with the triplets?" asked Emily.

"She reckons she married Derek on Myrtle's advice and then the tonic she gave him from Angelica after Donald was born (that's' their son) to, shall we say, cool his ardour, had the opposite effect. He went off with Sylvia from the hairdressers and to cap it all, the horse he bet on, after speaking to Ruby, came in at 100 to 1. Now, he and Sylvia are living in a houseboat on Windermere, happy as Larry. Of course, it's all in 'er head, but there's no tellin' her. So, she spends her time gossiping and holding seances with her cronies. Considers herself a bit of an amateur medium. She's not quite right if you ask me, which is probably the real reason why Derek left her. Now that two of her victims have died, she is probably feeling a bit bereft of a target. So, Emily dear, I'm afraid you're it."

"So," said Lou, "In a nutshell, there is a nutter, who talks to the dead, gunning for Emily."

"Well, yes!"

"I've got to call Mike. This is hilarious!" and she disappeared upstairs to find her phone.

"Emily, don't look so worried. The Wells

sisters all lived to be 100 despite Carla's curses."

"She cursed them!?"

"Only metaphorically I'm sure!"

That night Emily lay in bed, glad that Louise was in the next room. Carla filled her thoughts. Why her, Emily? She hadn't done anything wrong. Was it going to be the same whenever she went into the shop? She didn't want to have to drive all the way into town every time she wanted some milk etc. Yet she couldn't face being snubbed each time she went in the store. What was she going to do? Then with a glow of relief it came to her – on-line shopping. She would get it delivered. First though, she needed a phone line.

In the morning, the landscapers arrived with topsoil and a lorry load of plants. By lunchtime, the garden was really taking shape. The drive was now complete and once the landscapers had gone, she would be able to drive up there for the first time and be self contained in her own private little bit of Britain. To pass the time she suggested to Lou that they explore the woods at the back. So, the two of them climbed over the stile at the back of the garden and followed the dirt path amongst the tree roots as it wound into the wood. Having looked at a map of the area Emily knew that the wood ran along the side of the village and stretched up and over the top of the hill and that there were a number of rock outcrops along the ridge. Working their way uphill whenever they found a path leading that way they eventually broke out of the trees. Walking a little higher up the incline the path led them to a set of steps hewn into the rock. With Lou panting a little, they reached the top and sat to admire the view.

Beneath them at the other side of the wood were the rooftops of Greater Blessing and to their right, next to the church, the gable end of Wishing Well Cottage. Scanning the rest of the valley they could see the road as it came over the hill and Emily watched as a bus crested the rise and dropped down to stop in the bus stop behind her garden. It then continued away from the village, appearing and disappearing as it wound its way along the lane. Looking to the left of the village she could see Lesser Blessing in the distance. It was tempting to watch the sun set but even though there was no green canopy to the wood yet Emily didn't want to be trying to find her way, in twilight, with a pregnant Lou. So, they climbed down and headed back to the cottage.

Dave and his team hadn't quite finished yet, so they went inside. Emily took Louise's coat and was just hanging it up along with her own when Lou gave a shriek from the kitchen. Dropping the coats Emily flew down the hall calling for her friend.

"Lou, what's wrong? Are you okay?"

As she arrived in the kitchen Emily let

out a scream and nearly leapt into Louise's arms. There, by the fire, was Myrtle!

Emily went white and Lou helped her into a chair. Myrtle just smiled, oblivious to the effect her presence was having. "I thought I'd better come and make sure that you know about the well blessing so that you 'ave enough time to prepare."

Emily continued to stare at Myrtle who was absent-mindedly caressing the handle of the cauldron hanging on its hook over the fire.

"It takes place every year on the vernal equinox. Oh! Dear. You'd better get that fixed," she muttered, examining the wrought iron handle of the cauldron. "It's t'only thing big enough to feed t' whole village. I'd take that t't blacksmith reight away if I were you. Well, that's all I came to say. I'll let misel' out. I've done all I need to do. Don't look so worried. You'll see, all will be well in t' morning."

Emily and Louise listened to her go. When the front door closed Louise ran into the front room and peered through the window. When Myrtle disappeared out of the gate she returned to the kitchen where Emily was mumbling, "She's gonna die. She's gonna die, tonight. I just know it! Don't leave me Lou. Lou, are you listening to me?"

Lou wasn't really. Lou was staring at the cauldron. The handle, which had been curved and hooked through a hole in the side of the rim,

was now straight and no longer fully supporting the cauldron. "Do you think the woman gave
birth to Uri Geller? Just look at that Em. How
did she do that? It was fine last night. I saw it
with my own eyes." Lou sat down heavily beside
Emily.

"Shit, Em! Who are these people?"

CHAPTER
ELEVEN

E mily slept fitfully. Dreams of death and cauldrons filled her head. She felt that she was falling down a dark hole grasping a ladder as she fell. Every rung seemed to melt in her hands, and she could not pull herself up. There was something that she desperately needed to do but she didn't know what. Some enormous task! Everyone was depending on her, but she was failing. Falling and failing!

When she woke it was still dark, but the birds were singing. Dawn wasn't far off. Feeling exhausted and unnerved, vague memories of the dream going round and round in her head, she thought of Myrtle. Was she dead already? What did she want of Emily? Why had the sisters chosen her? Why Emily Hope? What had she done? What was she expected to do? Looking for solace, it soon arrived in the shape of Kevin. Her bedroom door nudged open and in he strode rumbling a cheery greeting. He leapt up onto the bed and nudging his head against her face began to purr loudly. An occasional vibrato trill accompanied the purring, lifting Emily's spirits and making her laugh in acceptance of her fate, whatever that turned out to be.

When she headed down to the kitchen Lou was already there eager to go out and find out if Myrtle had died. "You don't have to come. I could go buy a newspaper. These things get round very quickly in small places like this."

"No. I don't want to know! I really couldn't face it if she were dead."

"Well, she either is or she isn't. You knowing or not knowing isn't going to change that. If I find she isn't dead, then you will be able to stop fretting." With that she picked up her bag and headed for the door.

* * *

Grant took his little package and headed into town. He had wrapped it carefully as befitted its mission. Soon he would know where Emily was. Then he could go and find her. Then he would get her back. Then his life could get back to normal.

* * *

Emily waited impatiently. She put the kettle on then started on last night's washing up. Thirty minutes later Lou hadn't come back.

Forty-five minutes later and she still hadn't come back. What was she doing? She hadn't gone round there had she, but then she didn't know where Myrtle lived. It wouldn't take much for her to find out though. It was going to look mighty suspicious if she started asking around and then Myrtle was found dead. All Emily could do was pray. She did not want to talk to the Police again.

An hour and a half later Lou returned. She hadn't heard anything, much to her obvious disappointment. She had been into the store and bought a paper. There were no other customers and Carla had said nothing other than the price of the paper. There had been no hint though that she was keeping anything to herself. Lou couldn't help feeling that if Carla had known Myrtle was dead then there would have been some hint of smugness about her. She had then had a stroll round the village and gone for a coffee in The Little Teacups Café to see if she could overhear anything of interest. Behind her newspaper she had listened intently. A number of people had been in for breakfast but few of them appeared to be local. The only two possible locals sat separately reading their papers and saying nothing. The waitress, now sporting green hair, had been very chatty. She knew that Lou was staying at Wishing Well Cottage and asked whether Emily would be killing any more bushes. Lou was tempted to say no, just people, but decided to keep that to herself. It appeared that Emily was in enough trouble already.

"So, you didn't get your tea-leaves read then?" asked Emily.

"Damn, she reads tea-leaves? I knew I should have given up coffee for Lent!"

"Have you any idea what you would like for lunch? I figured we'd drive into town and go to the supermarket and stock up."

"How about a pub lunch? That way we can hang about here, maybe sort a few cupboards and drawers, see what other delights Angelica has hidden about the place." Emily looked doubtful. So, with both hands pressed to the small of her back Lou put on a pained expression, played the pregnancy card, and said, "I really don't fancy driving all that way Em!"

So, Louise got her wish. At lunchtime they went to stake out the pub. Lou plonked her coat on a chair at a table in the centre of the room and told Emily to sit whilst she went to the bar. Emily sat and watched nervously as Lou, back pain forgotten, chatted up the bar staff. As she sat there on her own Emily started to get paranoid. Was she imagining it or were people whispering about her? Looking round she couldn't be certain. When she caught anyone's eye, generally they smiled back. Eventually Louise brought over the drinks. "Course, if no one has actually been round there this morning it could be days before anyone finds out!"

Emily picked up her glass. "What's this?"

"Treble G 'n T. I thought you could do with a stiff drink!"

Glowering at her friend she took a large gulp. Then another! Just as she was finishing off the glass, and considering going for an orange juice, an elderly lady with silvery-blue hair and a pale yellow jumper and matching cardigan paused by their table. Raising herself to her full five foot two, she sniffed and growled at Emily, "You come 'ere, throwin' yer money abou'. No respect! Tha' peony was o'er 80 year' old. You just rip it up withou' a thought." Wrapping her cardigan around herself and hitching up her bosom she stomped out the door as the whole pub stared at Emily. Lou was on her feet in pursuit when Emily grabbed her arm.

"Please, Lou, don't. I've got to live here."

Lou stopped in her tracks and instead stared down the audience as she said, "Hopefully word will get round that the peony is alive and well and minding its own business. It now has its own detached lawn and a spectacular view of the rest of the garden as befits its elderly status." Meekly her audience returned to their drinks.

Emily took another swig, "Who'd have thought that shifting a few plants would cause such bad feeling. Do you want another drink? I know I do."

By the time they left The Three Wells pub Emily was three sheets to the wind. Louise was at first amused and then irritated as Emily decided to take her shoes off and paddle with the ducks. Not wanting her friend to make a spectacle of herself in the middle of the village green she was relieved to see Anna heading out of the store and called her over. Together they guided Emily back to the cottage and put the kettle on for some coffee.

When Lou explained about Myrtle and the cauldron and Emily being convinced that she would have died during the night, Anna said that she was due to go round there anyway and would go and find out.

By the time she returned, two hours later, Emily was somewhat morose but, having downed several cups of coffee, more sober than before. The reason that Anna had been so long, was that she had had to get a neighbour with a key to unlock the door and then she had had to call the doctor and the undertaker. Myrtle, it appeared, had died in her sleep.

Emily threw up!

CHAPTER TWELVE

E mily had another fitful night. Again, her dreams tormented her. She woke irritable and hot, unable to remember what they had been about, feeling annoyed with herself, but not knowing why. As she sat up her brain rapped its fists against the inside of her skull and her stomach grumbled, demanding something it could hurl!

At breakfast she announced to a surprised Louise that she wanted to go to church. It was right next door, and it would be a good way of getting to know the villagers, hopefully those of a more forgiving nature. She wanted Lou to go with her.

At first Lou thought that she was joking but soon realised that although Emily would not admit it, she was looking for more than acceptance by the God fearing of Greater Blessing, she needed to make sense of the bizarre occurrences that were taking over her life. She was seeking answers to something deeper, something she couldn't understand but something her subconscious knew all about.

To find out what time the service started they strolled down the path to the blue and white board outside the church. Sunday Service 11:00 it stated. They were about to turn away when a deep but gentle, slightly-sing-song voice asked, "Can I help you ladies?"

Turning, they found themselves in the company of the vicar of All Saints Church.

"We were just looking to see what time the service is," said Louise.

"Oh good. I am so pleased that you will be coming. I take it you are Emily and Louise." He smiled, "Anna, my housekeeper has been talking, I hope you don't mind. I've been meaning to come round and introduce myself. The name's James, James Meacher, and yes," as Lou started to smirk, "I'm aware that it rhymes with preacher." He laughed, "Listen, I must go, things to do, congregations to minister to and all that but if you feel the need to talk, share a pint, exorcise the odd ghost or two or three.........you know where to find me." With a grin and a wave, he set off up the church path, his gangly legs splaying his cassock in all directions. Were those track shoes he had on underneath?

"I think I'm going to enjoy this church service," mused Lou. As they headed back to the cottage, she nudged Emily, "He wasn't wearing a ring you know, and he's right next door!"

"Lou, right now I have enough going on in my life without any... complications and besides, he was just being neighbourly."

"You think!?"

At five to eleven, with the church bells cascading melodically, they headed across to the church. There was lots of nodding and smiling from the villagers as they all made their way through the porch, collected their hymn books and took their seats. Emily hadn't been to church since she was a little girl, but the atmosphere was familiar. She and Lou took a pew at the back and smiled at those sitting nearby. Lots of heads turned to look at them and an approved muttering bubbled gently around them. As the service progressed, they gained voice as they familiarised themselves with the hymn tunes, Lou letting rip in her usual uninhibited way.

The sermon dealt with new beginnings and uncertainty and having faith in oneself and the Lord. Emily and Lou listened intently; James certainly had a way with words and such kind eyes. When the blessings were reached, the congregation was asked to remember Myrtle and all the good work she had done in the village. Many a happy couple had Myrtle to thank for bringing them together in her own 'inimitable way' a phrase that produced knowing amusement from many and the odd disapproving 'sniff' from others. When the service was over the congregation spilled out into the sunshine and several people stopped to say hello to Emily and welcome her to Greater Blessing. One or two said that they were looking forward to the 'well blessing' the following weekend, which prompted Emily to seek out Anna.

Anna smiled when she saw Emily and Louise and beckoned them over. She was talking to a couple that were about Emily's age. The man was medium height with dark hair and a happy beaming face that bore a strong resemblance to Anna's, and the woman was slightly stocky with a rosy cheeked complexion and a friendly open manner. Anna introduced them.

"Emily, Louise, this is my son Jeremy and his wife Sally. Jeremy, Sally, this is Emily, she has just moved into Wishing Well Cottage, and this is her friend Louise."

"Hi, call me Jez. I hear you have had one or two surprises lately," said Jeremy grinning.

"Yes, you can say that again! Now I hear I am supposed to be hosting a 'well blessing', whatever that is!"

"You'll love it. The villagers trail round from well to well and a blessing is said at each one finishing with your well where everyone eats, drinks and has a thoroughly good time. Its great fun," enthused Jez.

"And I am supposed to cook?"

"Erm, yes. I was going to break that one to you gently," said Anna. "The usual fare is a hot pot and fresh bread and the guests provide desserts. Don't worry, I'll come round later in the week and explain all about it. You might want to go to the butcher though and order the meat – he'll know what and how much. Don't look so worried. All will be well. You'll see!"

A hot pot! Emily had never cooked a hot pot! She had no idea where to start, and fresh bread, did that mean she was expected to bake?

They chatted for a while and Anna explained that the well ceremony usually took place on the vernal equinox, March 21st. This year however, as it clashed with Good Friday, they were going to have it a day late on the Saturday which was better anyway because more people could attend. So, in 6 days time Emily would be feeding the entire village.

"Can I stay," asked Louise smiling angelically, "and bring Mike? He so loves big parties and if he knows that you have gone to all the trouble of slaving over a hot cauldron, I just know he won't want to miss it."

"Oh, you're staying alright! I'm definitely not doing this on my own. That way, if it's a disaster you'll be just as much to blame as me and have absolutely no right to gloat!"

"I'll get him to bring his camera," she said with glee.

Sally asked Emily if she would like to join her reading group. They usually met on alternate Tuesday evenings and over a bottle or two of wine discussed a book they had read. It would be a good way for Emily to get to know some other people in the village. There wasn't one this Tuesday, but she was welcome to join them the following week. Emily agreed and Sally said that she would call for her on her way there.

Back at the cottage Emily went to look at the cauldron. She was really going to have to get that fixed. She didn't even know where the blacksmith was. She didn't even know if there was one in the village. Something else she needed to ask Anna. Tomorrow she would make a determined effort to get done all those little things that she kept putting off. Things like getting a phone line installed!

After a couple of sandwiches each Emily and Louise decided to go for a walk. As they left the house via the back door and approached the well a deer raised its head with a jolt and stood transfixed, staring at them from the centre of the lawn. Emily and Lou stared back not knowing who was the more surprised. Large liquid brown eyes returned their gaze, all three beings frozen breathless in the moment. Then, within a heartbeat, the deer bolted for the wall. With one bound it disappeared into the wood and was gone, leaving the garden less perfect but more precious for its passing.

They followed it into the wood, hoping to see it again, but there was neither sight nor sound. Again, they made their way to the top of the hill and climbed onto the crag to look at the view. Together they sat on the cold limestone and watched the clouds roll by as the wind cooled them off.

"Emily you are so lucky. This village is terrific and the people so friendly. Well, most of them anyway. This would be a wonderful place to bring up children." Then seeing the look on Emily's face, "Oh, Em. I'm sorry. It'll happen for you. You'll see. We just need to find you the right man."

"I'm scared Lou. I don't know where to start. There has never been anyone else but Grant."

They sat for a while longer admiring the view and watching the birds circle the treetops. Since their last visit the woods had taken on a light green hue as new leaves started to grow and unfurl. There would soon be a heavy green canopy and the whole valley would look vastly different. At their feet tiny plants peeped from the rock crevices and insects busied themselves. Emily wondered what the plants were. Choosing the plumpest looking plant, she picked a small sprig. Hopefully, she would be able to identify it from Angelica's vast knowledge store.

"I don't think you are meant to pick wildflowers these days," muttered Lou. "What's the phrase? 'Take only photos, leave only footprints'."

"Oh! Well, I've picked it now!"

"I'm sure on this one occasion your education is justification enough, and sticking it back isn't going to undo your crime!"

"Perhaps I could take up sketching. It would be lovely sitting up here paint brush in one hand, palette in the other..."

"Feet holding down canvas as the wind whips it back and forth. What are you like! Besides, you know you can't draw. I really don't see you in a smock knocking out masterpieces, certainly not if you have to cart a load of stuff all the way up here. You know, you could just bring a wildflower book with you. And besides, I think that particular one you just picked, had it not been callously deprived of its young life, would have turned out to be a daisy!"

Emily stared at it, then tossed it into the wind.

CHAPTER
THIRTEEN

When Emily woke it was raining again. There would be no trips up the crag today. Still, she could make a start on all those tasks she had set herself and, importantly, get the cauldron mended.

By the time Louise appeared she had eaten two slices of toast and was on her second cup of tea. She had used her mobile to arrange for BT to install a phone line and much to her surprise there was Broadband in the village, so she had ordered that too. As Lou poured herself a bowl of Cornflakes Emily swung the broken cauldron out from the hearth and with great difficulty hefted it off the bar. It was heavier than she expected and very awkward to manage due to its broken handle. Going into the front room Emily found a ball of string and took it back to the kitchen. Ten minutes later, and the loss of another fingernail, she had secured the handle to the cauldron adequately enough to carry it.

When Lou had finished her two bowls of cereal, three slices of toast and a huge mug of coffee the rain had eased off slightly, but not much. Donning waterproofs and clutching umbrellas they set off for Anna's house on their quest for a blacksmith. Anna let them in and invited them to remove their coats saying that she was just about to put the kettle on. Emily said they had just had breakfast and Louise said, that would be lovely. So, removing their dripping jackets they hung them on pegs in the porch along with their umbrellas and went through to the living room. Anna's cottage was much smaller than Emily's and more deserving of the term. The living room had a small fireplace with shelves on the left of the chimney breast and cupboards on the right. A gas fire stood in pride of place in the hearth. The cottage was much cosier than Emily's and cleaner. She really must give Wishing Well Cottage a good clean.

"So, you live here on your own then," asked Lou as Anna handed her a cup of tea.

"Yes, Geoff, my husband, died a few years ago..."

"Oh, I'm sorry, I had no idea!" said Lou.

"... and I bought this...well, Jeremy had left home by then and I didn't need such a big place for just me."

"It's lovely," said Lou. "I'd love a place like this, a real country cottage."

"We came about the cauldron. Myrtle said to take it to a blacksmith. Is there one in the village?" asked Emily.

"Ah, the blacksmith!" Anna's face crinkled into a wide grin, comprehension dawning, and she laughed out loud. "She told you to take it to the blacksmith. Of course! All becomes clear."

Lou and Em looked at one another for help but got none. Anna continued to grin but refused to say anything further. Sketching a quick map of the village she marked the blacksmith's yard. It was at the end of the village on one of the lanes that ran round the back of the main street. It would be quite easy to find.

By the time they finished their coffee the sky had cleared, and the air was pleasantly fresh. Back at Wishing Well Cottage they collected the cauldron. Carrying it between them they headed out the front door. At the fork in the path, they nearly lost an arm apiece as Lou headed for the green and Emily the car. "It's not that far if we cut through," said Lou, "I am all right walking."

"There is no way that I am walking through this village clutching a cauldron! We are driving round."

* * *

Following Anna's directions Emily coasted the last few yards down the lane and came to a halt beside an entry marked by some rusty iron gates. It wasn't the most impressive entrance. Doubtfully, they peered into the yard. The only clue that they were in the right place was a pile of horse droppings at its centre. A selection of stone buildings with grimy opaque windows ran round the periphery. Paint was peeling on various doors that didn't look like they had been opened for a very long time, and might fall off their hinges if anyone tried. Tufts of grass sprouted here and there where the walls met the cobbles. Off to the right a horse's bottom could be seen sticking out of a doorway. Hefting the cauldron out of the boot they walked into the yard.

A sulky and superior looking teenager in full riding habit eyed them suspiciously as they approached the horse, the other end of which was now visible. "Albert's in there," she said looking them up and down, eyes coming to rest on the cauldron.

Inside the building, a large furnace blazed fiercely, roaring and radiating heat. Silhouetted against the glow was an awesome sight for female eyes. Emily and Lou stopped dead, the cauldron swinging between them. Briefly they tore their eyes away to glance at each other, eyebrows raised, before continuing their admiration. So, this was what Anna had been smirking about.

The blacksmith, a well-proportioned

statue of a man, removed a glowing horseshoe from the furnace. His back to the door, he was unaware of the Chippendale groupies behind him. Placing the shoe over the end of an anvil he proceeded to shape it, his glistening muscles rippling through his body-hugging vest. His strong hands, a sheen of light hairs sparkling as he gripped the hammer, deftly worked the metal as he turned it to and fro, expertly using the flat surface and the graduated end of the anvil to create the desired curvature and thickness. All the while the furnace hissed and roared, heating the air and adding to Emily's unnecessary glow. As he dunked the shoe in a bucket of water to cool it, Emily's cheeks turned crimson. Lou nudged her, a salacious grin on her face. Steam hissed out of the bucket enveloping the man in a cloud of vapour, partially shrouding him from their view as he turned. The scene was ethereal. Emily could not believe her eyes. Greek gods were not myth! There was a living breathing one here in Greater Blessing.

The steam evaporated and with it, Emily's fantasy. As he stepped towards them, Schwarzenegger biceps flexing, she saw to her major disappointment that not only did has physique match Arnie's, but also his age! The man must be in his 60's if not 70's. Emily gaped as the man spoke. "What can I do for you luv?" Lou sniggered and tried to raise the cauldron, Emily's paralysed arm weighting it down. Lou explained about needing the cauldron fixing before the end of the week and pushed Emily back to the car.

* * *

On the way back to Wishing Well Cottage they stopped off at the butchers to order meat for the well blessing. Emily didn't have a clue what type of meat or how much or even how to ask. She was too used to buying by sight. On the odd occasion she bought some mince for a chilli her decision was based on price and a visual guess as to what looked enough. So, much to her relief, Anna was right, the butcher knew exactly what and how much meat and said for them to pick it up on Friday.

* * *

Back at Wishing Well Cottage they found a parcel on the door mat, redirected from Emily's old flat. Surprised, she took it into the kitchen to study it. She peered at the post mark but couldn't read it. She didn't recognise the writing which had been printed childishly and there was no return address on the outside. She hefted it in her hand and then shook it, one ear cocked.

"Will you be detonating it any time soon or shall I put the kettle on?"

"I haven't ordered anything, and it isn't my birthday! I can't think what it can be."

"Well one sure fire way to find out is to open it. It's a parcel not a Masonic puzzle."

"I know but…"

"Just open the damn thing, preferably outside, just in case", and, pointing at her abdomen, "Your god-son incubating here."

"I don't like mysteries."

"Yes, you do. You want to solve the mystery of what is in there before you open it. Admit it."

"God-son! You mean I am going to be god-mother? Really? Oh, Lou. Thank you."

"Don't take it personally. Any millionaire will do. You just happen to be handy. Get it open."

After giving Lou a quick teary hug, she turned her attention back to the parcel and reluctantly started to open it. After much popping of bubble wrap a cardboard box and a note fell out. The box contained a mobile phone. The note was from Grant! 'I miss you so. Please, please call me.'

Emily was about to call and tell him what she thought of him when Lou grabbed her arm, "Don't. Don't you see what he's done? The phone is switched on. He has used it to find you. He has used your mail redirect to find you. If he wants, he can track the phone. He's bought it. It's his phone. He can legally track it. We've got to get rid of it, keep it moving, get it away from here!"

"How, how, how?" stammered Emily.

A quick bout of blue-sky panicking and Lou said, "I know, the bus stop. We can put it on the bus. No, we'd need to get on board to leave it there."

"We could get on, ask where it is going to, drop it into the used ticket bin, and get off again."

"Good plan. When's it due?"

"I think the next one is about 3 o'clock".

"Bad plan. That's no good. We need to get rid of it now. We could drive it somewhere…"

"Yes, come on. We can think as we drive," said Emily grabbing her car keys.

They climbed into the car and Emily turned the ignition. Nothing happened. She tried again, still nothing. She really must get a new car. She was a millionaire why was she still driving this unreliable heap of garbage! Staring through the windscreen in frustration, her eyes locked on the only moving thing on the village green. Slowly working its way round towards the cottage, along with several men in green outfits, was a dustbin lorry. Emily and Lou looked at each other, then leapt out of the car. Emily grabbed the wheelie bin, threw the phone in, and started dragging it down the drive, newly laid chippings scrunching noisily. The phone bounced and thudded as it rattled about in the bottom of the bin.

"You need to put some rubbish in there. They aren't going to empty an empty bin. They can't help but notice the phone. Quick, go inside and empty the bins."

Emily ran into the house fumbling with her keys in the lock. In the kitchen she flipped up the pedal bin lid and yanked at the plastic liner ripping it. Cursing she picked up the whole bin and ran out of the house. Lou lifted the wheelie bin lid and Emily tipped the rubbish in burying the phone. Parking the bin at the bottom of the drive she smiled nonchalantly as the first bin man strolled up, trying desperately to slow her heavy breathing.

"Morning ladies."

"Morning."

"Morning."

Emily and Louise held their breath as the bin man wheeled the bin to the back of the lorry, hooked it in place and pushed a button. The bin was lifted into the air then tipped up depositing its contents into the back of the lorry. He brought the bin back and parked it in front of Emily giving her a wink, "You two really need to get out more. You know, I am sure the recycling plant does tours if you are that interested. I could make enquiries and get back to you. No? Shame!" and he gave them another wink and grinned as he walked away.

As the lorry moved on, they headed back to the house but looked back anxiously as, just past the church the lorry stopped and operated its crusher, compacting its contents.

"If the phone is crushed and stops working there is nothing we can do about it, but if not, then it will look like it has gone all round the village, slowly, like the postman would have done, before moving on. So, Grant won't be able to pin-point where you live," said Lou satisfied. "Right. Kettle on."

CHAPTER
FOURTEEN

C arla drew back her bedroom curtains and peered across the green. The early morning sunlight was just starting to filter through the tops of the trees. It glinted off the weather-vane at the top of the church adding sparkle to the morning. She glanced left and right, taking in the scene. She always liked this time of day, before the village was awake, when everything looked fresh. Just then, something flashed in the nearest tree, something green and piercing. Two eyes, just visible amongst the newly sprouting foliage, in an otherwise camouflaged body, stared back. As Carla froze, their eyes locked, and a shiver slithered its way up her spine. Kevin was watching her. She wrapped her cardigan tightly round herself and stepped away from the light, back into the gloom of the bedroom. He knew!

That damn cat knew!

* * *

It was a glorious day. Sunlight streamed through the windows of Wishing Well Cottage. A myriad of dust particles danced merrily in its rays, which also highlighted the dirt round the leaded glass bringing the garden into soft focus, which unfortunately wasn't the effect she wanted. Emily's 'To Do before Saturday' list was growing. She had a million and one things to do and the more she did, the more she found she needed to do.

The most pressing thing on her mind was the hotpot. The whole village was depending on her to feed them and would judge her for ever-more as a result. For her to mess up Greater Blessing's annual ceremony was unthinkable. If she wasn't going to be an outcast it needed to be perfect. She needed Anna's help. Once BT had been and installed her phone line she would go and see Anna.

The engineer arrived about 11am and by 1pm the cables had been installed and she had a phone. It would be the next day before her broadband would be up and running.

* * *

After knocking on Anna's door and arranging a time for Anna to go round and instruct her in the delicate art of hotpot making Emily walked over to the store for some milk. Carla was unusually gracious, obsequious in fact.

"You'll be needing some vegetables for the hotpot. I've put some aside for you. You can collect them whenever you like. The Wells woman grew her own, but I don't suppose you're into all that."

"Thank you," said Emily, "but I'll be ordering them online."

There was a sharp intake of breath and Carla's face turned puce. Trying to hide her discomfort she took Emily's money and dropped it into the till, shutting its drawer louder than she intended. Emily walked out the door to the impatient tapping of bright red fingernails.

* * *

Back at Wishing Well Cottage Emily decided that they really needed to do some cleaning and check out what crockery and cutlery she had for Saturday. They cleared the kitchen table and stacked on it all the plates they could find in the cupboards, including those from the herb room. Altogether there were 53. Next, they collected all the cups and glasses and then the knives and forks. "I'd better get some paper plates and plastic cutlery, napkins etc." said Emily.

When Anna arrived, the kitchen looked like a junk shop. "Is that for Saturday? Sorry, didn't I tell you? The pub provides all that. They will bring it over in boxes that morning. You just need to provide hotpot and bread."

Over a cup of tea, she explained how much and

of which vegetables, what herbs and what seasoning to use. If Lou and Emily would peel the vegetables, light a fire in the hearth, fill the cauldron half full of water and heat it to get the water simmering and the stove hot she would be over about 9am to show them the rest. Together they would make the bread dough on Friday, so it was ready to stick in the oven Saturday morning. They must draw the water from the well for both the hotpot and the bread. All Emily needed to do was get the ingredients Anna listed, before Friday afternoon. Oh, and dress the well.

"What," said Emily, "How do I do that?",

"I don't know. Angelica always did it. I just remember it always looked nice. I didn't really take much notice. It was all symbolic though. The tradition goes back hundreds of years. Lots of fertility stuff, new birth, green shoots, all that kind of thing."

"Well, who might know?" asked Lou.

"I don't know. There isn't anyone left. I suppose Al might," smirked Anna, then seeing their puzzled looks, "the blacksmith." She looked at Emily suggestively, then at Louise and was surprised and disappointed that they patently did not share her view of him. "The blacksmith? The Wells sister's great nephew! You don't know! They had a brother, Eli, but he died years ago. His grandson is the blacksmith and a fine specimen of a man too. Anyway, fantasies aside, he might be able to help, but he never really got involved, so I doubt it." Then, after a bit more thought, "Actually James, the vicar, might know. He does the blessing. I'll ask him."

* * *

Kevin sat, paws curled under him, on the warm slate tiles at the back of the store. He was nicely comfortable. The sun was heating his back and the outhouse chimney was sheltering him from the breeze. Best of all, from here he had an excellent view through the skylight into Carla's storeroom. At this time of day, now the weather was warmer, the skylight would usually get opened unless of course it was raining, which it wasn't. Kevin only had to wait. Kevin was comfortable and content. Anticipation could be so satisfying.

* * *

Emily got a bucket of water and a sponge and went out to clean the windows. She took one look at the sticky net of cobwebs and went back in to find a brush. She then set about sweeping away the winter's accumulation before washing off the grime with the sponge. She had no idea how she was going to do the upstairs windows. She didn't remember seeing a ladder anywhere. Still, she could at least do the inside. That would improve things a bit. As she struggled to get rid of the streaks on all the individual leaded lights she got more and more fed up. She didn't fancy doing this again. Lou would tell her to get a window cleaner. After all, she could afford it. She went back in to change the water.

At first, she couldn't find Lou, but then she heard laughter coming from the front room and went to investigate. Lou and James Meacher were pointing and laughing at the photos on the wall over the sideboard. "That's the year the fox brought the hunt through the garden. We heard them before we saw them and we barely saw the fox it was so quick, but then we had 15 hounds piling over the wall, yapping and barking and scattering people and chairs all over the place. I think we got one horse too before the hunt was brought to a halt. Then there was an horrific squealing of brakes and scrunching of metal from the road at the back as two cars just missed the hounds but ploughed into each other. No-one was hurt fortunately, and the fox got away too, but there was quite a stink about it at the time. The papers had a field day as you can imagine."

"James has come to advise us on the well-dressing. Apparently, he is a bit of an authority on the matter," said Lou.

"Oh, I wouldn't go that far, just interested in local history, old traditions, that kind of thing."

"We've found a photo of the well. See, that's what it should look like dressed."

Emily looked. The well was garlanded in what appeared to be several layers of fresh and dried plants. It all looked very pretty and also quite intricate. She doubted that just any old plants would do. As Anna had said, it probably all had some symbolism attached. So, no pitfalls there then for a naïve outsider who had already annoyed half the village by simply moving a peony bush. It looked like she would need to do some in-depth research to identify the plants and the nuances of their usage.

"James, I don't suppose your interest in local traditions extends to poring over ancient texts on plant usage does it? I think I am going to need all the help I can get with this well-dressing."

"What, an excuse to ferret through all those tomes and mysterious jars in the other room and find out what Angelica and her sisters were really about all these years, you bet. When can I start?"

"So, this herbalism, with all its lotions and potions, doesn't go against your religious principles?" asked Lou.

"No, most of modern medicine is derived from herbs. So long as what they were doing did no harm and their intentions were good, I have no problem with it. When I first came to this parish, there were rumours about the sisters, hints that what they were doing was 'unnatural', that they were a coven of witches casting spells etc., but having got to know them, and I confess I was a bit wary at first, I can confidently say they didn't have a malicious intent between them, unlike some in the village! I admit that odd things did seem to happen: things that appeared to be more planned than coincidence would seem to allow. However, if they were deliberately controlling events it is beyond my understanding. All three turned up for church regularly, which is more than I can say for most of my parishioners. I got lectured once when I intimated that manipulating events with the use of herbs etc was not part of the Christian teaching. I was told that God made everything on earth and in Heaven. It wasn't for us mortals to question how it all worked. 'You should know better than that vicar,'" he said wagging his finger, in a passable impersonation of Angelica that made Emily laugh out loud.

"That was brilliant. Lou, it's a shame you never met Angelica so you could appreciate how good that was. Do you do other impersonations?"

"Actually, I can do most of my parishioners, but I don't advertise the fact. It wouldn't go down well in some quarters. I wouldn't want to be known as The Irreverent Reverend."

"I'll bet you have a real job delivering a solemn sermon to all those po-faced parishioners," grinned Lou. "You'd make a great stand-up."

"As a matter of fact, and I don't tell many people this, I do have a routine I'm working on. I perform on the Comedy Caravan circuit. We tour various clubs around Manchester." James blushed slightly and then said, "Would you ladies like to come some time?"

"Try and stop us." Said Lou, and Emily nodded.

Together the three of them went into the herb room and started hunting through Angelica's mountain of books and notes, frequently studying the photograph to identify the plants. Gradually they built up a list and found dried versions of the herbs hanging from the ceiling or stored in jars. Occasionally one of them would read out a fascinating bit of folk lore or ancient myth. All sorts of fascinating facts were unearthed, such as Zeus's cup-bearer, Ganymede, being given Tansy to make him immortal, Rosemary being revered for sheltering the Virgin Mary on her flight to Egypt, maidens putting Borage into the cups of their favoured knights to give them courage when going into battle.

By the end of the afternoon, they had assembled a good selection of herbs and made a list of those they hoped to find in the garden to add some fresh greenery. The party was broken up abruptly when James remembered that he still had a eulogy to write for Myrtle's funeral the following day. As he left, Kevin strolled through the door and headed down the hall to the kitchen where Emily found him sitting by his bowl, smugly awaiting his reward.

CHAPTER
FIFTEEN

Emily came down to streaky windows, streaky on the outside but still mucky on the inside. Just great! There was no way she was going to get them all done by the weekend. She rifled through the recycling and found various 'flyers' that had come through the door. A couple of phone calls later, and the promise of a hefty tip for re-arranging his schedule, and a window cleaner was on his way. Problem sorted. Money may not be able to buy happiness, but it could get you clean windows; inside as well as out it seemed.

Her broadband was now working so she placed her shopping order. Things were under control. The garlands for the well were taking shape and, with Anna, Lou and James' help, everything should be okay. She was starting to relax. If no other members of the Well's family materialised at the funeral she felt, for the first time, that she could settle contentedly into her new life here in Greater Blessing.

* * *

It was another fine, fresh day with barely a cloud in the sky and only a light breeze to sway the very tops of the trees, just perfect for Myrtle's funeral. Emily and Louise were dressed smartly as befitted the occasion, Emily in a black skirt and jacket with a cream blouse and Louise in a dark blue dress with lace trim, the nearest she could get to black in maternity wear, and a camel-coloured coat. Sitting at the back of the church they had a good view of the congregation.

Gerald was sitting on the far side leaning heavily against one of the stone columns and peering up into the rafters. Emily pointed him out, "You remember me telling you about Gerald, the estate agent, well that's him over there."

"Probably checking for woodworm before he values the place," whispered Lou.

"And there, right down at the front is the absolutely gorgeous undertaker I was telling you about."

"Mm, from what bit I can see of him through the sea of low-lighted perms and black lace and feather fascinators, not bad. Not bad at all young Em. I was getting seriously worried you'd lost your lust! Thought I was going to have to hide myself away in your front room and mix you up a lurv potion, sneaking out at night to pick some winter savory, grinding it up in the old pestle and mortar with some caraway and coriander, or does it need steeping? Anyway, a bit of trial and error and 'hey pesto' as a herbalist might say."

"Sssssh!" whispered Emily, as James began the service.

It was the end of an era. Myrtle was the last of the well-loved Wells sisters. It was incredible that the three of them had all lived to be 100 years old. It was remarkable that all three had been christened, married and had their funeral services here in All Saints Church. Each sister had served the church in her own special way. Myrtle was no exception. She was known as a bit of a matchmaker and there were many happy couples who had Myrtle to thank for bringing them together. Indeed, the plant myrtle is said to represent Venus and Love and is often incorporated in bridal wreaths. A fact he had found out only the other day. He went on to tell how Myrtle was always willing to lend a sympathetic ear to other people and was never shy of offering practical help, taking in evacuees during the war, and turning the village hall into accommodation for people bombed out of their homes in Manchester and Liverpool. In the 50s and 60s she set up several charities offering marriage guidance as well as refuge shelters for abused women and children and was amongst the first to recognise and offer a refuge to men. Her own marriage to Arthur was as solid as a rock. The pair were said to be inseparable. He died a few years ago leaving Myrtle to carry on without him. Now they could be together again.

* * *

As the coffin was carried down the aisle, on its way out of the church, Emily's knees felt like jelly and her insides leapt with joy and other feelings not seemly in a church. Her undertaker was, as the lead pall bearer, nearest to her and Louise, and getting closer with every step. Lou grabbed her hand and squeezed it in enthusiastic approval. Yes, he did look like a rugby player in a suit and with the solemn and intelligent countenance of a Nobel Prize winner. Wow! The only down-side as far as Lou could see was that he handled dead bodies for a living.

Slowly they shuffled their way out of the church with the rest of the mourners and got as near to the grave as the large crowd would allow. They hung their heads as James said a final prayer and Myrtle's body was lowered into the grave. People then filed past, scooped up a handful of earth and dropped it onto the coffin. Emily tried to make out who, if any, were relatives. She knew that none of the Wells sisters had had any children. In the church she had spotted Albert, the blacksmith, and again briefly outside, but he was no-where to be seen now.

The crowd was beginning to disperse. Emily and Lou were just thinking about going when they spotted six black top hats moving through the crowd towards them. Emily's heart skipped several beats and almost stopped completely when 'her' undertaker gave her a sly wink as he passed. She couldn't believe it. Had she imagined it?

"Oooh, Em. He likes you. I'll have a chat with James. Find out if there are any likely demises amongst his sick parishioners. Find out when the next funeral is likely to be. We must keep this flame alive!"

* * *

Back at the cottage they had a wander round the garden. Carrying their reference material, they set about identifying likely plants to add to their garlands for the well-dressing. Lou almost jumped for joy when she spotted some borage, actually in flower, which is chiefly why she was able to identify it, and proudly pointed it out to Emily. "Apparently we can put the flowers in drinks, and I'll bet if we put them in ice-cubes they would look terrific."

Next, they found what they believed to be Lemon Balm. It was supposed to have tiny pale-yellow flowers in summer, but that was no help in March. However, as they weren't feeding it to anyone, they didn't think it was too heinous a crime if they were wrong.

They were just off-loading armfuls of

greenery onto the table in the herb room when there was a screeching and banging at the front door. Together they hurried into the hall. Emily yanked the door open before the glass was put through. The barrage stopped but the screeching doubled in volume as a furious Carla pushed her way in and headed for the kitchen.

"Where's that bloody cat. I'll wring its scrawny neck. The evil little bastard's trying to put me out of business. Don't think I don't know what it's been up to, that scheming little monster." Stopping dead in the kitchen, with Kevin no-where to be seen, she turned on Emily, "So, my veg isn't good enough for Miss Millionairess. No, she has to have it delivered. Buying on-line indeed! She can't possibly lower herself to carry her shopping home."

Lou had been gathering herself for a fight and this was a fight worth having. An angry Carla, just ripe for goading, couldn't be resisted. "Please, have a seat; I can see you are upset. Do tell us all about it, "she said soothingly.

The wind removed from her sails; Carla sat. Emily sat too, determined to enjoy the show.

"Would you like a cup of tea?" asked Lou pleasantly.

"Well, I... No!"

"Okay then. What has our little hero been up to?" prodded Lou.

Hackles rising again, Carla spat, "You know what!"

"Know, how could we know? He is a cat. He doesn't confide in us," purred Lou as she held her hand, palm upwards, and extended one finger, claw like, and inspected it before scratching behind her ear.

"Mice," screeched Carla, "That's what. He's been dropping mice through my store-room sky light. Mice droppings everywhere, just when the health inspector called! If that gets round the village, I'll be ruined. Fortunately, everything was covered, but I've had a warning and a re-inspection's booked, but I could be closed down and all because of that bleedin' cat."

Lou looked shocked, "Well, we are terribly sorry. Yes, it would be dreadful for you if that got round the village. Simply dreadful, wouldn't it Em? A careless word here or there... gossip probably spreads like wildfire in a small village like this." She leaned forward conspiratorially, "I hear that the twin-set and pearls brigade have a record-breaking communication network. I'll bet you can get a rumour the length and breadth of this village in under 30 minutes, even with tea and scones. However," and she put her hand on Carla's knee, "you have our word, doesn't she Em, that Kevin, at least, won't say a word."

Carla spluttered and, incoherent, she stormed out of the house, slamming the front door. In the silence that followed there was a "Perrrrup!" and Kevin unfurled and sat up. Shaking the dust off himself he peered over the top of the Welsh dresser, stretched and then jumped down, via a chair back, to the floor. He rubbed round Lou's ankles and then went and sat on Emily's lap. As she stroked his back he purred loudly, and his satisfaction spread to envelope them all. "Oh, Kevin, did you really? I guess we'll never know but we sure want to believe it."

CHAPTER SIXTEEN

A t 10am her Tesco delivery arrived. She put it all away in the kitchen and then turned her attention to the garden. She was going to have nearly all the village traipsing round to the back of the house. She needed to ensure that it was accessible, and that people would not be trampling on areas she cared about. She also wanted them to see that the peony bush was alive and healthy; it was just starting to sprout new shoots and although she told herself that their opinion didn't matter, deep down she cared what they thought. She had a stroll round the garden following the route her guests would take. They would come through the front gate, up the drive and round to the right of the house. She moved the bins to one side and parked them neatly next to the outhouse. Several edging stones were lying out of place on the path. She manoeuvred them back into position with her feet. Working her way round the house she tidied as she went, ripping out over-grown foliage and pushing other bits out of the way or tucking it into the lattice work on the end wall. She gathered up some fallen branches and threw them on the compost heap, then thought better of it and dragged them to the wood store by the back door for firewood.

Next, she had a look at the well. She folded back the wooden cover and lifted it off revealing the bucket hanging beneath the rim. Yuk. It needed a scrub! After a sustained effort she managed to untie it.

When Lou appeared, she found Em hard at work in the kitchen scrubbing out the bucket. She took one look at it. "You aren't going to use that are you? It looks like it is lined with lead!"

"Oh!" said Emily. "Is that bad?"

"No, its perfect, if you want to give everyone lead poisoning. Although I doubt the amount of contamination from one annual exposure is going to kill anyone. Still, I'd use a plastic bucket if I were you."

As the day progressed the house and grounds were slowly tidied up and the possibly public areas cleaned. The outhouse washroom and toilet were made respectable with a good stock of toilet paper and a stack of clean towels, a can of air freshener and a dispenser of soap.

The floor was cleaned, the hedgehogs having moved out for the summer, and a small prettily coloured mat put down. Emily planned to add a small vase of flowers on the Saturday morning. Slowly she was beginning to like the idea of hosting the village.

The window cleaner had done a good job and the whole house seemed brighter. She and Lou had worked hard, and every room felt welcoming, as if the whole building approved of her presence. Emily wandered from room to room. For the first time, she actually felt at home and was quietly amazed at how much her life had changed in such a short time. Looking back on how reliant she had been on Grant she could not believe how different she was and how much more confident she felt. Here she was, Emily Hope, about to cater for an entire village, in the grounds of her own home and yes, she was actually looking forward to it. Of course, she had help, quite a lot actually, but whereas the old Emily would have voiced a string of concerns the new Emily was equally convinced that 'all would be well'. Is that really how she felt or was she just lapsing into the vernacular of Greater Blessing? That phrase seemed to have seeped into her soul. Absent-mindedly her fingers sought out the chain around her neck and traced it to extract the warm periapt from where it nestled against her skin.

Lou was excited. Mike had sent her a text

to say that he would be arriving straight from work instead of the following morning. Emily was delighted; another pair of hands would not go amiss. There was still plenty to do. Perhaps Mike would get the deckchairs out of the outbuilding. She had found them under a tarpaulin and the couple that she had inspected seemed to be sound. They just needed dusting and airing. If the weather remained fine then they could be put out early, a quick dust and the breeze would do the rest. There were also half a dozen trestle tables and some chequered oilskin tablecloths that would be ideal. Probably they were always used for the well blessing catering.

Anna had said that the pub provided the crockery and cutlery, but she thought she would go over when it opened and check in case there was anything else she was expected to do that she hadn't thought about. Also, it would be a good way to introduce herself to the publican. She realised that she had no idea whether the people she had seen serving behind the bar were the owners or just staff. Remembering her last visit to The Three Wells pub she also desperately wanted to replace the probably bad impression she had made of herself with the normal, sensible, articulate, essentially sober version. In fact, a pub lunch would be a well-deserved break. The pair of them had been working hard all morning. Not having to sort out lunch would be great.

* * *

Grant met up with his mate, Jonathan, for lunch. Jonathan had an A4 sized brown envelope for him. Whilst waiting for their food they removed a large piece of paper from the envelope and unfolded it, spreading it flat on the table. Printed on the paper was a map. At its centre were the two villages of Greater and Little Blessing. Superimposed on the map was a wiggly black line snaking back and forth with time stamps at various locations. Tracing the line and studying the time intervals it appeared that the phone had been driven to Little Blessing where it had sat in two locations for approximately 30 minutes. It had then been driven to Greater Blessing where it had travelled slowly round the village, stopping momentarily at various locations. It had then travelled rapidly for 7miles before becoming stationary at what the map proclaimed to be a Waste Disposal Site. The men were impressed. Clever! Had the villages been larger, then Emily's ploy may have worked. Grant still didn't know where Emily was, but now he had a much smaller search area. A bit more detective work and it was just a matter of time.

* * *

As Emily and Lou approached the pub Emily spotted Carla hiding behind a rack of postcards outside the store and decided to try and make amends. She told Lou to go find them a table in the pub and walked up to Carla.

"Carla, I'm sorry about yesterday, and I am sorry about the mice. Are you sure it was Kevin? Did you actually see him dropping mice through your sky light?"

"Well, no, but it must 'ave been 'im. Who else would have done that? He and Angelica, all the Wells lot, they all 'ad it in for me. He 'ates me that cat."

"Carla, you're talking about him as if he is a human being. He's a cat. They don't 'ave it in for people'."

"Don't you believe it! He knew that inspector was coming. 'Ee did it deliberately."

"But isn't it possible that the mice found their own way in? They seem to be able to get through the smallest holes. What makes you so sure it was the sky light?"

"Because the dead one beneath the sky light didn't climb onto the work top on its own."

"Well, it could have died of natural causes or, if it had come through the sky light, got injured when it jumped down and then died," suggested Emily.

"It don't take Miss Marple to figure out that no fall from a skylight is going to inflict puncture wounds. That mouse had teeth marks and its fur was all wet. It was that damn cat and you know it!"

"Well, if he did do it deliberately, I'm sorry, but it is nothing to do with me."

"Oh yes it is," snarled Carla stepping forward and jabbing her index finger in Emily's face so that she stepped back defensively, "You've been chosen. It has everything to do with you!" At that she turned on her stumpy heels and marched back inside the store setting the post card rack spinning in her wake.

Stunned and unsettled Emily went to find Lou. She had tried, but Carla obviously wasn't going to let her be friends, and what on earth did she mean? Inside The Three Wells Emily spotted Louise, the only customer, perched awkwardly on a stool trying to reach the bar over the top of her expanding abdomen. She was deep in conversation with the man behind the bar. He was tall with dark curly hair and a weather-beaten complexion, warm eyes and a ready smile, which he turned on Emily as Lou beckoned her over.

"This is Richard, the owner of The Three Wells. Richard this is Emily, my very good friend, and the new owner of Wishing Well Cottage and the host to be, of Greater Blessings' Well Blessing, and I am so glad I was sober for that. Richard here is going to come over on Saturday morning with a whole load of crockery etc and I have offered him Mike's help with that. We just need to set up the tables ready. He will draw us a plan of the usual layout. So, tell us what usually happens."

"Well, the parade starts about 11.30 at

Fare Well, that's Myrtle's cottage, and the first part of the ceremony takes place there. Everyone takes a drink from the well and then stuff is thrown down it and a blessing said. I am not sure what they throw down, presumably herbs and the like. Obviously, nothing that is going to contaminate the well water. Then the vicar leads the parade round to Ruby's place, Bode Well, carrying a floral wreath. More prayers, more drinking of the water and more throwing down some herbs and blessing it for another year. Finally, they all troop round to Wishing Well for about 12.30 where the final ceremony takes place and then we all get to eat, drink and make merry."

"Drink! Am I supposed to provide that too?"

"No. I provide that. I'll bring over a barrel or two. They all get one drink each with their hotpot and bread. They all then tend to spread out onto the green in front of the pub having paid their respects to the last well and continue their drinking at their own expense and my profit. It's a busy old afternoon for me, and evening. It'll probably be a bit noisy. You'll see."

"The bucket for the well, does it matter if I don't use it to pull up the water? It was disgusting. I have cleaned it, but it looks like it is lined with lead..." said Emily.

"Yes, I can see why you'd think that, but I do believe it is pewter."

"Really?"

"Yes. I don't think the Wells sisters had their lives cut short by being slowly poisoned."

"Phew, that's a relief. So, the bucket is okay to use?"

"Yes. Besides, yours is one of three and the buckets, to my recollection, all look the same."

* * *

After lunch they continued with the housework, wanting it to look its best, not just for the Well Blessing but also for Mike's arrival. This would be the first time he had seen the cottage and having told him so much about it they wanted it to be perfect. As the afternoon wore on the light began to fade so Emily went to put the outside light on and make sure she had left enough room for Mike to park his car. She switched the porch light on and was about to open the door when she realised that there was a figure on the doorstep. Was Mike here already?

"Lou, he's here," she yelled over her shoulder.

She yanked the door open to greet him and was shocked to find herself staring into the face of the undertaker. Several emotions coursed through Emily's confused body. Her mind could not handle all the input and several questions presented themselves all at once. Every other time she had seen him he had been dressed from head to toe in black, apart from a white shirt of course. His grave expression had been solemn and his countenance one of reverence and concern. Now he was beaming and wearing a chunky V-neck with the sleeves rolled up, jeans and a pair of expensive looking tan shoes, but, most incongruous of all, carrying a cauldron. Her cauldron! Emily's tongue refused to work.

"Hi, he said. I'm Alex. I thought you'd probably want this for Saturday and tomorrow being Good Friday, well, I'm not open."

Emily continued to stare, getting more and more flustered by the second. Thankfully, Lou appeared at her side and invited him in. After an initial amount of confusion, it turned out that he wasn't, in fact, an undertaker. Being the only male relative left, of the Wells family, he was the chief pallbearer. His grandfather was the Wells' sisters' brother. He was their great nephew. The reason he had Emily's cauldron was because he was the village blacksmith, or rather farrier. He made horse-shoes and in particular racing plates, which was why old Albert was standing-in when they turned up with the cauldron. Albert was retired but liked to keep his hand in which was good because Alex was away quite a lot. He had just been out to Dubai fitting racing plates to some very expensive horses.

"So, those strong hands don't spend their days manhandling dead bodies, then?" asked Lou much to Emily's horror.

"Err, no!"

"Lou, the doorbell is ringing," said Emily pointedly, "I think your *husband* just arrived."

"Okay, I'll leave you two to get... *acquainted*," and with that suggestion embarrassing both of them she left the room, humming what sounded like 'Love is a many splendoured thing!'

"She's quite a character your friend," ventured Alex after what seemed like hours to Emily's screaming brain which was repeating 'say something, say something, say something' over and over and blotting out all constructive thought!

"Yes, I'm sorry," managed Emily.

"Oh, don't be.

A noise from the hall and Lou burst in dragging Mike. Introductions followed and the tension eased. Alex explained that, apart from returning the cauldron, he had come for help with the dressing of the other two wells as it had now fallen to him. He had never done it before as the sisters had previously each done their own. Emily and Lou agreed to help as best they could. As the afternoon lapsed into evening the four of them fell into easy conversation, although Emily contributed little. Just when she was thinking that maybe she should invite him to tea, but wondered if that would seem too pushy as they had only just met, or that she was thinking it was time for theirs and was wanting him to go, Alex announced that it was time he left; he hadn't realised it had got so late. Relieved to have the decision taken away from her she then made a stupid show of acting surprised that it was so late, despite having got up 30 minutes before to draw the curtains and put the lights on.

"I'll just pop this back for you before I leave. It's a bit heavy," said Alex as, with one tanned hand, he deftly lifted the cauldron back onto the bar over the fire, the glow from which defined every muscle, vein and hair of his strong wrist and forearm. Emily took in every detail.

Having let Alex out the front door she returned to the kitchen.

"Does our Emily have a crush?" teased Mike.

"She sure does, and big time!" said Lou with glee.

"Oh, was I that obvious? That was awful. I feel like I'm 14 years old not 28. I don't believe this. What must he think!"

"I'm sure he thought you were perfectly delightful," said Mike grinning. "Now, when are you seeing him again? It's important Lou and I know how much time we've got. If we are going to teach you how to talk then we'll need to work out a training schedule. Don't look like that. Talking is important. Prospective husbands like that. Most household tasks don't need it, but it can be vital for shopping, making sure you understand what food he likes, not being conned when you get the car serviced etc."

"Don't you two gang up on me I feel bad enough as it is. He must think I'm a right idiot."

CHAPTER SEVENTEEN

Emily woke early. Restless, she got up and decided to go for a walk, partly in a futile effort to get away from herself. Thinking back on the previous evening she could not honestly say that she had said or done anything *that* embarrassing but she cringed every time she remembered how awkward she had felt and how disappointed she was with her performance. Lou hadn't helped. She gave Kevin his breakfast and, leaving a note on the kitchen table to say where she had gone, pulled on a thick coat and a pair of trainers and let herself out the back door.

She climbed over the stile and set off up the path through the woods. The trees were really bursting with new leaves now and the rising sun was having difficulty penetrating the thickening canopy. In a week or two it would be really quite dark in here even once the sun was overhead. The winter carpet of wet leaves and pine needles was drying out and the path felt quite springy underfoot. The odd twig snapped as she stepped on it and she had to watch where she put her feet, stepping over tree roots that snaked across the path. In the tops of the trees, birds were calling out to one another announcing her progress through the wood. As she climbed higher the sun climbed with her and by the time she emerged from the trees it was fully daylight and she had a magnificent view of the valley with the higgledy piggledy rooftops of Greater Blessing disappearing beneath a veil of green. Soon the village would be hidden for the summer with only the church visible from the hilltop.

As she sat in silent contemplation mulling over the events of the previous evening, she realised that if Alex had found her *that* awful he needn't have stayed as long as he had. He could have just left the cauldron and gone, but he hadn't. Admittedly he had wanted help with the well blessing, but it hadn't taken all evening to ask about that and she hadn't blown it completely, they were going to see each other again. There was time to make amends. There was also time to compound her stupidity; lots of it. No. Stop it. This time she would be ready. It had come as a total shock finding him on her doorstep. This time he would see the real Emily, the mature, vivacious, attractive, confident Emily. Having gained a little perspective, she felt better. Yes, she actually felt she could face him again.

Leaving the crag, .and believing herself to be the only person out and about at this time of day, she was surprised to see a gangly figure jogging uphill towards her. The figure, it seemed, was as surprised as she because he visibly jumped when he saw her, misplaced his footing and nearly went full length before regaining his stride. He stopped running and strode the remainder of the way to where she was standing. Minus cassock, and this time sporting shorts with 'hi-viz' fluorescent side panels, an old T-shirt with 'Believe in Change – Pennies for Heaven Appeal' and a pair of trainers, was James the vicar.

"You gave me quite a start there. I don't normally see anyone at this time of day," he gasped.

"You surprised me too. Do you often go running up here?"

"Yes. I'm in training for the Three Peaks later in the year." Bending over, he rested his hands on his knees and in between breaths said, "I don't suppose...you'd care to sponsor me, would you? ...I'm raising money for the local YDU, St. Peter's. Sorry, Young Disabled Unit. It's a 20 bedded unit for young adults who need physical care, either temporarily until their own homes are suitably equipped, or, if necessary, long term."

"Yes, certainly. Bring your form round sometime."

"Actually, I was hoping to use the well blessing to gather sponsorship... I'll wait until after the ceremonies, obviously...I just wanted to make sure you didn't mind me... 'touting for business' so to speak, on your land."

"No, no. You might as well get as many people as possible."

"Right, thanks. I must get going... keep moving... this breeze quickly chills you when you stop... I can't afford any injuries. See you tomorrow." With that he headed off along the ridge gradually dropping out of sight.

* * *

Back at the cottage she was surprised to find that it wasn't yet 8:15. Lou and Mike probably wouldn't be up for ages. Even knowing that there were two other people in the house, the place still felt strangely empty. Now that Lou was part of a couple again Emily felt isolated, a bit of an oddity in her own home. It would not be long before she was left on her own, and she had an unwelcome foretaste of what life was going to be like when Lou and Mike went back home on Monday. In the ensuing silence she heard the distant sound of a swinging cat flap and, as if in answer to her telepathic distress call, a furry beacon of comfort came trotting into the kitchen and rubbed round her ankles. He allowed her to pick him up and bury her misty-eyed face in his fur. She sat in a chair by the hearth and cuddled him until Kevin decided he'd accomplished his mission and it was time for his reward. He went and sat by his dish. He was right. She felt better. Grinning, Emily fed him and then proceeded to organise breakfast for the rest of them.

Lou and Mike finally surfaced about 10:30. First Mike, and then Lou, strolled downstairs. Emily raised an eyebrow and smirked at the pair of them.

"What?" said Mike, "Just getting re-acquainted, haven't seen each other for over a week."

"No need to explain yourselves to me," said Emily, "Coffee?"

"Any chance of a cooked breakfast? Bit of an appetite for some reason!" grinned Mike.

"Yes, I was just waiting for you to arrive. It's been keeping hot. I just need to do the eggs. How many do you want?"

Emily fried a couple of eggs. She then opened a door on the range and produced bacon, sausages, hash browns, mushrooms and tomatoes. Dishing it out onto a plate she added a dollop of beans from a pan and the two eggs and handed the plate to Mike.

"Your cooking's improved. I'm quite impressed. I'm really looking forward to seeing what you can do with a cauldron."

She fed Lou and herself and asked what they would like to do with the rest of the morning, bearing in mind that they were both going to help her make bread in the afternoon whether they liked it or not.

Having shown Mike around the house the previous evening Lou was keen to show him round the village. Having cleaned away the breakfast things the three of them set off. The weather didn't look like it knew what to do with itself, so they took brollies just in case. They strolled across to the pond first and said 'hi' to the ducks who, disappointed that the trio hadn't brought any bread, quickly got back to minding their own business and dredging the bottom of the pond for edible wildlife.

"Nice looking pub," said Mike, "Any real ales?"

"I'm sure we can finish our tour there and you can find out. In fact, we've volunteered your help. Richard, the publican, is providing the drinks for the well blessing as well as glasses, crockery etc., and could do with a hand taking it over to the cottage and will no doubt be glad of a hand pulling the odd pint. Sound like something you could manage?" said Emily. "Whilst we are talking about it would you mind getting the chairs and tables out of the out-building tomorrow? You'll need to be up a bit earlier than today though."

They ignored the store, had a look at the treats in the bakery window, did a bit of window shopping at the couple of gift shops and the charity shop and strolled to the end of the main street before crossing over and heading back past the café, estate agents, dentist and sundry other businesses. When they reached the church Emily automatically turned into the graveyard. She enjoyed walking along the winding chipping covered paths and she was keen to show Mike the Well's sisters' graves. For some reason it was important to her that he saw them. They were probably of no relevance to him but to her they were all part of the story that was Wishing Well Cottage. The three sisters that she barely knew had all become part of her life and she couldn't escape that. She led the three of them up the path and round the back of the church. The odd snow drop was still in bloom here and there, but they were now vastly outnumbered by daffodils glowing golden under the trees, despite the overcast sky. She turned to share her delight with her companions. Annoyingly Lou and Mike were deep in conversation and appeared oblivious to their beautiful surroundings and her. Emily felt excluded. As they looked up they both smiled and increased their pace to join her but the path wasn't wide enough for the three of them so Emily continued in the lead.

When they reached the plot at the back of the cemetery where the three graves sat side by side, Emily hid a tear. Why was she here? Why had she been 'chosen' and for what purpose? Were Carla and Anna's intimations to be believed? Anna: they needed to get back. The pub would have to wait.

* * *

Anna turned up armed with a couple of extra mixing bowls and quickly got them all organised. When Mike returned from his mission to draw water from the well she even managed to rope him in and, once he had got the hang of it, appeared to secretly enjoy the physical side of needing dough. It took most of the afternoon and by the time they had finished the kitchen was shrouded in wholemeal flour. The only bits of the floor not affected were the patches where they had each been standing. The four of them also had a light brown dusting giving the whole scene the appearance of an old, faded photograph. The dresser now had an assortment of bowls covered in an equally varied assortment of clean damp napkins and tea towels: anything they could find in which to store the dough whilst it rose. "Ideally," said Anna, "the dough should have been made in the morning, but I really don't think there would have been time. You will have enough to do, baking it and making the hotpot. Right, if you don't mind, I'll leave you to it. I'll be back about 9am. Have the range lit and start baking the first batch of bread about 7am. Each batch will take 30-40minutes. You'll probably need to experiment to get it right. Apart from the colour, if you tap one, it should sound hollow. If you get the veg peeled and chopped and the water in the cauldron simmering, we can get the hotpot going when I arrive." With an amused glance round at the state of the kitchen she said, "Have fun," and left.

They looked at the mess, and then at each other, and were just contemplating where to start the clean up when there was a complaint from the top of the dresser. An agitated Kevin was pacing back and forth, his landing platform having been covered with bowls of dough. Emily looked around for something to act as a platform for him. Seeing nothing at the right height she walked over, bent forward and braced herself against the wall. A dusty Kevin jumped onto her back and then the floor emitting an approving 'perrup'. He then shook himself producing a small cloud before setting off across the kitchen floor leaving tiny paw prints all the way to his dish, which he eyed with disdain. It too had a dusting of flour. Emily emptied and washed it before refilling it. Contented, Kevin tucked in.

Having cleaned the kitchen and moved the bowls of dough onto the kitchen table to keep Kevin happy they headed over to The Three Wells where Emily bought them all dinner and introduced Mike to Richard who let him have a go at pulling a pint, something Mike had always wanted to try.

"Simple things," said Lou, smiling as she watched her husband behind the bar.

"Yes, but we love them anyway," grinned Emily.

"Pleasures I meant."

They had an enjoyable meal, sampling the steak and ale pie, the lamb shank and shallots, and the chicken in tarragon, followed by a selection of desserts. They couldn't decide which to have so Emily ordered one of each and three spoons. They finished off with coffee and liqueurs.

Outside, it was a lovely clear night and the three of them spent some time sitting on the bench by the duck pond staring up into the heavens amazed at what they could see without the light pollution they were used to in the city. So many stars! They swivelled their heads and followed the tip of The Plough to locate The North Star and, as their eyes grew more accustomed to the dark, gazed in wonder at The Milky Way.

CHAPTER
EIGHTEEN

E mily woke with Lou shaking her and telling her it was time to get up; she had tried knocking but got no response. Realising what day it was Emily staggered out of bed and got washed and dressed as quickly as she could. Before she knew it she was on her hands and knees fire lighting. Soon she got the range going and had a fire under the cauldron. She balanced a tin tray, the nearest thing she could find to a lid, across the top of the cauldron, to help it heat up quicker.

Lou had started dividing the risen dough and placing balls of it onto baking trays. As soon as she thought the range was hot enough, she put in the first batch. Emily started peeling potatoes.

Mike appeared, looking somewhat dishevelled, just in time to sample the first batch of bread which, having been put back to bake a little longer, now looked slightly burnt. Together they sat down to sample their fare. Juggling and blowing, they each managed to tear open and butter a hot bap. As Mike, Emily and Lou sank their teeth into the hot bread they 'oohed' and 'aahed' and 'mmmmed' and congratulated each other. The bread was a success. They agreed that Lou should carry on baking the bread. She had done such a good job with the first batch, discounting its slightly burnt appearance and, it had to be said, taste. However, it only needed the timing refining slightly and all would be well. Mike would be in charge of the garden, laying out the trestle tables and deck chairs under Richard's supervision as he was the only one of them who had attended previous well blessings. Together they would serve the drinks. Emily would be in charge of the hotpot.

James and Alex turned up just before Anna at 9am. They had come to gather the garlands from the front room as they were to dress all three wells. This had to be done by 11am as the first well blessing started at 11:30 and James needed time to change.

"Glorious day for it," said James. "I checked the forecast. It's due to be clear skies all day."

"Of course, it's the well blessing," said Alex, as if anything less would be unprecedented.

"Look, aren't Lou's baps great?" said Emily, then seeing their faces, gestured pointedly at the table as the men exchanged amused glances and the women sighed in mild despair. "I was going to offer you one but not anymore. There's work to do, go get on with it."

Anna helped Emily peel and chop the last of the vegetables and tip them into the cauldron which was now boiling nicely. She added some seasoning and gave it a stir. They then set about frying the chopped meat in batches and adding it to the cauldron. By 10am the hotpot was simmering nicely, and Emily had become adept at feeding the fire just enough to keep it so. Lou was on her fifth batch of bread and they decided it was a good time for a break.

Emily went out into the garden to ask what drinks were wanted and to see how the well-dressing and other preparations were going on. Alex and James had finished the well and to her disappointment left to do the other wells. Inspecting the well she was pleased to see how pretty it looked and impressed that the garlands they had made looked professionally finished, hung symmetrically and most importantly of all, as far as she could tell, were indistinguishable from those in the photograph. Delighted, she went to talk to Mike and Richard who were setting up two barrels on stands and stacking plastic pint glasses on the table next to it. At the other end of the table were plates, forks, napkins, 4 large jars of pickled red cabbage and some squeezy bottles of HP sauce. Finally, there were two large tureens and a couple of ladles. Seeing her looking at them Richard suggested that she take them inside to warm as they were what the hotpot was served from.

* * *

Grant was up early. Having looked out the window and checked the forecast on his Blackberry he had decided to take the Midget. It would be a bit fresh with the top down, but it would do him and the car good to 'clear away the cobwebs' so to speak. A fresh day for a fresh start!

* * *

Alex and James were on their last well. The two men had only ever been on 'nodding terms' in the past as they had had no cause to either socialise or meet professionally, but as the morning wore on, they found that despite their different back-grounds conversation flowed easily and each felt comfortable in the other's company. It was only when James returned to Bode Well Cottage from having changed ready to officiate at the well blessing that Alex remembered that James was the vicar. 'This time last year,' he thought to himself, 'I would never have believed that I'd be flower arranging with the vicar!'

* * *

Jess dragged a couple of wonky cast iron tables out onto the pavement in front of The Little Teacups Café and then arranged some chairs with padded floral seat covers at each. Next, she stood a couple of menus on the tables but thought better of it, laid them flat and anchored them with condiment baskets. There was only a light breeze, but it wouldn't take much wind for the menus to take off and lead her a merry dance up the street. She then watered the tubs either side of the door, tidied up a bit of the dead foliage and removed a crisp packet that had got wedged behind one of the tubs. Satisfied that the café front was presentable she went back inside to wait for custom. She wasn't expecting much. There was rarely any to speak of on the morning of the well blessing, but the afternoon was likely to be busy.

* * *

Emily went to get changed but realised that she hadn't enquired as to what was, if any, the dress code. She dashed back downstairs but Anna had gone. She ran out the front door but there was no sign of her. On her way to Anna's cottage, she bumped into one of the villagers that she had seen in the church. "Excuse me, are you going to the well blessing?" asked Emily.

"Yes," said the woman.

"Please. Is there a dress code? I'm not sure what I should wear. Only it isn't quite warm enough for a dress. Would jeans and a smart jumper be okay, only I don't want to offend anyone."

The woman thought for a moment, pushing her glasses back onto the bridge of her nose, multiple rings glinting on bright red nailed fingers. She pursed her lips considering, then smiled revealing the wrinkles radiating from her mouth now highlighted by the cracks in her foundation where her lipstick bled, "Smart casual," was the reply. "Yes, jeans would be fine. With a smart jumper, that would be perfect."

"Oh, thank you," said Emily. "I really want to make a good impression. Gotta go, got to keep an eye on the hotpot. See you later."

As Emily turned away the woman smiled thinly, "Oh, I'm sure you'll make *just* the *right* impression!"

* * *

At 11.30am the All Saints' Church bell sounded the half hour and James began the service at Bode Well Cottage. He started by welcoming everyone, glancing round the packed garden and making eye contact with the various people gathered. Most of the faces he recognised, but some were new. Most of them belonged to the village or were friends of villagers, brought along for the spectacle. Some were there out of curiosity to witness the historical tradition, and no doubt some were there for a free lunch, although traditionally the free lunch crowd only turned up at the last of the wells. He proceeded by saying a few words about the Wells' sisters in general and their sad passing after 100 years. He made note of their selfless service to Greater Blessing and how over the past 70 odd years they had kept the traditions of the village alive, traditions which went back at least 350 years. Every year the three wells in Greater Blessing were blessed in order to ensure their water supply. That tradition was now being continued by their great nephew, Alex Wells, and the new owner of Wishing Well Cottage, Emily Hope, both of whom he hoped would have the villagers' support in their new role. He then led them through a short prayer asking for a continued and plentiful supply of fresh water from the well. As he did so he scattered a handful of herbs into the well, followed by a sprinkling of liquid from a small glass stoppered bottle. As he brought the prayer to a close there was a murmured 'Amen' and the garden was silent for a moment.

"Right, bring your glasses. For those of you that haven't brought one there are some on the table over there."

Alex lowered the bucket into the well. There was a splash and a gurgling sound as it filled and then a creaking sound as he turned the handle bringing the dripping bucket back up. Next, he took a small ladle and dunking it in the bucket he gave James the first glassful. As the throng filed past, he ladled water into their glasses so that everyone had a drink from the well. A trail of people then followed James out of the garden and through the village to Fare Well Cottage. Finally, Alex himself had a drink and arrived, just in time for the second well blessing, as the last chime of 12 sounded from the church clock.

* * *

Grant turned off the main road at the crossroads that was Little Blessing. He pulled in at the petrol station which appeared to be derelict although there looked to be a workshop that was probably in use during the week. The pumps were ancient. He didn't even recognise the petrol they professed to serve. Looking at his map he got his bearings and realised that he could see most of the village from where he sat. The few houses were fairly non-descript and he really didn't think that Emily would choose to live here. He could not imagine what she could afford, even here, if she did. Spotting a woman walking her dog he got out of the car and crossed the street. Keeping his distance from the setter's slobbering mouth he explained that he was looking for a friend who had recently moved either here or Greater Blessing. Had any young woman moved here recently? The lady seemed a little suspicious that his friend hadn't given him an address but eventually conceded that none of the houses in the village had been sold recently. So, unless the woman was lying, Emily wasn't here. He got back in the MG and pointed it towards Greater Blessing.

* * *

At Fare Well Cottage Alex had time to reflect as he repeatedly hauled buckets up the well and ladled water out to the long, long line of people. It hadn't really sunk in before that this cottage, and Bode Well, were now his and his status in the village had been elevated to, well, he didn't know what exactly. These people were all treating him as lord of the manor. He was both amused and a little alarmed. His great aunts had been the village 'elders', for want of a better term, and it hadn't occurred to him until now that he would be expected to replace them! Thankfully, he did not have Wishing Well Cottage as well. He wondered if Emily was nervous. His role in the festivities was nearly over. Hers was about to begin. He truly hoped all would go well. The villagers were wonderful helpful people, but they could also be unforgiving enemies. He really wanted them to accept her.

* * *

Kevin sat on the roof of the outhouse. From here he had an excellent view of the back garden and well and, if he swivelled his head 180°, the whole of the village green. He saw Lou and Mike head back inside when they saw the procession of people following the vicar past the church. He led them through the garden gates and up the drive. Kevin noted one or two of them glancing in relief at the peony bush which was sporting some healthy looking bright green shoots. He also took note of those who exhibited visible signs of disappointment that it had survived and exchanged a knowing glance with his companion.

* * *

Emily gave the hotpot a final stir, rolled down the sleeves of her jumper, made sure the periapt and its chain hung straight, gave her hair a quick comb in the mirror in the hall, and went out to meet her guests. Together with Lou and Anna she stood and listened as James began.

He welcomed them all to Wishing Well, the third and last of Greater Blessing's wells. With the blessing of the last well, not only was Greater Blessing's water supply secured for another year but the safety and prosperity of the village and its inhabitants. For legend had it, and here he departed from his reverend delivery of the service and, employing a voice of heathen prophecy and doom, warned, "The village will fall, and its inhabitants be cast out in poverty." The crowd laughed. "Mock not, it has been foretold!" As the laughter died, he raised his glass, "Ladies and gentlemen I would like to introduce you to the new owner of Wishing Well and ask that you welcome her to Greater Blessing. I think it came as a bit of a shock to her to find she was hosting the well blessing, but she has risen to the challenge, she has opened her garden to us all and, with water from the well as is tradition, produced bread and the hotpot, and most amazing of all, willingly accepted her new role. Would you all please thank Emily Hope. Emily, where are you?"

Emily, embarrassed, stepped forwards and walked over to the well. James smiled at her but seemed momentarily taken aback, but then recovered himself. Looking round at the crowd she became aware that they were all staring at her. All the smartly dressed people were staring at her. Nearly everyone was in a suit of some sort, or their outfits bordered on evening dress. Greater Blessing's most important annual ceremony and she, the host, was in jeans, jeans and trainers. Looking instinctively to Alex for some sort of approval she noted that he too was now in suit and tie and even Mike and Lou were smartly dressed. No-one was wearing jeans. Fingering the periapt for solace she noted that this drew resentful looks from one or two, alienating her further. Then, her attention drawn by the sun glinting off a pair of glasses as they were slid back up a heavily 'pan-caked' nose, Emily's gaze came to rest, with instant recognition, on the woman she had consulted in the street. The woman gazed back from the anonymous comfort of the crowd with a sickly-sweet smirk of satisfaction on her malicious little mouth.

After what seemed like an eternity to Emily, James came to her rescue, "Right, time to eat, drink and mingle. Richard, if you would be so kind..." and he pointed at the beer kegs.

"Thank you all for coming. God bless Greater Blessing!"

Emily dashed inside the house closely followed by Anna. "That bloody woman," moaned Emily, "She said jeans would be fine. What have I done that they hate me so?"

"Never mind now. Just go and change whilst I fill these tureens and get some hotpot out there. Go, go!"

* * *

Grant could not believe how quiet Greater Blessing was. There wasn't a soul about. He drove slowly down the main street looking for inspiration in his search for Emily. Crawling round the green he took in the pub and the duck pond and the church. If she had bought a house here it would be something small and these were all either businesses or large properties, and attractive ones at that. Unless she'd got a flat over one of the shops it would most likely be something small tucked away down a side street somewhere. He needed to narrow down his search. He needed to ask someone. Continuing back down the high street his eyes came to rest on a window with several pictures of houses for sale. The estate agents, of course! He coasted to a halt just past it and got out.

The man behind the desk got up and greeted him, "Hello, how can I help you?"

After his encounter with the suspicious dog-walker in Little Blessing he revised his story. "I am trying to find a friend of mine. I've come all this way and stupidly left her address and phone number at home. I feel like a right idiot. She bought a house here recently so I was hoping you might be able to help me. Her name is Emily Hope."

Gerald looked Grant up and down and took in his expensive looking clothes, his strong and able physique, his good looks and his interest in '*his*' Emily and *hated* him. As a professional salesman he kept his true feelings in check and replied smoothly, "I am sorry, I would like to help you, but it is company policy not to give out clients' details. I am sure you understand." Grant briefly tried pleading, one man to another, but Gerald just shook his head and politely refused whilst smiling his best professional smile. As Grant headed out the door and across the street towards the store Gerald picked up the phone. Speaking to his partner who was out on a viewing he arranged to leave as soon as the other man got back to the office.

* * *

Emily ladled out hotpot to what seemed like a never-ending stream of people, muttering occasionally to people's comments that she hadn't had time to change before, as there had been so much to do. The frantic wardrobe changes had left her flushed and sticky and now, despite the sun, she was beginning to feel chilly in the blouse and thin suit jacket she had finally opted for. Still, the feedback from the hotpot appeared to be good and the whole event seemed to be successful. Everyone, well the majority anyway, were enjoying themselves. A number of people congratulated her on the wonderful job she had done and marvelled at how she'd managed to dress the well just right. She explained at length that the well was really Alex and James doing but no-one seemed to care. The well was hers.

Having refilled a tureen with the last of the hotpot she took it outside, fed James who had just returned, having changed into civvies, and finally helped herself to a plateful. Leaving those who wanted seconds to help themselves, she went off to get herself a drink. Mike was in his element and it was obvious that he was taking the quality control aspect of his role seriously. He hadn't yet started slurring his words, but Emily knew him well enough to know that he had had much more than his allocated 'one pint each'.

Strolling round the garden she spotted James, sponsor form in hand, methodically ambushing her guests. Alex, in turn, had been ambushed by a group of young women all of whom appeared to be competing for his attention. Her momentary annoyance was relieved when he looked up and sent her a silent SOS with his eyes. Amused, she left him to it. Turning, she was momentarily blinded by the flash from Mike's camera. The beer having run out he was amusing himself by hiding in the shrubbery and surprising people. She chatted to several people in turn, graciously accepting their compliments on a job well done. One or two guests, though, pointedly avoided her. On her second circuit of the garden, she bumped into Anna and Lou who were deep in conversation. Anna was most apologetic for not telling Emily that the well blessing was always a 'Sunday Best' type of occasion but that she shouldn't take her mistake to heart, really only the ones who *wanted* to be offended would be. Emily was now suitably dressed and looked lovely, if slightly blue of complexion.

"Yes, I'm frozen," said Emily rubbing her hands together and blowing on them, "and these heels weren't meant for grass, but they were the best I could find. Damn, I've lost another nail." Seeing Emily suddenly look pensive and realising where her thoughts were taking her, as she inadvertently glanced towards the hotpot, Lou said, "How many have you got left?" Emily held out her hands. "It's okay! You only had 7 at breakfast. Relax! Though I admit, I can't account for the eye of newt and the tongue of frog that were in those jars by the rosemary."

* * *

As the festivities continued in the garden and some of the guests started to spill out onto the green and over to The Three Wells in search of further refreshment Kevin sat and watched and kept his own council. He was alone now, his companion having gone off on a mission of her own.

* * *

Carla looked up as the smart young man entered the store. She gave him her most helpful smile and asked how she may be of assistance. He returned her smile and said he was hoping she could help him. He felt such a fool, but he had come to visit a friend and stupidly left her address and phone number at home. He thought that the post mistress might know where she lived. She had only moved in recently. Did she know her? Her name was Emily Hope.

"And you are?" queried Carla, matching his charm.

"The names Dobson, Grant Dobson," he replied in his best 007 voice.

Carla almost laughed out loud at her good fortune, the timing really couldn't have been better had she planned it, but instead, she giggled girlishly at his flirtatious impersonation. "Really, I shouldn't be doing this, it's not very professional of me, but you seem such a nice young man, it can't do any harm," and she smiled conspiratorially, "I am sure Miss Hope will be delighted to see you. Don't let on it was me who told you, but she lives over by the church at Wishing Well Cottage. You can't miss it. The whole village is there for the well blessing." As he left, she was slightly sorry that she wouldn't be there to 'see the fireworks' but she would certainly hear about them. In the meantime, she could imagine, and it made for a very satisfactory afternoon.

* * *

Jess was in a good mood. Business was slow, which made a pleasant change as she was usually rushed off her feet. It could change at any moment of course but in the meantime, she was enjoying herself. She had just finished a very satisfying cup of tea with an even more satisfying arrangement of tea leaves decorating the bottom of it. Life, it seemed, was about to take a turn for the better.

Movement outside the window caught Jess's attention and she looked up from her book at the possibility of a customer. There was a grey shape at one of the tables outside. It didn't really look like a person though. Puzzled, by being unable to make out what she was looking at, she came out from behind the counter and went outside. Sitting on one of the tables was a large silver tabby. As she approached it jumped off and trotted a few paces up the street, stopping briefly to brush its arched back against the wheel of a red sports car.

'Wow, an MG midget, and in very good nick too,' thought Jess as she walked over and ran her hand along its nicely rounded wing. Doing a circuit of the car she admired the condition of the chrome work and was impressed how neat and tidy the vehicle was. When she reached the driver's side, she couldn't resist the temptation. She opened the door and got in.

* * *

Going against the trickle of people leaving Wishing Well Cottage Grant found his way round the back. He was baffled. Was this really Emily's house? Her car and those of Mike and Lou were parked out front but there was no way she could afford this. Was she living with someone? He tried to think what Mike and Lou had said. Yes, he was fairly certain they had said that she had *bought* a house, but then would they tell him if she had moved in with another man. Surely they would just have said she had moved, got somewhere else to live or some other phrase rather than stating that she had *bought* a house. Could he face it if she had found someone else? Patting the small box in his breast pocket he really didn't think he could, but he had to see her. He had to know. There were such a lot of people about. Where was she? An arm was wrapped round his shoulders and a beery greeting breathed in his ear, "Grant, what are *you* doing here? Let me get you a drink." It was Mike and he was steering him over to the drinks table.

"No, thanks. I'm driving. Where's Emily?"

"Dunno! Probably chatting up Alex. Let me get you a drink. I have a secret stash."

Grant extricated himself from Mike's embrace and left him filling a glass. Threading his way through the crowd he spotted Emily over by the well talking animatedly to a tall, dark haired, clean-shaven, slimly built man wearing a shirt and tie and, Grant looked closer, yes, an out-of-date suit. Mentally he dismissed him, if this was Alex, well...then he noticed the interaction between the couple, how familiar they seemed with each other and how at ease in each other's company. Grant felt a stab of jealousy. He hadn't expected this. He really hadn't expected it. The man leant forward, putting his hands on Emily's shoulders. Grant thought he was going to kiss her. He felt sick. Instead, the man spoke in Emily's ear, then set off towards the house. Grant couldn't hear what he said over the rest of the noise in the garden. Emily was alone. Now was his chance. He strode across the lawn, not knowing what he was going to do or say. He didn't care. She was there. Finally, there. He couldn't stop himself.

As if sensing his approach Emily turned. With a mixture of shock and horror frozen on her face she stared open mouthed. She didn't need to speak. The look on her face said it all. She really didn't want to see him. Grant slowed to a stop in front of her as she recovered enough to demand in a low but angry voice, "What are you doing here? How dare you turn up now, you money grabbing shit! You didn't want me when I had nothing. Nothing! You threw me out. Well now, I'm throwing you out. Get out. Get out of my garden," she yelled, shoving him in the chest. He grabbed her wrists in defence.

It all happened so fast. Her expression changed to one of alarm focussed not on him but over his shoulder. He was grabbed and spun round to his right. Instinctively he moved his arms to block the attack. His left arm was arrested briefly, caught in something as he turned, then released too late to deflect the punch. It struck him forcefully on the left temple and was followed up immediately with one to the right side of his chest. Through intermittent flashes of light, he heard someone screaming, "No, Gerald, No." Staggering, he focussed on his assailant and steadied himself, anger and humiliation competing to fuel what was to come. In pain, and incensed, he launched himself at the estate agent who now stood apparently bewildered by what he had done. Grant cannoned into him and took him a good 3 metres through the air before the pair of them landed heavily on the grass and commenced pummelling and kneeing each other. Amongst the blind rage he heard shouting and screaming and the odd encouraging shout, for which of them he didn't know. Then hands were separating the pair of them and hauling them to their feet, and then Grant and Gerald stood there, glowering at each other, with the villagers of Greater Blessing looking on in disapproval. Suddenly, Gerald turned and limped out of the garden, smoothing down his soiled suit and surreptitiously inspecting his knuckles as he went. Then someone large took Grant by the elbow and marched him out to the street. He could hear Emily crying.

* * *

Not knowing what else to do Grant headed slowly back to his car. At first, he didn't notice her. Her red hair was almost a perfect match for the MG's paintwork. Shocked that someone would have the audacity to sit in his car he was almost polite as he said, "What are you doing?"

Jess, caught out, felt innocence was the best ploy. She turned and smiled at him. Shielding her eyes from the sun she looked him up and down. Good body. Well dressed. Not *bad*. Then, batting her eyes, positively beamed. "I'm sorry. Is this your car? Did you buy it like this, or did you do it up yourself? It is in really good nick. The chrome and bodywork are perfect." She chose this moment to open the door and extend one shapely black stocking leg. Swivelling her hips, she brought the other leg out to join the first and stood. Grant had to step back. As he did so he turned to face the sun and now Jess saw the swelling bruise on the side of his face and the cut next to his eye which was slowly dripping blood onto his shirt collar.

"Oh, wow! What happened to you?" and she reached instinctively for the side of his head.

Angry with her, whilst at the same time

wondering - tights or stockings, no tights - skirts too short, and thinking of Emily and feeling fickle, he brushed Jess's arm aside and got into the car. Inserting the key in the ignition he turned it. A pain shot up his arm and the world 'phased' and he slipped into momentary oblivion.

When the ringing in his ears subsided and he was able to focus he found Jess was holding his head in both hands and gazing at him earnestly. "You look ghastly, you're going nowhere," and she pocketed his ignition key. "You gave me a right scare there." Grant cradled his right hand. It was swelling up quickly and a bruise was starting to form on the back of it.

When his colour started to return Jess helped him out of the car and took him into the café and to a table by the counter. "You really need to get that seen to, you sit there, and I'll call you an ambulance."

"No, I'll be fine, it's just a bruise. Look," and he opened and closed his hand a couple of times stifling a wince as he did so. "Have you got any ice?"

After a bit of thought she produced two choc ices wrapped in a tea towel and placed them on the back of his hand. Seeing that he was adamant about not going to hospital she made them both a cup of tea.

* * *

Emily was distraught. She was sitting on

a chair in the kitchen with Lou holding her hand and trying to tell her that it wasn't that bad. It wasn't her fault. No-one could blame her. She hadn't started the fight. She couldn't really blame Grant either. It was Gerald who had started it. Grant was only defending himself.

"Yes," said Mike, trying to be helpful, "See," he said, "I've got photos," and waved his camera dangerously close to Emily's drippy nose.

"Mike!" snapped Lou, "Put that away."

"I was only trying to cheer her up. I've got a *brilliant* one here..."

James tactfully steered Mike's arm away and positioned the camera so he could see it. He then took the camera over to Alex. When Lou looked up the three men were peering intently at the camera and sniggering silently like a bunch of naughty schoolboys. Following her gaze, Anna got up and joined them. Then Lou wandered over and Emily found she was on her own. 'What were they all finding so amusing?'

She got up and went to join them rubbing the side of her neck as she did so. There was a lump. Moving her hand back and forth she traced the extent of it. She had a raised wheal round the side of her neck. 'What on earth?' Then it struck her. The periapt was gone! "Haaah!"

At her sharp intake of breath, they all turned her way.

"The periapt has gone. I've lost it!"

Seeing Emily's neck, Lou clasped her hands to her face as a memory flashed before her eyes. "Something flew through the air when the fight started," then she looked with horror at Emily... "It went down the well...!"

"What? No!" Emily dashed outside and they all followed.

Most people had left, but a few were still wandering round the garden or sitting chatting on the deck chairs. They looked up now in expectation of further entertainment as Emily burst out of the house and hurled herself at the well. Violently knocking the bucket to one side she leant over the edge. The others arrived and followed suit, blocking out the light. Yelling at them to get back she peered into the depths but with the sun disappearing behind the trees there was nothing to be seen. Someone produced a torch from the kitchen, but its weak beam died along with the battery. With lots of suggestions, from the crowd that had gathered, they then tried lowering down a candle but that set fire to the string, and with flame racing towards his hand James had to drop it. They checked the bucket, just in case, but it contained only water. Bereft and having provided enough of a spectacle for one day Emily went back inside and shut the door.

CHAPTER NINETEEN

As she did every morning, Emily pulled back the curtains, inspected the weather and surveyed her garden. There was always something new to see: a green shoot here, a flower there, birds large and small, even the odd heron and bird of prey, not to mention the deer, but none of them received the reaction that this morning's novelty visitor produced. There at the well, fishing-rod in hand, like some giant garden gnome, was Gerald. Emily blinked at the scene. What was he doing? How did he know? Then she remembered; word travelled fast in this village, and the lost periapt would be big news. She was about to throw open the window and yell at him that he had done enough damage and to get the hell out of her garden when she suddenly couldn't be bothered. She redrew the curtains and climbed back into bed. Sticking her head under the pillow she shut out the world. She had nothing she need get up for today and she hated garden gnomes, this one in particular.

Drifting in and out of sleep she let the morning pass, thoughts and dreams intermingling until the church bells woke her and she realised it was Sunday. Having been to the church once she felt obliged to go again. The villagers would be bound to notice and disapprove if she were absent. She looked at her clock and realised that there was no time to get dressed and run over there and, turning up late would surely be unacceptable as well. She would go next Sunday. Then she thought about James. What would he think? Uncertain, she got up and had a look out of one of the front windows. The church bells were now silent, and the church doors firmly shut. No, it was too late. She couldn't stand the thought of them all turning to look as she snook in late. Irked, she slunk back to her room and disappeared under the covers once again.

When she finally crawled out of bed she determined not to look out of the window. She couldn't bear it if Gerald was still there. Thinking back on the day before, she had to agree that the well blessing itself had been a success. The preparations had all paid off, the food was good, it seemed that they had got the well decorations 'just right' and James' research had found the right herbs to sprinkle down the wells for the blessings. If it hadn't been for the sabotage, which wasn't her fault, the event would have been perfect. So, did it really matter that she had been wearing jeans? Maybe she should start a new trend, a new tradition, bring the ceremony into the 21st century. After all, it was her garden and her well. If Alex agreed, the village would have to lump it. *That* humiliation mentally dealt with she felt somewhat better. The loss of the periapt, however, was another matter. She felt strangely naked without it.

* * *

Lou and Mike were getting concerned. They had been up for ages, and even Mike, who was suffering slightly it had to be said, was up and about. It was unlike Emily to spend this long in bed but then it had been an exhausting stressful week and what with the dramas of yesterday they could understand her having a lie in. They had just decided that Lou should go knock on her bedroom door when they heard her coming down the stairs.

"Hi, sorry," she said as she entered the kitchen. "Have you found what you need for breakfast?"

"Breakfast? We're all ready for lunch," said Mike systematically opening and closing cupboard doors. "Good sleep?"

"Yes and no. Couldn't face life with a gnome in the garden! Has he gone? I daren't look," said Emily running a hand through her tousled hair.

"Yes, but I reckon he'll be back. He was most apologetic about the periapt and determined to make amends," mused Mike. "So far he's brought up two mugs, a pair of huge 1970's sun-glasses and, of course, a candle on a piece of burnt string." Then he smiled sweetly at Emily, "You know what I fancy...some kindly millionaire to treat us to Sunday lunch and a hangover cure. *Well*, there is *nothing* here," he said closing his last cupboard.

"Uh, oh!" said Lou who was standing by the window. "Your gnomes back."

"That's it. Lunch is on *me*. Besides, I've got to face the villagers some time and I'd rather not do it on my own. Get your coats on."

* * *

As they crossed the green, they spotted Carla on hands and knees in the shop doorway, Marigolds angrily scrubbing away at the step. She glanced round briefly at them and glowered, soapy water splashing everywhere, the smell of lemon strong in the air.

Emily pushed open the pub's heavy oak door, took note of its well-worn beading, stained glass panels and shiny brass finger plate, and smiled. She felt a real satisfaction knowing that she had a real connection to the pub and all its history and the generations of people who had walked through this door for the last 3-4 centuries. She realised that since the well blessing she'd gained a sense of belonging. She felt at home.

Inside, the pub was filling up fast and they managed to grab the last table. Leaving Lou guarding it, Emily and Mike went to the bar and ordered two roast beefs and a roast chicken, two pints of Stella and an apple and mango J2O. Richard finished serving a customer farther along the bar and then came over to say hello. They thanked him for yesterday and said they would bring the crockery and glasses over when they had washed them. He told them not to bother washing them as they would go in the pub dishwashers. They only needed to put them in the plastic racks he'd taken them over in and carry them back. Mike said they hadn't found them all yet as they were scattered all over the garden. They told him about Emily's new garden feature and Richard reckoned that Gerald had found his calling in life; it suited him well, no pun intended. "Hopefully, he'll get your necklace back and if not, well," and he grinned at Mike, "the U-tube royalties should pay for another. Do you get royalties on U-tube?"

Emily looked puzzled and Mike looked alarmed and pulled a 'put your foot in it now' face at Richard.

"Drinks on me. Must get on. Busy, busy," said Richard and abandoned Mike to serve his customers.

Emily stared at Mike, "U-tube? So, am I to assume there is also a *video* clip of yesterday's humiliation?"

As denial at this point was clearly out of the question, he decided that valour was the better part of discretion and said proudly, "Yes, and it's ab...so...lute...ly brilliant. It clearly shows the periapt going down the well which means that we know where it is and that searching the entire garden isn't necessary. Grant is exonerated. Although it was his hand that caught it and sent it flying through the air and into the well, it clearly wasn't his fault. Gerald started the fight. Grant just defended himself. Your face was a picture. I wanted to show you, but Lou didn't think it would cheer you up at all..." Glancing round the pub he continued, "Everyone thought it was hilarious..."

"So, yesterday evening whilst Lou and I were at home you, and I presume Richard, James I'll give the benefit of the doubt to, and Alex were over here happily showing video clips of one of the most humiliating incidents in my life to the people I had already made a fool of myself in front of, and a bunch of total strangers!"

"Well, to be fair, most of them, if they hadn't been there to see it had already heard about it."

"Great! Just great! Thanks."

And with that she picked up her drink and headed over to their table. Before she reached it however Carla appeared through the door spitting feathers, though probably fur would have been more fitting. Her face inches from Emily's she hissed, "He's done it again. That soddin' cat o' yours 'as done it again."

"What?"

"He's pee'd in my shop doorway."

"When?"

"Last night."

"How do you know it was him? Did you see him?"

"No, but I know."

"*How* do you know," interjected Mike, "It could have been someone leaving here. After all, it was quite a night last night. The place was packed. Young men...convenient doorway...it's not nice but...you know..."

"It was 'er blasted cat!"

"You can't know that..." pleaded Mike trying to calm her down, aware that the spotlight was now on the three of them, but, completely oblivious to the audience now hanging on their every word Carla screeched, "Just you smell it for yourself. My entrance stinks!"

The vacuum, caused by the collective intake of breath, snuffed out one or two unfortunately placed candles. One man coughed and spluttered as the bitter he had inadvertently snorted came back down his nose and another man's howl of laughter blasted the head of his Guinness onto his mother-in-law's tiramisu.

Even those that hadn't realised what Carla had said were soon laughing too, purely from the contagious hilarity of it, whether the reason had been explained to them or not. The reason no longer really mattered. As Carla faded through the door, the pub was in uproar.

With mixed emotions Emily sat and waited for her food. Amused that Carla's attack had backfired but aware that this would only increase her sense of injustice Emily couldn't help feeling slightly worried. How far would Carla be prepared to go to get revenge? How warped did you have to be to believe that a cat was plotting against you? The really worrying thought though was that Emily suspected it might be true and where did that leave her? How many loose screws did it take to become completely unhinged!

When they walked into the kitchen all three of them automatically looked for Kevin. He wasn't hard to find. Sitting regally on the chair by the fire he waited for his subjects to approach him. Was it their imagination or did he look smug?

"Hey, Moriarty," said Mike, "Nice one. Respect!" Like a sovereign bestowing favours Kevin raised his chin and allowed Mike to scratch his neck. Favour bestowed, Kevin jumped down from his chair crossed the rug in front of the fire and jumped up onto the opposite chair. There to everyone's surprise sat another cat, a serene silver tabby. Kevin circled behind her to sit by her side, his tail curled companionably round her body. The two cats sat side by side and returned the humans' gaze, the newcomer looking directly at Emily. For a moment no one spoke. No one seemed willing to voice what they were all collectively thinking.

Mike was the first to react. Slowly he strolled over to the two cats, crouched down and held out his hand to the new arrival. She sniffed it briefly, then without breaking eye contact with Emily rubbed her head against his hand a couple of times. She then sat back and waited. It was clear that Emily was required to react. Warily she went over and knelt on the floor in front of the two cats. She stroked Kevin on the head and then with her other hand reached out and stroked the other cat. Two clear green eyes looked at Emily, fathomless black pupils dilating to two perfect huge discs. Emily was the first to look away as the cat's gaze penetrated her soul. Emily knew but couldn't acknowledge it, couldn't accept what she felt in her heart. It was too ridiculous for words! With nothing she wanted to say but desperately needing to do something she went and picked up Kevin's dish, found another small dish and filled them both with cat food. Placing them both on the floor she was relieved when both cats arrived and started eating.

"So, looks like you now have two cats,"

said Lou keen to break the tension.

"Well," said Mike, "an obvious name springs to mind."

"Don't," snapped Emily, "Don't even go there!"

The back doorbell rang making them all jump. Emily went to answer it and returned with Alex who had been tidying up the back garden and just noticed that they had all returned. Gerald, apparently, had disappeared as soon as Alex turned up, much to Emily's relief.

Alex needed the plastic crates which were in the kitchen. Taking them outside the three of them found that he had stacked most of the glasses on the trestle tables but was running out of room. Together they searched the garden gathering the rest of the crockery, glasses and cutlery and packed them into the plastic crates. It was amazing the variety of places people had found to deposit items. The odd glass or two were tucked into crevices in the stone wall and plates littered the grass amongst the deck chairs. Thankfully there didn't appear to be any breakages. Despite Emily providing bins for her guests, they found paper napkins wedged under hedges and in the branches of trees. Two hours later the crockery had been returned to the pub, the deck chairs and trestle tables stacked back in the out-buildings and the litter bagged and binned. Discounting the flattened lawn and the odd footprint here and there on the flowerbeds the garden was back to normal.

"Right, I'll be off then," said Alex.

"Oh," blustered Emily, "Do you not want to stay for tea?"

"Thanks, that would be really great, but I need to pack. I'm off down to Gloucester first thing in the morning. Work."

"Really," said Mike, "What are you doing down there?"

"Fitting horseshoes."

"Don't they have their own blacksmiths down there?"

"Yes, but I'm a specialist. I do racehorses. I have some *very* influential clients."

"Such as?" asked Lou.

"Sorry. I can't tell you."

"What? Why not? We won't tell anyone. Please, please."

"Afraid not. Part of my reputation is based on my discretion. I'm not jeopardising that even for you lovely people."

"But it's a bank holiday tomorrow," said Emily.

"Yes, which is why I want to travel down early morning to miss the traffic. Emily, perhaps we could go out for a drink next weekend, when I'm back... and you two...nice to meet you. Hopefully, we'll get to meet again. Must go," and with that he left, leaving Emily looking at a very long week.

CHAPTER TWENTY

W hen Emily went down for breakfast, she was surprised to hear Lou and Mike apparently arguing and they were attempting to do it quietly. It was obvious that they didn't want her to hear. As a result, she found herself tiptoeing down the hall, concern for her friends over-coming her reluctance to eavesdrop.

"I really don't think we should," said Mike.

"She has a right to know."

"At this point, I don't think it would be doing her any favours."

"Okay, suppose we don't tell her, and later she finds out. It's got to be her decision."

Emily marched into the room, "What's got to be my decision. Tell me!"

Lou and Mike looked at her and then at

each other. Mike shrugged his shoulders and conceded to Lou's judgement.

"Okay, sit down," said Lou. Emily sat. "Yesterday, whilst we were clearing up the garden Mike found something on the lawn, trampled into the grass: trampled into the grass where Grant and Gerald were punching each other." At this point Lou pulled a small dark blue box out of her dressing gown pocket and placed it on the table in front of Emily. As Emily stared at the ring box Lou continued, "Mike got a text this morning from Grant. It's his. It must have fallen out of his pocket during the fight. He didn't want you to know he'd lost it."

Emily couldn't speak. Grant had come to propose! No! She couldn't handle that. Not now...not now she was finally feeling settled... feeling she actually belonged... and besides... there was Alex...! She reached out and slowly but firmly pushed the ring box, the decorative thin gold line circling its lid a promise of quality within, back across the table. Even if he genuinely didn't know about the lottery win...did he really want to get married...did he now want to have children...did he really want her or just their relationship?

"Emily, just talk to him! If you really want it to be over between the two of you, you need to talk to him. If that is *really* what you want, you need to tell him that it is over...face to face. Are you sure that is what you want? You two were such a great couple. I'm sure if you just talked to him...and gave him a chance," pleaded Lou.

"He really doesn't know about the lottery and he's miserable without you," added Mike. "He realises you are upset and angry with him and he is trying to make amends, but you aren't giving him a chance."

"If it really is over then you owe it to him to tell him to his face, because he isn't going to believe it and he isn't going to leave you alone until he does."

"No, I'm going for a walk. Sorry," and with that she grabbed her jacket and headed out the back door. As she crossed the lawn with its area of flattened grass, heading for the stile, images of Grant and Gerald rolling about on the ground flashed unwanted into her mind, tormenting her; distasteful images reminding her of her public humiliation and adding to her resentment. Of all the times he could have chosen, why had he chosen that moment, of all moments, to turn up?

She trudged determinedly uphill, pounding out her anger, dark thoughts beating each other up. Should she see him? Should she try to humiliate him the way he had humiliated her. Perhaps if she turned up at his work and made a scene... told him what a lousy money grabbing low life he was...hunting her down...fighting... rolling around on the ground like some grubby little schoolboy. Perhaps if she went to the next motor club dinner in some 'in-your-face', 'knock-dead' designer number and told them *all* how their golden boy had abandoned her, on the worst night of the year, in an unreliable car, when she could have frozen to death. Told them how he'd kicked her out of their home and changed the locks. Then, when she'd won the lottery, all of a sudden, he wanted to get married!

As she emerged from the trees and sighted the crag, she was surprised how quickly she had climbed the hill. Slowing to regain her breath, she found the last few metres quite an effort and quite warm. Divesting herself of her jacket she pulled at the neck of her sweater, in an effort to cool down. As she reached the top and collapsed onto a rock, her anger dissipated as she relaxed into her exhaustion and her breathing returned to normal. Staring round at the view she felt distanced from her problems. Grant seemed a long way away. Did he really want her back? Was he really going to propose? Were Lou and Mike, right? Did Grant really not know she had won the lottery? If he didn't and he had come to propose...how did she feel, then? He had made an impressive effort to track her down. He wasn't to know about the well blessing and that their meeting would be so public. After all, what had he done wrong? He hadn't started the fight and, as Mike said, Grant was only defending himself. He'd given Gerald a right pummelling. Couldn't blame him for that. In fact, she'd have liked to have done that herself. Hah, two men fighting over her. She'd never had that before. Then he'd been escorted off the premises. Poor Grant...

Eventually she put her jacket back on and made her way back down the hill. She was calmer but still undecided what to do.

* * *

It was Lou and Mike's last day. They planned to leave after lunch. In Emily's absence, and knowing that there was nothing for lunch, Mike had been to the bakery. There was a pasty each and a selection of sticky cakes. Mike had been looking at the map. He suggested that they took the food, crossed the road at the back of the house, headed across the fields and down to a river. It looked like there were some rock outcrops and judging by the contours probably a waterfall. It could be a lovely place for a picnic. What did she think? Lou looked keen so, despite having only just got back in from a walk, Emily agreed.

Opposite the bus stop, on the other side of the road, was a stile. Stuck into the ground beside it was a post with a wooden public footpath sign at the top stating Spring Falls 0.5 miles, which was encouraging. They climbed the stile and set off diagonally across the field as the sign indicated, dodging cowpats as they went. The field sloped gently, and they spotted a gap in the hedge at the other side and another stile alongside a five-barred gate. As they approached, the ground round the gate got boggier and boggier, soil and cow muck churned up by multiple hooves. Reaching the stile was going to be difficult. None of them were wearing wellies. The ground on the right of the gate was a bit higher and not as trampled and therefore drier. This allowed first Mike and then Lou and Emily to reach the gate. One at a time they side stepped from right to left along its lowest rung, the gate dipping alarmingly as the pregnant Lou slid gingerly along, a puddle of stinking liquid mustard waiting eagerly below. Lou's nose wrinkled.

"Your face," laughed Emily, "you look so disgusted. In 3 months' time the pair of you will be up to your armpits in stuff just like that."

Following the public footpath signs, they crossed another three fields and stiles, occasionally disturbing the odd bird and rabbit, setting them to flight. As they climbed over the last stile, they joined a new path and turning right, followed it through bushes. They could now hear water rushing and splashing somewhere ahead. The path wound down amongst rocks and the shrubbery opened out to reveal a large slab of limestone. Several large boulders surrounded it, trees and shrubs fighting for space amongst the cracks. To the right, looking up the valley, more tumbled boulders held back the foliage and there, running down the centre of this small valley, carving its way through the rock, was a spectacular stream. Great sheets of water poured over smooth limestone ledges and dived into deep clear pools to come up bubbling and splashing exhilarated by the headlong rush. Looking downstream the water fell into wider and shallower pools as the valley levelled out and the river gained in majesty on its long journey to the sea.

Looking about, it was obvious that others had been there before them. The remains of a fire could be seen blemishing part of the rock and there was the inevitable squashed beer can tucked into a bush alongside a ripped carrier bag. They found a rock each to sit on and sat down to enjoy their picnic. The pasties met with everyone's approval and it occurred to Emily that the bakery was likely to be too easy an option if she wasn't careful. She must do some more on-line shopping. She also needed to do something about her nails. What would Grant think? Woah, why did she care what *he* thought?

"So, what are you going to do when we're gone?" asked Mike.

"Good point. Hadn't thought that far ahead... Need to do some shopping, and I've got the book club tomorrow night. I'm quite looking forward to that...get to know a few more people."

"Oh, yeah, Sally seemed nice," added Lou. "Hopefully there will be other women our age there for you. Anna's lovely but it would be good to have a friend your own age in the village."

"So," said Mike, this Pills & Swoon club, what are you reading?"

"Well, I don't know yet. I'll find out tomorrow."

"I can just imagine," and he turned to Lou, put an arm round her waist, and stood, pulling her to her feet. Looking deep into her eyes he put his other hand behind her neck and tipped her backwards, awkwardly, as she wasn't currently built for 'dipping', and then, in a husky voice said, "*As he took her forcefully in his arms, his strong embrace overpowering her slender resolve, he gazed deep into her eyes. Her heart fluttered. She gasped, a gentle sigh emanating from deep within her soul escaped through the crimson prison of her pouting lips. Her mind swam, her body melted, and she slipped through his strong surgeon's fingers to land with a painful splatter on the pointed toes of his Cuban heeled snakeskin boots.*" He sat Lou back down laughing.

Taking up the theme she continued, "*Disgusted by the mess, he shook first his left and then his right foot, wiped his heels on her prone figure, slung his stethoscope over his shoulder, buttoned up the front of his white coat, winced whilst he extricated his chest hair, and then strode off into the silent night of the hospital...*"

Mike leapt to his feet and headed dramatically across the rock, back of hand to forehead, "*Devastated by his shallowness Virginia got to her feet and waded after him. "Lance!" She knew in her heart that he didn't love her, that he just wanted to dip his manhood into her virgin plunge pool, but she couldn't help herself. She loved him and would stoop to any depths to win his love. Ever since childhood, when her father had beaten her repeatedly and told her how useless she was, she'd dreamt of a moment like this. She was ready. This was her moment. She knew how to plead pathetically. She knew how to use her low self esteem to win over the Lances of this world."*

Not to be outdone, Lou got to her feet, acting out the movements as she spoke, *"Encouraged by the others in the casualty waiting room she plunged recklessly after him catching her diaphanous skirt on a fire extinguisher, ripping it from hem to hip. With one tanned thigh flashing as she ran, she stumbled down the sterile corridor panting seductively, her heaving bosom fighting to escape her tight bodice. With a tearing of taffeta her neckline descended revealing creamy pink flesh from nape to navel. At this moment, her jet-black hair, released from its bonds on the top of her head, cascaded and fell about her neck, her modesty tantalisingly contained. "Lance. Don't leave me. I can't live without you. I'll do anything you want. Anything!"* Lance turned.

Mike, looking lecherously at Lou, narrated whilst Lou acted, *"In slow motion she shook her head, her voluptuous black hair swinging seductively and wafting gallons of perfume through the antiseptic air. Batting her doe-like eyes, against the lead weight of her mascara, she flashed her electric blue contact lenses at him. How could he resist! As the remains of her dress fell off one shoulder and then the other, he pushed her roughly into the broom closet."* Mike grabbed Lou by the shoulders and kissed her passionately before all three dissolved into laughter.

* * *

Grant was trying to figure out how he was going to get to work the next day. Having spent most of Saturday night awake, not knowing what to do with his hand to give him some relief from the pain, he had spent most of Sunday morning in Accident and Emergency getting it first X-rayed and then plastered. Typical boxer's injury they had said. He'd fractured a metacarpal. So now he had a hand he couldn't use for the next few weeks. The pain had settled some, now that the bone was immobilised and protected and provided he kept it elevated in the sling. He didn't actually need to go to work as the hospital had signed him off, at least until his out-patient's appointment, but there were things he needed to deal with. He needed to go to work if only to make it possible for him not to go to work for the next week or so, such as passing on information to others, cancelling appointments, finishing the report he was writing. There were also things in his personal life like getting his ring back and his MG.

Jess had been great. She had completely blown his initial impression of her. The red hair, the multiple studs in her ears and the too-short skirt had been a visual turn off for him. In some respects, he had even dismissed her as a worthy human being, assuming her to be not very bright and, having found her sitting in his car, not very trust-worthy. Normally he wouldn't have given her the time of day, despite his physical reaction to her legs as she wielded them out of his car. He preferred classier, less obvious, well groomed women, women made-up to look naturally beautiful. Jess by comparison was, well, trashy! Her actions though had rapidly changed his mind. She had done the sensible thing by taking his keys off him. There was no way he could have driven. He didn't have the strength to hold the wheel whilst he changed gear and he had been in danger of passing out had he needed to grip the wheel at all. At her insistence he had phoned round until he had found a mate to come pick him up. Whilst they waited, she had made him a cup of tea, apologised when he spluttered on the unexpected leaves in his cup and fed him cake, saying the sugar would do him good. Then she had very deftly helped him to put the top up on the midget and said she would keep a good eye on it until he was able to collect it. She had treated his precious car with impressive respect and the conversation they had had regarding it resulted in him trusting her completely. He was even slightly amused that her hair matched the paintwork.

It had been over two hours they had spent together waiting for Steve to come pick him up. As there were few customers, they had chatted about all sorts of things. He had explained about Emily, and the fight, and was keen to point out that he didn't normally get into fights. In fact, he hadn't had a fight since he was at school. It all happened so fast. Why had the estate agent attacked him? Was he Emily's boyfriend? Was it his house? Emily certainly couldn't afford it.

Jess stared at him. "You don't know, do you?"

"Don't know what?"

"It was in all the papers, well, the local ones anyway..."

"What was?"

"She won the lottery. One point two million or something like that," said Jess.

Grant was stunned. Then slowly it sank in. "She thinks I want her just for her money. I threw her out and then she wins the lottery and now I want her back. Oh, shit!"

That night, as he had struggled to get undressed one-handed, he had realised that the engagement ring was missing. He had texted Mike.

CHAPTER
TWENTY ONE

It was a miserable day and Emily was feeling slightly apprehensive although she didn't really understand why. After the frantic events of last week, this was the first day she had had on her own. With nothing she needed to do she was feeling slightly at a loss. There were lots of things she could do, but nothing she actually felt she wanted to do. Was this a foretaste of what her life was going to be like? All those years of not wanting to go to work, of desperately wishing she had the freedom to do what she wanted, when she wanted, and now that she had it...she was slightly afraid that she wasn't going to know what to do with it.

During breakfast she decided to make a list. There were lots of things that needed doing. Yes, she would make a list, two lists, immediate everyday things like shopping and another long-term list for projects. Firstly, she needed food and various other items, like toilet rolls. Her guests had got through more than she had expected. She had had to bring down the ones from the bathroom. She suspected that most of her guests had used the facilities purely as an excuse to nosey inside the house. Still, she couldn't blame them for that. She would have probably done the same. She also needed to get her nails fixed. She wasn't sure how far she was going to have to travel for that. She didn't fancy going all the way back to her old salon. She needed somewhere nearer. She'd ask Anna, but then that wasn't her kind of thing. She started her lists and then left them on the table ready to add to them as she thought of things. Then she went and got dressed before doing her on-line food shop.

The morning passed slowly as she tidied up the house and stripped the bedding off Lou and Mike's bed before sticking it in the washing machine. She added various items to her two lists, one of which was to systematically work her way through the house tidying each room whilst having a sort through. She was sure that there must be lots of stuff that could go to charity.

She found a tin of beans for lunch and a left-over bap and was just washing up when the doorbell rang. It was James, come to see how she was doing, thinking that she might be at a bit of a loss after the excitement of last week now that she was on her own. She was most apologetic for not having been to church. He said that he hadn't spotted that she hadn't been there amongst the sea of faces but, with a glance skywards, he said it wasn't him she needed to apologise to. He hoped she didn't mind him calling. He hoped she also wouldn't mind, but she'd said she would sponsor him, and what with the fight, he hadn't managed to present her with the sponsor form.

Of course, she would sponsor him. She was sorry but she had quite forgotten. In fact, she'd been thinking that maybe she would like to do something useful with her money. Instead of just giving it away, she was wondering if she could use it to actually generate more money. Did he have any ideas?

He thought for a moment then said, "Well, it depends on how much you are willing to invest and what time and effort you want to put in. You could just put money in a high interest account and then pay the interest to the charity of your choice or you could go the whole hog and set up a charity business providing a service or selling goods. You don't have *that* much money, so the latter probably isn't a viable option. Let me have a think."

She made them both a cup of tea and told him all about Gerald, spending every daylight moment that he wasn't working, fishing for the periapt. She was desperate to get it back, if only to get Gerald out of her garden. They chatted at length. Going over the well blessing, they discussed what had gone well and what they felt they could improve on for next time. Emily filled in the sponsor form and James joked that he'd wanted to get in quick before Alex got back. When Alex had heard what James was doing, he decided to join him. They were going to train together, and no doubt Alex would also be along with a sponsor form.

Emily asked him what had made him take up running and he explained that it initially had been a way of keeping fit after he left the fire service. He explained that he had been medically retired after injuring his back. It was no longer disabling but his back was no longer up to the demands that rescue work might impose.

"So, you weren't always a vicar then. What made you decide to join the church?"

"Well, no great vision or profound experience if that's what you're getting at, I just always had the feeling that there was something more, that we weren't alone, that there was something greater aware of what I was doing..."

"Oh, I know what you mean. I had that, but that was my mother. She always seemed to know what I'd been up to," laughed Emily, "Sorry, I didn't mean to mock. I guess I've always just had an open mind when it came to religion. So, what was it like being a fireman, or firefighter, or whatever the politically correct version is?"

"Well, boring a lot of the time. You spend hours on end equipment checking and drilling, and the rest trying to keep fit and just find a way of passing the time. Then there are the false alarms and repeat false alarms; ones you know full well are just a waste of everyone's time, but you have to go anyway, just in case on this one occasion it's a real fire, and then there are the real fires, some tragic, some that haunt you forever more. Anyway, I don't do that now."

"So, is this your first parish?"

"No, I had an inner city one first. That was temporary though, filling in whilst the vicar was recovering from a car accident. He was off for 18 months. It did me good, let me make mistakes and learn from them before starting afresh here, with some experience under my cassock."

"So, how did you hurt your back if you don't mind me asking?"

"Oh, nothing dramatic. We were just damping down and making safe, huh, after a fire in some bed-sits. A floorboard gave way under me and I fell through up to my hip. I twisted and landed badly. They had to carry me out, and the rest is history. I'm fine now, just can't support any weight reliably. So now, I serve the community in a different way."

"Isn't it amazing how small events can turn your life in a whole other direction," mused Emily. "Well, I'm glad you are alright now.

* * *

Just after 7pm Sally called for Emily to take her to the book club meeting. Together they walked to the other end of the village and a little way up one of the side streets that encroached slightly on the wood below the crag. The houses were all set amongst the trees, most in their own grounds, but Sally led the pair of them to the centre of a short terrace of five houses that backed onto the hillside. It was apparent that the properties all had cellars and attics, giving them four floors, and making them quite substantial houses. Large lumps of limestone formed gate posts and solid limestone walls held back small gardens which separated the houses from the road. Squarely cut granite steps led the way up to each of the five front doors. As Emily and Sally waited for the door to be opened, they were joined by another book club member. Sally introduced her as Cheryl. Cheryl hadn't lived in the village for long either and it was good to have some new members.

The door was opened and the three of them were ushered in. Dave, the owner, greeted them and then introduced them to everyone. Now Emily had joined there were fourteen people in the book club. They didn't usually all turn up and so far, their arrival made nine. Emily's two bottles of wine were well received: especially Angelica's red that she had found in the cellar. Not knowing what it would be like she had also brought a bottle of Tesco's 'The Best' white. However, Angelica's wine had an excellent reputation, and everyone was keen to have a glass, albeit a small one. When everyone had a glass and was seated Dave suggested that they each said a little about themselves so that the two new people could get to know everyone. Emily's heart sank. She hated this. She wouldn't hear a thing anyone said until after she'd had her go as she would be too busy trying to work out what she was going to say, and what *was* she going to say? 'Hi, Emily, I'm Nuevo riche.' 'Hi, Emily Hope, Millionaire.' 'Hi, I'm Emily, I'm the one who made a complete fool of herself at the well blessing. I'm the one men fight over!' 'Hi, I'm the one with the crappy nails.' She was busy inspecting them when she got nudged. It was her turn. "Hi, I'm Emily.

"I think we all know who *you* are," said Dave, "who here didn't go to the well blessing? Who didn't enjoy the hotpot"

"Yes, you did a terrific job."

"Well done."

General congratulations and mutterings of approval rippled round the room. Emily blushed.

"Well, welcome to the book club," said Dave.

The last two people introduced themselves. Cheryl, the other new person, was a nurse at the St. Peter's YDU, and Andy was an accountant. They seemed very nice and Emily determined to remember *their* names; the rest she would just have to listen out for as she had no idea what they had said. Glasses were topped up and Mags, who Emily concluded was Dave's wife, explained that they had just read Bram Stoker's Dracula. They had chosen it because out of all the books that they had read they hadn't read any horror. So, why not read a classic that everyone was familiar with but not in the original version.

They had all enjoyed it and commented on how atmospheric it was at the beginning. Different people highlighted different aspects that they had admired and there was some questioning of the intricacies of the plot as different people remembered different things. Emily was relieved that the discussion wasn't too academic and despite not having read the book she enjoyed listening to the varied opinions and marvelled at the way they had all enjoyed it in different ways. It was Donna's turn to choose the next book. Donna was a mother of three boys who worked from home designing greetings cards. She was quite slim with very rich ginger coloured hair. She had a ready smile but seemed rather excitable and anxious which Emily found a little off-putting. She had chosen Dostoyevsky's 'Crime and Punishment' for their next book, to murmurs of approval. One or two of them had read it previously and were happy to read it again, reporting it to be a very good book. It sounded rather serious to Emily.

As the evening wore on, discussion turned to the well blessing. They all seemed keen to chat to Emily about her new role and how she was finding life in the village. Having enjoyed several glasses of wine she was feeling relaxed and comfortable in their company and confessed her distress at Carla's attitude and behaviour towards her. She couldn't understand why the woman was so antagonistic towards her. She knew there was no love lost between Carla and the triplets, but Emily had been nothing but polite to her. The only possible thing she had done to cause offence was to buy her groceries on-line. She told them all how Carla had put some vegetables to one side for her for the hotpot and Emily had refused them, but her main reason for buying on-line was because Carla made her feel so unwelcome in the shop.

At that point one of the women, short dark hair and with a pair of blue framed reading glasses perched on the end of her nose, exclaimed thoughtfully, "When was this?"

Emily thought a bit, "Last Tuesday."

"My Harry said that – he's a recycling operative – when he emptied the bins at the back of the store, on Wednesday, there was a whole load of perfectly good veg in the recycling. He thought it was odd because it was in better nick than most o' the stuff she generally 'as on display."

"What," said Dave, "what are you imply-ing?"

"I'm just saying it seems odd that she put aside veg for Emily, Emily refuses it, and then a whole load o' perfectly good veg gets thrown away. Why not just put it back on the shelves … unless, there is something wrong with it…?"

"You don't thing she'd poison the veg for the hotpot. She'd be poisoning the whole vil-lage. She might be a little unhinged, but she isn't that far gone. Apart from the criminal side of it, that store is her livelihood."

"It just seems extremely odd to me," said glasses woman.

"What if she just wanted to *ruin* the hot-pot – make it *taste* bad," suggested Sally tucking her hair behind her left ear, "that wouldn't do anyone any harm, but it would spoil Emily's achievement. How could she go about doing that?"

This started a lively discussion as to how you could tamper with vegetables to make them taste bad without it being noticeable when you peeled and chopped them. You would have to find a way of getting whatever it was in-side either by cutting a tiny hole, injecting the substance or soaking the veg. What could you use that would have the desired effect? Salt, bak-ing powder. It would need to be something that wouldn't stain or cause deterioration, leak or smell. Someone suggested carefully picking out the eyes of the potatoes, injecting salt, and then putting the eyes back, but no one knew whether or not the salt would affect the potato and turn the flesh black, and, anyway, how many potatoes had eyes these days?

Then a voice of reason asked whether Carla was really that nutty as to sabotage the well blessing just to get back at Emily.

"I don't know," said Emily, "Carla is convinced that Kevin, that's Angelica's old cat – he came with the house – is plotting against her. She believes that he deliberately dropped mice through the storeroom sky light when the health inspector visited..."

"Yes," laughed Andy, "and that he deliberately pee'd in the shop doorway."

"You know, she's been losing it for a bit. Her and her cronies are always whispering together. There has been bad blood building for years. The Wells sisters tried to ignore it but Carla was convinced that they were witches and spread all sorts of rumours about them when her Derek went off with that other woman. She blamed them, but lord knows why."

"Yes, I heard that since Angelica died, she hasn't dared hold a single séance," mused Donna.

"She holds séances?" asked Cheryl.

"Oh, yes, has done for years, always passing judgement and claiming the dead aren't happy with this or that. I believe she was charging for her services at one time, until she claimed to have been contacted by the deceased uncle of a family, over Holm Firth way, wanting them to dig in their back garden for some unspecified item that he had lost, only to have the guy send them a post card from the Costa Del Sol six months later saying he was alive and well and living there with a masseuse from Pontepridd. In the meantime, the family had dug over virtually their whole garden looking for some heirloom that was going to make their fortune. As you can imagine they weren't too happy and not only demanded their money back but were wanting compensation for the state of their garden and, of course, 'emotional distress'!"

"And now," said Emily giggling, "you are saying that she daren't hold any séances because all her enemies have passed over, and she is afraid that all three of them will be waiting to have a go at her from the other side. Fantastic!"

There followed lots of amused suggestions as to how a séance might be conducted by Carla and some general discussion as to whether it was possible for the dead to communicate. This led to various guests relating their own personal ghost stories whilst other members of the group were adamant that ghosts didn't exist. Then to everyone's shock Cheryl, the newcomer, stunned them all by announcing in a serious and matter of fact way, "I see dead people."

Everyone stared at her, as the hairs on

the back of their necks stood up, and something cold appeared to possess the room. "I'm a nurse, it's an occupational hazard," she said, then smiled wickedly as comprehension dawned on them all and they started to laugh in relief at her sick joke.

"You really had us going there," laughed Dave, as he topped up Cheryl's glass.

By the time they all left it was well after midnight. Sally and Emily wove their way back up the high street trying to talk quietly in the deserted silence.

CHAPTER
TWENTY TWO

L ou and Mike were having breakfast and dis-
cussing Emily and Grant. Mike had spent the
previous evening at Grant's flat having returned
his ring. Grant was pretty morose. Life was prov-
ing rather difficult with only one useful hand
and he was in varying degrees of pain. He had no
food in the house and no clean clothes and his
MG was in Greater Blessing. The only good bit
about his life at the moment was that Mike had
brought his ring back, but that was useless now
as he had completely blown his chances with
Emily. He had made a complete fool of himself
and he had humiliated her in the worst possible
way. Apparently, there was now an 'Alex' and
as if that wasn't enough, he now knew that she
had won the lottery. He couldn't even offer her
financial security. He felt he had nothing to give.

Even the ring, which had cost him over a grand, now looked cheap in his eyes. Emily thought him a money grabbing good for nothing. She was wrong, but he could see why she'd think that.

Lou and Mike didn't know what to do for the best. The only thing they could do was to tell Emily how miserable Grant was and that he had only just found out about her money. He really had not known. After Mike had gone to work Lou phoned Emily.

"Hi, Em."

"Hi, Lou. How are you both?"

"We're fine. I'm just calling to let you know that Mike saw Grant last night and he's pretty miserable."

Emily was silent.

"I just wanted you to know that he now knows you won the lottery, and he is also really sorry for making such a scene at the well blessing. Oh, and he broke his hand. It is now in plaster and he can't drive, which is why his midget is still parked in Greater Blessing high street in case you happen to spot it there."

"He broke his hand?" Emily felt slightly sick, and she realised that her feelings for him weren't completely dead.

"Em, will you do something for me?" asked Louise.

"Of, course!"

"I've e-mailed you Mike's clip of the fight. I want you to watch it."

"Oh!"

"Promise me you will."

Reluctantly Emily promised. To change the subject, she told Lou all about the book club meeting and how she'd enjoyed it and about the lovely people she'd met that were such fun.

* * *

Carla did a double take. She had nipped upstairs to change her jumper, having spilt milk on it from a split carton, and glanced out of the window. She thought she was seeing double, but on closer inspection she found she wasn't, there were now two pairs of eyes watching from the tree opposite. Kevin was no longer alone. He had been joined by a silver-coloured tabby. Unnerved she drew the curtains and sat on the bed to think. She couldn't do anything about the cats, but without the protection of the periapt...

* * *

Emily tried to avoid the moment, but Lou's insistence that she watch the video played on her mind and eventually she decided to just get it over with. At first, the image moved about wildly as Mike honed-in on the action. Then, as he focussed in on the three main characters, Grant, Emily and Gerald, it settled down to a lopsided, full colour, blow by blow account in excruciating detail. The camera followed Grant across the lawn with Emily and James in the background by the well. She remembered that James, who could be seen shouting into her ear, trying to make himself heard above the noise in the garden, was telling her that the outhouse toilet had run out of paper. As he disappeared from shot, she turned and saw Grant approaching, the expression on her face clearly unwelcoming. She started shouting at Grant and then to her horror she saw herself start punching him in the chest. She did not remember doing that. If anyone had told her, she would not have believed them. He grabbed her wrists to fend her off. Then, her eyes grew large as Gerald stepped into shot and blocked both her and Grant from view. At this point the camera position moved jerkily as Mike obviously tried to get a better shot. Now, all three were visible. As Gerald grabbed and spun Grant, the look of surprise and then bewilderment on Grant's face as Gerald punched him, cut Emily to the quick. Grant tried to turn to face his attacker, but his left arm was restrained. As it came free something shiny shot through the air tracing a sparkling silver arch from Emily's neck, to the well, clearly dropping inside. The periapt had gone down the well. Now the camera moved backwards, and the actions were shaky and blurred before settling on Grant and Gerald rolling about on the floor, kneeing and punching each other. There was no sound, but each blow resonated in her chest as Grant absorbed every punch. The shot became crowded and muddled as several people stepped in and hauled the two men to their feet. At this point the clip ended abruptly, and Emily realised that she had tears running down her cheeks. Poor Grant. None of it had been his fault. First she, then Gerald, had attacked him. All he had done was defend himself. He had come bearing a ring, presumably he was going to propose, and what had she done, pulled that ghastly face at him and started punching him in the chest. He had finally come to do what she'd wanted him to do for years, and she'd assaulted him, hadn't given him a chance. She played the clip again and made herself watch every miserable detail.

* * *

Alex was just downing a glass of water and taking a breather. It was hot work, and this particular horse was being particularly difficult. It was large and skittish and tensed violently every time the shoe singed its way into the hoof, nostrils flaring at the smell. He wondered what Emily was doing, alone now in that big house. Was she thinking of him at all? Did she like him? She had seemed keen when he had suggested going out for a drink, but was she just being friendly, wanting to make friends in the village? Then there was James. She obviously liked him too and had actually spent more time with him. The two of them seemed to get along very well. He didn't know, but what he did know was that Emily was occupying more and more of his thoughts. It was Wednesday already, but the weekend seemed a long way away.

* * *

Emily had just had a visit from two elderly sisters. One was 89 and the other 92 years old. Longevity, it seemed, was not just confined to the Wells family. They had come for their ointments and like the old man before them fully expected Emily to continue to meet their supply. Her 'payment' this time was a large, very wrinkled paper bag full of home-made biscuits.

"Ooh, thank you," said Emily glancing inside the bag, "I just love pistachios."

"No dear, they're almonds," said the elder of the two and then, with a meaningful look around the room, "You really need to get to know your nuts."

As they left, Emily peered inside the bag again. She could see now that she had been wrong, the slight green tinge of the 'pistachio' was actually blue! She screwed the bag shut again and popped it in the bin.

If more and more people were going to turn up, she needed to know what she was going to do and she needed advice. After some thought she decided that the most likely person to give her advice would be the local GP and as she hadn't registered with one since she'd moved perhaps, she could 'kill two birds with one stone'. She found the address in the Greater Blessing newsletter which came through the door once a month, apparently, and contained all sorts of useful local information.

Walking down the high street she spotted Grant's MG. She must have passed it with Sally but hadn't noticed it in the dark. Now, she felt a wave of sadness as she saw the familiar red vehicle with Grant's motor club badge on the radiator grill. She patted the black hood and felt the metal supports through the water-proof cover and remembered the times she had popped the shiny metal studs of it, hurriedly helping to put the roof up as it started to rain during some picnic or other that she and Grant had been on. All that age ago. In another lifetime it seemed. A life when she was happy to be bounced about in a draughty car, getting cold whilst her hair was blown to smithereens, just because it pleased Grant, and making him happy mattered.

The GP surgery was a modern building with a sign saying, 'parking at rear', and small lawns either side of a smooth path that curved in a gentle 'S' to a wide entrance porch with automatic doors. The waiting room had several groups of chairs and a couple of tables stacked with magazines and a disarray of health leaflets. In the corner was a selection of children's toys which looked surprisingly new, and clean. The end wall was a dark red making the green of the plants, standing in pots in front of it, very vivid. The space was warm and welcoming. Emily presented her NHS card at the reception desk and said she would like to register with a GP. Having answered the required questions and completed the medical questionnaire she opted for a female doctor and then asked if it was possible to make an appointment to see the GP about a non-medical matter. The receptionist was rather taken aback by this so Emily explained that she wanted to ask about Angelica Wells supply of 'medicines' to the villagers. This was greeted by an amused smile and an appointment for 2pm the following day and a, "Dr Hartley will be delighted to talk to you, I'm sure."

* * *

Kevin watched as Emily sat thoughtfully by the fire sipping a cup of coffee and flicking through a photo album of her and Grant. The album was a mixture of their holiday in Jersey last summer and various social events leading up to Christmas, including a weekend at Grant's parents, their Labrador puppy starring in nearly every shot. She wondered how Jackie and Tony were and whether it had taken Grant as long to tell them of the break-up as it had taken her to tell her parents. She had got on well with Jackie. It was strange not seeing her and Tony anymore. It must have been 4 months since she had seen them. She hoped they didn't blame her.

She ran her fingers over Grant's smiling face, imagining the feel of his holiday stubble, and stared into his carefree eyes as they smiled delightedly back at her. She remembered taking the picture as Grant rowed them across a boating lake. What was the name of the park? She couldn't remember. He was laughing as he could see the large wake heading their way from the tour boat which had just passed. She took the picture a split second before the wave hit their stern tipping her into the bottom of the boat and drenching her. They'd been so happy. How had it all gone so wrong?

Kevin jumped up onto her lap giving her no time to close the album. After a series of noisy purring circles and a pincer mark or two from his needing claws he successfully drew her attention away from the photos. She lifted him slightly to remove the album and then allowed him to settle on her lap. Together they sat, silently enjoying each others company, deep in their own thoughts. As the light started to fade, she got up, put the light on and drew the curtains. She heard the cat flap and soon the silver tabby came and stood besides Kevin. "Hi, Cat, where've you been? Ready for some food?" She filled both their dishes. They ate and then settled down together on the chair to the left of the fire, a tangled heap of furry limbs, pink pads and fluffy tails. Could such a delightful pair really be as disturbing as her thoughts? Every time she looked at the newcomer, she had the strange feeling that the cat new more about her than she did about the cat. Every misgiving though seemed to be followed up by the thought, 'all will be well', which was disturbing enough in its own right. She shrugged her shoulders in resignation. After all, whatever was going on, it seemed to be in her favour.

CHAPTER
TWENTY THREE

J ess was busy daydreaming. *She and Grant were driving along the Amalphi Coast in the MG. They had the top down, and the sun was beating down on their backs. They'd had lunch outside a small café in Sorrento* – she wiped the table top and straightened the cruet, stacking the sugar sachets neatly into the plastic holder – *The Italian waiter had been flirting with her and Grant had been annoyed – mildly, he wasn't the jealous type – they had sipped their Pinot Grigio and exchanged witty banter as they ate their calamari* – Jess had no idea what calamari was but it sounded just great – *now they had parked by the side of the road in the shade of some olive trees and Grant had spread a travel rug on the ground. As the sun settled on the horizon, spreading a golden light across the sea, Grant pressed his lips to hers...*

"You alright love, you look quite peaky?"

"Oh, sorry, didn't hear you," said Jess. Flustered, she forced a smile at the elderly gentleman who was standing in front of her holding a flat cap, greasy silk lining uppermost, a look of irritated concern on his weather-beaten face, "What can I get you?"

"A Chorley Cake and a pot o' tea, please, and I don't want any o' your leaves; they only get under me dentures." He wandered inside. Jess picked up the cloth and then the bottle of spray cleaner. Swinging it 'six-shooter' like round her extended finger a couple of times she grabbed it, finger on trigger, and pointed it at the old man's back. Having fired a couple of shots of cleaner in his general direction she followed him inside.

* * *

Emily had tried to have a lie in, but feline stomachs wait for no man, or woman. The combined effect of eight pummelling paws was difficult to ignore. Emily opened her eyes. The two cats were staring at her. Seeing she was awake, they jumped off the bed and headed for the door. From experience she knew that the only way to get a lie in was to go downstairs, fill their dishes, and come back up. Her training now complete, she obeyed. As she returned to the stairs, she noticed an envelope on the mat by the front door. Turning it over she recognised Grant's company's frank. As she made her way back upstairs, she ran her thumb under the corner of the flap and ripped open the envelope. Sliding back under the covers she opened the folded printed sheet.

Dear Emily,

I am so very very sorry for ruining your well blessing. I really didn't mean to cause any trouble. Can you ever forgive me? I just came to talk to you as I miss you so.

I was stunned to hear that you have won the lottery and I am really pleased for you. It is a lovely house you have bought, and the village seems really nice.

In case you notice the MG sitting in the high street I had to leave it. No doubt Lou has told you by now that I broke a bone in my hand and can't drive. It is a nuisance but it will heal.

You appear to be happily settled, and I hear there is another man in your life now. I wish you well.

If you can bear to see me again, I would like to call round when I come to pick up the car. I want to apologise, not only for last weekend but also for the way I treated you. You have no idea how sorry I am. I can't deal with the thought of never seeing you again. I was so, very very stupid. Your love was the best thing in the world, and I threw it away.

All my love,

Grant xxx

Emily brushed away a tear. *Grant* was written in a child's hand. He had obviously struggled to sign the letter with his left hand, unable to hold a pen in his right. Was he giving up on her? Another man? What had Lou and Mike told him? Or, did he think she and Gerald!...Ughh!

Having wasted the morning lying in bed pondering what to do about Grant, she nearly missed her appointment with the GP. Hurrying down the high street she tried to ignore Grant's car but couldn't. Thoughts of him filled her mind. Could she really take him back? Did she want that? Or, was she just feeling sorry for him? The wacky waitress with the coloured hair was clearing crockery from the tables outside the Little Teacups Café. Emily smiled as she walked by. The girl's smile dropped from her face once it was apparent that Emily wasn't buying.

At the surgery, Emily sat on a chair in a corridor, the antiseptic smell making her feel nervous even though she wasn't there as a patient. Eventually the door was opened, and she was ushered in by a tiny bustling woman whom Emily judged to be in her late 50s. Her hair was cropped and sculpted into a no-nonsense bob which complimented her round face making her look younger than she actually was. The woman appeared delighted to see her, excited almost, as she offered Emily a chair and asked her how she could help. Emily explained about the house and how all Angelica's belongings had been left for her and about the 'patients' that kept turning up. She was worried that she may poison someone, and she wasn't sure if any of it was legal.

The doctor laughed. "I am so glad you have come. Angelica was a law unto herself. She had several 'run-ins' with we GPs over the years. In fact, we'd all be delighted to come to your house and see what she was up to and what was in those concoctions."

"If you want, please come. Then you can tell me what to do. I don't want to upset anyone else in the village by withdrawing their medicines, but I also don't want to be responsible for killing anyone," said Emily.

"Well, I have to say, that we aren't aware of anyone coming to grief over her ministrations, and a number did get better, but whether they would have got better anyway is difficult to say. Plus, placebos can work very well for some people, especially if delivered with a bit of tea, sympathy and understanding that Angelica did very well and we, unfortunately, don't always have time for. "

So, Emily arranged that the GPs would visit and give their opinion as to whether she was the proud owner of a holistic pharmacy, or a poison pantry. Dr Hartley, Claire, would let her know when they were all available. Friday evening was a possibility although Emily was secretly hoping that Alex would ask her to go for a drink that evening. She thought he might have called sometime during the week to arrange it, but he hadn't. Maybe it was for the best if she was re-examining her relationship with Grant. But then, she couldn't see Grant moving to Greater Blessing and she had no intention of going back to her old life in Manchester. As she wandered back down the street, she realised that she was biting the remains of a nail. Inspecting her hands she decided that, Grant or Alex, she needed to smarten herself up.

Passing the café, she was hit with inspiration. The waitress, with all the studs, must get her hair done somewhere a bit more inspirational than the perm parlour, with the sixties advertising board and yellowing window display, which she had seen next to the bakery.

"Hi," said Emily, "I hope you don't mind me asking but I was just wondering where you got your hair done. They do such a good job. You see, I need my nails doing, and I was hoping they might do those too, or if not, you might know somewhere that does?"

The waitress looked at her own bitten nails and laughed, "No, they don't do nails." So, thought Jess, the love of Grant's life is asking for my help. This needs thinking about. "If you give me your phone number, I am sure I can find somewhere and let you know."

"Oh, right, thank you," said Emily. "That's

really good of you," and she wrote her number on a piece of paper and handed it over.

* * *

By the time evening arrived Emily had more or less made up her mind to see Grant. She still cared about him, and him turning up on the day of the well blessing had just been lousy timing. As for what had happened previously, well, they had both been at fault. She had said some dreadful things, things she didn't really mean or things that didn't really matter that much, but which she had used as ammunition simply because she knew it would hurt. Probably he had done the same. She shouldn't have expected him to take her to the airport and miss his motor club dinner. Maybe she could have asked work to postpone her trip to India until after New Year. If she had just altered one of those two things, then none of this would have happened.

There was a long, drawn-out moan from the chair at the other side of the fire as the silver tabby stretched and rearranged herself. Before settling down again she looked at Emily, head slightly on one side. The old lady's words replayed in Emily's head, 'but do you love him?' Then she remembered Grant locking her out and her heart sank. Could she forgive him for that?

She tried watching some TV but couldn't concentrate and just ended up flicking between channels. Maybe Lou was right, she needed to see Grant and tell him to his face, one way or another. She did miss him, but why was she so un-certain? Before she could change her mind, she wrote him a quick e-mail.

Grant,

Thank you for your letter. Let me know when you come to collect your car and if you want to talk that is okay. Sorry about your hand.

Emily.

She read what she had written. It was suc-cinct and business like. She was not committing herself to anything. Before she could change her mind, she hit 'send'. *That* done, she felt a little better. Now the ball was back in his court, all she had to do was wait.

CHAPTER
TWENTY FOUR

A t 9am the phone rang. Emily's heart
skipped a beat; she wasn't ready to speak to
Grant yet. Palm a little sweaty, she picked up the
receiver, "Hello?"

"Good morning, is that Emily?" said a female voice.

"Er, yes."

"Hi, it's Claire... from the surgery ... Dr
Hartley."

"Oh, yes, sorry," said Emily, "I was expecting someone else. What can I do for you?"

"Would it be possible if we GPs came
round tomorrow morning, say 11 o'clock? It is
about the only time the majority of us can make
it."

"Certainly," said Emily relieved, thinking
of Alex, that the doctor had not suggested an

evening. "I look forward to it. See you all at 11, then."

She needed to tidy up. The front room was in a right mess since the preparations for the well blessing. She stood in the doorway and surveyed the room. There were dried leaves and seeds all over the floor, crumpled into dust where they had been trampled on. On the table in the centre of the room various books were open and stacked precariously where they had been discarded in the hunt for pertinent knowledge. Bits of garden twine remnants lay where they had been cut, faded flower heads on broken stalks shed pollen dust into the cracks in the old table, and bunches of unused herbs lay in sad heaps on the table, on chairs and on the floor. The room had a patina of dust covering everything and the air was heavy with a musty perfume.

She started by clearing one side of the large table. She then sorted out the books, picked out all the bits of twine, scissors, jars, knives etc. and what she thought to be useful bunches of herbs, and put them to one side. Then, taking a hand brush she swept all the debris on to the floor. She did the same with the chairs and other surfaces. Using a long-handled brush, she swept the mess into a heap in front of the door before shovelling it into a large bin bag. Having taken the bag and emptied it onto the compost heap she dusted, then vacuumed the room. Impressed with her efforts she was spurred on to clean the jars on the shelves, keen to make a good impression on the doctors.

Having tidied the room she then wondered about the best way to show them what she had, and what her 'patients' were expecting of her. She retrieved the notebook Lou had found with all the ointment instructions and put it on the table. Ointments 1-56 were listed. She climbed on a chair and took down all the numbered jars. There were 29 in all. Obviously not all the ointments were in use. She gave them all a dust and spread them in numerical order across the table. At one side she displayed the weighing scales and various measures and tools. Then she hunted through Angelica's notebooks to find the 'medical records' and put them on the table.

She arranged the chairs in a little group by the fireplace with a cushion or two to brighten up the scene and finally put a bunch of dried flowers in a vase on the windowsill. The room now looked homely, smelled pleasant, and was a clean, welcoming space. She did a bit more book tidying and shelf re-arranging so that it was more pleasing to the eye. Another look round the room and she decided to clean and lay the fire. It was turning into a lovely little consulting room and she realised that she was getting quite carried away with her 'role' as medicine woman. What *was* she playing at?

Turning her attention to the hall she

dusted, vacuumed and tidied. When she was satisfied that it was clean, she searched the house
for items that would colour co-ordinate and displayed them, a picture here, a vase there, to
brighten up the entrance. Pleased with herself
she went and got some lunch. Just when she
was thinking that things were under control, she
remembered the cellar. Apart from noting the
racks of wine and various unknown substances
stored down there she hadn't really investigated
it properly as the light was so poor. There was
only one dull bulb at the bottom of the steps.
She had shone a torch round the rest of it and
noted that there were other light fittings, but
she just hadn't got round to getting or fitting any
more bulbs. After lunch she would pinch some
bulbs from elsewhere in the house and fit them
in the cellar. That way, she could show the doctors everything.

Lunch over, she went up to the attic and
removed the light bulbs. She took them down to
the cellar and, torch in teeth, pulled over a chair,
climbed up and fitted the first bulb. Having put
a bulb in each of the four light fittings she went
back to the top of the stairs and switched on
the lights. What a difference. The cellar seemed
much larger. It ran the length and breadth of the
house and was divided into three areas, one long
room and two alcoves fitted with shelves. The
end wall of the main room was one huge wine
rack, practically full of dusty bottles, all clearly

labelled by year. Emily did a quick calculation, there must have been close to a thousand bottles. She took one out at random and wiped the label. It was very faded, but she could just make out the handwriting – Wishing Well Winery - Elderflower 1968. 1968? Would it still be alright? The bottle she had taken to the book club had been from a batch stacked at the bottom of the stairs, dated two thousand and something.

Turning her attention to the rest of the cellar she noticed that, whereas her end was cut square into the rock, the far end was rounded and one of the columns supporting the ceiling was actually, yes, she was certain, a huge stalactite. The other column, which was composed of blocks of stone, had top and base continuous with the ceiling and floor. It looked like a column of limestone had been replaced with stone blocks. Briefly she wondered why. Maybe it wasn't as big or strong as the other one. Then Angelica's words came flooding back to her, 'cut from the limestone beneath our feet'. Is that what she meant, the periapt was cut from that very column? Inspecting the remaining column, she mentally compared the colour and texture of it against her memory of the periapt. It had the same shiny, almost translucent, creamy texture. It must be. She really needed to get the periapt back. Maybe Gerald would succeed. Whatever the rest of his faults she could not criticise his perseverance or his determination to make amends. He had been in her garden every evening this week and most of Thursday, his day off.

Wandering round, she found a box of old ornaments and some paintings, bags of clothes and old shoes, odd chairs and a folding table. Under an oilcloth was a stack of records and to Emily's delight an old hand cranked gramophone, complete with a tiny push out drawer full of needles. Lifting the lid, she saw the jointed shiny metal arm leading from the pick-up head to the speaker horn in its base and the 'His Master's Voice' logo under the lid, its hinged pocket holding two gramophone records. How neat, thought Emily, a self-contained record player and carry case. She took the angled handle and screwed it into the hole in the side of the box. Then she pulled one of the records out and placed it on the turn table and turned over the head of the pick-up arm to rest the needle on the record. Then she turned the handle. After several turns the turntable strained to move. She lifted the needle off the record and the record turned. After a bit of experimenting, she realised that the turntable needed to get up to speed before she lowered the needle. Amid some offensive crackling 'Daisy, Daisy, give me your answer do' could be clearly heard before the record slowed down. More handle turning got it going again but the whole machine was badly in need of oiling. The second record, to her surprise, was Frank Sinatra's 'Nancy', but sadly it was cracked.

Realising that time was getting on, she turned her attention to the shelves. Here there were jars of glycerine and petroleum jelly, beeswax and tonic waters, lanolin and rosewater and all manner of oils. One at a time she cleared the shelves, wiped them and replaced the contents, cleaning and grouping them as she went. She then swept the floor before putting a rug down to make the place look better and be a little less cold under foot.

When she finally went back upstairs, she was surprised to find that she had been down there as long as she had. It was dark outside, and she was famished. Still, it had been worth it. She would be happy to show the doctors around.

* * *

Grant was weary. Having got the bus to and from work for the past few days, he was thoroughly fed up. Just getting dressed and undressed was a challenge. He had quickly given up to shirt and tie and had opted for T-shirt and jumper. At work, the struggle to type one handed, whilst balancing the phone against the side of his head with a plastered hand that looked like a cobra ready to strike, was exhausting. Removing his meal from the microwave he cursed as it dripped on the floor. Having been nearly defeated by the packaging he had stabbed a bit too violently at the film lid and gone right through the base. He tipped it sloppily onto a plate and slapped the upturned carton against the plate a couple of times to get out the dregs. The only good thing about his day was the novelty bottle opener shaped like a buck-toothed monk, attached to the wall and designed for one-handed operation. Emily had bought it for him, just 'cos she'd thought it was cute. Emily had made life so much better in all sorts of little ways. With a satisfying fizz the cap came off and he downed half the bottle.

* **

Alex stopped at Knutsford services for a quick coffee before cutting across to the M62 to take him north of Manchester. He tried calling Emily again but after 6 rings her answerphone cut in once more, so, having left a message the first time, he hung up. Hopefully she was enjoying herself somewhere. By the time he got to Greater Blessing it would be a bit late to call round. He would pop by in the morning and see if she wanted to go for a drink that evening, or even a meal. As he sipped his coffee, he wondered whether Gerald had managed to retrieve the periapt from the well. If not, he thought he had a way to get it out. He didn't want to have to resort to going down there. It was do-able, but it was a bit narrow and the water level varied. At this time of year, the water table would be saturated.

* * *

Emily checked the doors were locked and the range was stoked up for the night and safe, and headed upstairs for bed. The two cats were already there, curled up together on the candle-wick bedspread she'd put on to protect the satin quilt from their claws. She slipped her nightie on in the bathroom, irrationally not wanting to undress in front of the two cats. She told herself not to be so stupid, but she still found the pair unnerving even though she was certain any 'intention' was benign. She climbed into bed and picked up her book. Part way down the page she realised that she had no idea what she had read. She started again. It was no good, she wasn't concentrating. She closed the book and put it back on her bedside table. Staring at her feet beneath the covers and the curl of the cats next to them she suddenly had a vision of herself growing old here in this huge house. 'Cat woman' sprang to mind and the accompanying vision, was not one of her wearing shiny black figure-hugging leather and stilettos. The image was completely sexless.

CHAPTER
TWENTY FIVE

T he morning came and the cats were gone. She got up and had a peer out of the window. Gerald wasn't at his post yet; it must still be early. Course, it was Saturday; it was a working day for him. She had a quick wash and pulled on jeans and jumper and went down and put the kettle on. She switched on the radio for some music and was happily singing away when the cats came in and reminded her of her previous night's vision. "Hi, you two, want some breakfast?" They purred appreciatively as she placed full bowls on the floor, and then tucked in.

She was washing up and just thinking she had about half an hour before the doctors arrived, when the doorbell rang. Drying her hands, she went and answered the door. To her surprise and delight Alex was standing on the doorstep.

Strangely, he was clutching a ball of string and a large magnet.

"Got a well that needs trawling?" he asked, dangling the magnet. I don't suppose your gnome has succeeded, has he?"

"Hi, No, come in." Emily looked puzzled. "The periapt is made of stone and the chain is gold. Gold isn't magnetic, is it?"

"No, but I suspect that the fastening on the periapt would have been fashioned by the local blacksmith and, is most likely iron. Shall we see?"

They went out into the garden and Emily watched as Alex fed the magnet down the well until the string went slack. He then pulled it taut again and dragged it from side to side, occasionally pulling it up so they could see if anything were attached. After the first couple of attempts Emily explained about the imminent arrival of the GPs and went back inside. She seemed to be collecting garden gnomes. This one however, was very welcome and a most attractive garden feature.

The doorbell rang. It was Claire and two other doctors. She was expecting five altogether. Claire introduced the other two as Mark and Peter. They were both older than Emily and she guessed they were in their late 40s. Mark seemed quite open and friendly, but Peter seemed a little reserved, maybe ready to disapprove of what she had to show them.

"Do you want to wait for the others to arrive?" asked Emily as she showed them into the front room.

"No, that's alright," said Claire, "We are all eager to see what you have here. You have no idea how long this has been a mystery to us all."

First, Emily showed them the ointments book and the row of jars. The three doctors poured over the pages reading out ingredients. They picked up the jars and removed their lids. Some were screw tops, others rubber bungs and muslin. The doctors sniffed their contents. Claire took a spatula and scooped out a small amount from one jar and spread it over her hands.

"Lanolin, that could be a problem," muttered Peter pointing at the book.

"No, look, further down, 'lanolin allergy – substitute glycerine'," said Mark.

* * *

It was a long winding journey through the country lanes. The bus took in every village, making detours that added 10-15 minutes every time, to a journey that, direct, would have been a total of about 30minutes. Instead, the total trip took nearly two hours giving Grant too much time to think about what he was going to say. Finally, Greater Blessing arrived. Grant stepped down off the bus at the stop behind Wishing Well Cottage and pushed his way through the kissing gate.

* * *

Alex held his breath. There was something shiny dangling from his magnet. Carefully, so as not to hit the sides of the well and knock it off, he pulled it slowly up to the light. Lifting it clear of the well he grasped the dripping periapt and inspected it. He had been right. The fastening was magnetic. Although helpful in its retrieval, this sadly meant that having been submerged in water for a week, it was showing signs of rust. Otherwise, it was all there, albeit with a broken clasp. He went in to show Emily.

* * *

The doctors were now looking through the 'patient' notes and were visibly impressed by how meticulous they were. The holistic approach to the patients' mental state was particularly useful. Emily had been afraid that it would be unethical for her to show them the notes, but the consensus was that the GPs were already treating the people concerned and it was in everyone's best interest to ensure that they weren't being harmed.

Alex appeared, a smug smirk on his face and a mischievous glint in his eyes. Her spirits lifted. Had he got it? He held out his hand and dangled the periapt for her to take. As she took it, their fingers met, and a sparkle of electricity jolted her senses. He smiled at her and she beamed back. The periapt, warmed by his hand, seemed even more precious than before.

Simultaneously the phone and doorbell rang. They laughed.

"That will be the other GPs," said Emily.

"I'll get the door, you get the phone," said Alex and headed left out of the room as Emily went right to answer the phone in the kitchen.

Alex pulled the door open, and the smile left his face, "Oh, hello."

Grant was completely taken aback, "Who are you?" he blurted, the memory of strong hands and over-powering arms coming crashing back as he remembered being marched off the premises on his previous visit, humiliated and powerless to resist. This was the man responsible.

"I'm Alex." He replied evenly. "Emily is busy right now."

This was Alex, *the* Alex that Mike had mentioned. He took in the other man's physical presence, his calm and confident manner and the easy way he wore his clothes, and felt humbled, "I just want to talk to her, apologise…"

"Now really isn't a good time."

Grant looked past Alex, up the hall, trying for a glimpse of Emily. Alex put an arm across the doorway. He wasn't going to let him in.

"But I…"

"Don't you think you've upset her enough?"

"Please, tell her I called," pleaded Grant as he backed off the step and reluctantly headed out to the street. Now what was he going to do.

* * *

It was Lou on the phone. She was ringing to say that Grant had called them. He had been trying to contact her, but he just got her voice-mail. He had e-mailed her but hadn't had a reply. She stared at the blinking red light on the phone, someone had managed to leave her a message. Lou said that Grant was going to visit her to apologise and to see her. He was desperate to make it up to her. So, said Lou, "he is likely to turn up sometime over the weekend".

When she went back in the front room, she found that Alex had let the other two doc-tors in. There was a quick re-cap going on of what they had found so far. None of the ingredi-ents Angelica was using were toxic, at least, not in the doses she was using. Most of the prod-ucts were tried and tested home remedies and reading the notes she had made on individual 'patients' it was clear that what she was pre-scribing was sensible. The majority were skin preparations or inhalations and the rest herbal teas. Provided Emily stuck to the recipes and didn't take on any new patients they didn't see any harm in her continuing to supply her cur-rent 'patients'. Together they made up a new batch of ointment No 23. The fact they had all made it together made her feel much more con-fident about giving it out and it would keep the old man happy.

When the GPs left, Alex and Emily inspected the periapt. Emily was horrified when she saw the rusty marks on the clasp. The chain she could get mended but the rusty clasp on the stone ...

"Don't worry, that's nothing," grinned Alex, "It's a bit more delicate than I'm used to but I can fix that." Seeing the look on her face he added, "metal work – its one of the things I'm really good at. These hands, you'd be amazed what I can do with them." Grinning at Emily he added, "Would you like me to fix it?" leaving her uncertain as to whether or not the comment had been suggestive. Then, as she handed over the periapt, he became all serious and took her hands in his. "Emily, I want to ask you out this evening, but before you answer there is something I have to tell you..."

She was puzzled. What could he possibly have to tell her? Was he married? Did he have an artificial leg? Were there bodies buried? What? He was only asking her on a date. He *was* meaning a date, wasn't he?

"Emily, when you were on the phone and I answered the door, the first time, it wasn't the doctors." He let this sink in and watched the possibilities race across her face until she settled on the most likely. He nodded, "Yes, it was Grant."

"Why didn't you let him in?"

"When he saw *me*, he kind of backed off and I didn't think that, with a house full, you'd want to talk to him and risk a repeat of before. He asked me to tell you he'd called. I'm sorry if I did wrong..." He was still holding her hands, the periapt absorbing their heat, uniting them.

Looking Alex straight in the eye, and with a deep sigh, she said, "No, you were right. I couldn't have handled talking to him then. I'll call him and arrange to meet. I need to tell him to his face..." She smiled, "Yes, I'd love to go out with you."

"Okay! I'll pick you up at 7pm. Do you have any dietary preferences, allergies I should know about? You aren't vegetarian. I know that, unless you were trying not to upset the villagers by eating your own hotpot."

"No, I'll eat anything. Where are we going?"

"It's a surprise!"

"What should I wear?"

"Whatever the hell you like, a plastic mac and wellies if that's what you feel comfortable in. It will be an honour to have you on my arm," and with that he gave an exaggerated bow and backed out the door leaving Emily laughing and feeling better than she had done in weeks, months even.

* * *

Having briefly hung around outside Emily's, not knowing what to do, his bus not being due for another hour and a half, he gravitated towards his midget. Having done a quick circle and satisfied himself that the car was alright, he wandered, on autopilot, into the Little Teacups Café. He sat himself at a table and inspected the shelves of teapots whilst he waited for Jess to appear. She soon arrived balancing a plate of cakes on her left wrist and holding cups, saucers, teaspoons, teapot and milk jug in her hands. Deftly she set them down on a table in the window and arranged them. The customers, a couple who were more intent on saying 'cooey' through the glass to their dog tied up outside, virtually ignored her. Spotting Grant, she smiled and raised her eyebrows. He raised his in agreement.

"Hi, nice to see you again. How's the hand?"

"Less painful than it was. I should have listened to you and gone to the hospital straight away. They had to manipulate it before putting this on," and he waved his hand about.

"Quite a cast," said Jess wide eyed, "I've never seen one like that before."

"No, it's a volar slab or something. It was agony the first couple of days but not so bad now the swelling is going down."

"So," ventured Jess, "What brings you here? You obviously can't drive yet."

Grant explained about coming to see Emily and how desperate he was to make amends. How he had managed to pluck up his courage to come back and face her, how he was willing to do anything to get her back, and how her door had been opened by some Incredible Hulk called Alex. The guy had been so damn civilised.

Putting her hand on his good one she asked, "Have you eaten?"

"No."

"Let me get you a cheese and ham sandwich and a mug of tea." She brought him tea and then quickly returned with a plate of sandwiches. She had cut the crusts off and left them on the side of his plate, like his mother used to do. "Ketchup or HP?" she asked, ready to squirt either onto his plate.

He smiled, "HP please." She squirted and he picked up a piece of crust and dunked it in the brown sauce.

"Thanks for looking after me. I must seem a right pathetic mess."

"Oh, you are, but I won't hold it against you. Anyone with a keen little sports car like that can't be all that bad."

"Would you like a ride, when I'm able to drive?"

"Thought you'd never ask! Was beginning to think I'd have to hot wire it."

* * *

She raced upstairs. What was she going to wear? She sat on the bed, nibbling her nails. Damn. Her hands were a real mess, and she was going out that evening. Perhaps if she looked on-line she could find somewhere. Fifteen minutes later she had 3 possibilities. The numbers written on a piece of paper, she went to pick up the phone and saw the message light was still flashing. She pressed play. The first was from Alex suggesting going out Saturday evening, obviously made on his way back from Gloucester yesterday, and the second was from a Becky Roberts... apparently Jess had given her Emily's number...she did nails, if Emily wanted to give her a call. Eagerly she phoned the number. To her amazement Becky was free that afternoon and did house calls, would 4:15 be okay. It was perfect. Bizarre! As Emily put the phone down, she secretly wondered if the situation might have been different had her financial status not been so well known. However, if it got her nails done, she wasn't complaining.

Whilst sorting out something to wear she pondered on Grant and what to do. If she was going to break up with him, she wanted to do it on her terms. She wanted to be able to control the situation. She wanted to be able to leave rather than have to force *him* to go. Much better if she went to him. Whilst the MG was here though, he had an excuse to come back. Thinking about it, she was probably still on the insurance and if he still had a spare key screwed under the wheel-arch she could drive the car over for him. Not wanting to phone, in case he answered, she e-mailed him with the suggestion. Was Sunday afternoon okay? She'd get a taxi back.

At 4pm Becky arrived, all chat and bustle. She was in her late 20s, pretty when she smiled, sour faced when she didn't. Emily studied her as she laid out the equipment on the kitchen table. Her make-up was flawless, if a little heavy on the eyes. Her perfect teeth were a startling white. At first glance Emily thought she was wearing a gumshield, her teeth were that uniform. Becky took one of Emily's hands in hers and studied it. "Gosh, these are a mess. I'm afraid I am not going to be able to repair them; they are too chipped. I think it best if we soak off the remaining extensions and then see."

When all the nails were bare Becky looked in her case and started hunting round frantically. When she finally stopped, she looked up at Emily most apologetic, "I am so sorry, I was certain I had enough with me, but I don't. I can't do your extensions today. I can get some more on Monday and pop round Monday evening..."

"What?" said Emily, "I'm going out this evening, what am I going to do? They look awful!"

"Well, there is one possibility. I've never used it before, but I can try it if you like. It will fill in the areas of pitted nail and make them look smooth. It won't make your nails any longer, but they will look neater." Seeing a slight spark of hope on Emily's face she disappeared off out to her car. Moments later she returned with what looked like a large nail varnish bottle. Peering at the label she said, "It does say you should do a test nail first and leave it for 24hours. What do you think?"

Emily looked at her hands. The ends of all her fingers looked like they had been stamped on.

"Shall I do one and we can see what it looks like. It has got to be your decision though, because as I said, I've never done this before and I can't give you any guarantees."

Reluctantly, but feeling she had no other choice, she agreed. Becky painted the first nail which quickly dried allowing her to add two more coats in quick succession. The nail was now smooth and a healthy pink colour. If all her nails were trimmed to the same length and treated, they would look fine. They couldn't be classed as elegant, but they were acceptable. She gave Becky the go ahead to do the rest. Half an hour later her nails were done, and she felt a lot better. Time for a shower, or rather a bath, she'd need to shave her legs; she hadn't had them waxed since she couldn't remember when.

At 6:55 she was sitting waiting, ready to go and feeling horribly nervous. Every sixty seconds she glanced at her watch, the watch that Grant had given her for her last birthday. What *was* she doing? Why was *she*, Emily Hope dating again? This was ridiculous. She had no idea how to behave. Thinking about it, there had never been anyone other than Grant and she couldn't even remember their first date. They had always been together. Now the thought of getting to know someone new terrified her. The doorbell rang and she nearly fell full-length, stumbling down the hall on heels she hadn't worn for weeks. She opened the door.

Alex stood there smiling, "You look beautiful," he said, "Would you do me the honour of dining with me?" and he held out his arm in a show of mock chivalry. She pulled the door to and linked her arm with his. By the gate, a dark limo waited, its engine purring quietly. She slid into the back seat and the driver closed the door. Alex got in the other side. As they drove through the village, chinks of light could be seen as the odd curtain twitched.

They drove for about half an hour before turning into the driveway of a large hotel, obviously a converted stately home. The limo made a circle on the gravel and drew up under a large stone entrance. They got out of the car and headed up the stone staircase to the large brass festooned doors. The door was opened for them and they stepped into a full height hall, a massive double stairway rising from its centre which split as it met the far wall doubling back on itself and giving a choice of routes upstairs. Emily's eyes followed the stairs up and round and came to rest on an enormous chandelier hanging in the centre of the ceiling. A Ceiling rose and plaster mouldings broke up the white expanse, the detailing mirroring the panels on the walls. Large oil paintings of various Venetian scenes adorned the panels.

"Well, what do you think?" asked Alex.

"I'm really glad I didn't wear my wellies, that's for sure," she whispered. Her coat was taken from her and they were shown to their table and napkins placed on their laps. "This is really nice, but it must be costing you a fortune. You didn't need to do this... I'm happy to pay my way." Now she felt uncomfortable. Was that insulting?

He could see what she was thinking, and laughed, "I'm touched by your concern for my finances and if you really insist, we'll go halves, but I don't splash out often and I think you're worth it."

"Thank you, but..."

"I can afford it."

"Really? Are you sure?"

"Emily, you haven't worked it out yet, have you? Who do you think inherited the other 1.2 million? Plus, two houses. Me."

She felt such a fool. Of course! Why hadn't it occurred to her? She hadn't even wondered about the other houses and Ruby's win.

"I'm sorry."

"Don't be. At least now I know you aren't after my money."

"Oh, I don't know, I'm starting to feel

like indulging my newly found liking for champagne."

"Really? Right then, let's celebrate our newly acquired wealth."

The evening seemed to fly by, and the conversation flowed easily despite Emily's initial fears. When the limo dropped her back home, Alex walked her to the door. She was debating whether to invite him in when he took the decision out of her hands. He told her he had had a wonderful time and would love to do it all again. He stepped towards her and just as she thought he was going to kiss her on the lips, he raised her hand to his mouth and looking straight into her eyes, splayed her fingers and kissed her palm. Then he was heading back to the limo. He stood by the car until she had gone inside.

Smiling to herself she hung her coat and bag on the banister and headed upstairs to bed. As she slipped off her stockings her fingers caught, snagging the nylon. She was alarmed to discover that her nails were starting to peel. Had they been like that all evening? Surely, she would have noticed. Hopefully, Alex hadn't. They looked awful. Flakes were starting to drop off.

CHAPTER TWENTY SIX

Emily had slept really well, and enjoyably, up until the point where she had woken up, at a very inconvenient moment. She wanted to call Lou but it was a bit early. She texted instead. 'D8 with A ace. Call me'. Then she remembered that she had e-mailed Grant and suggested returning his car. She logged on half hoping that he wouldn't have read it yet and she could put off seeing him. No, there was an e-mail from him. She waited for it to open, praying that he wouldn't agree to her suggestion.

Dearest Emily,

Yes, you are still on insurance and spare key still there. I would love to see you this afternoon. Just let me know what time to expect you and I will be there.

All my love

Grant

Okay. So, she would return his car this afternoon and that would be it. She wasn't looking forward to it, but it had to be done.

* * *

Above the store Carla was feeling pleased with herself, her patience was paying off. She had just learnt that Emily still wasn't wearing the periapt even though it was no longer down the well. She didn't know why, but whilst it wasn't round her neck its influence was less potent. Other information had come her way too. It all needed thinking about, but, not for too long...

* * *

Grant was busy cleaning the flat. Two bin bags of washing that wouldn't fit in the washing machine had been hidden in the wardrobe. He had cleared out the fridge, sprayed and wiped it and done a test sniff. Yes, it was acceptable. He poured a liberal dose of bleach down the sinks and toilet and then squirted air freshener in every room. When he started to cough, he decided that he also needed to open the windows as the combined smells were somewhat overpowering. He stripped the bedding from the bed knowing that *that* was too much to hope for but - just in case - and then worried that him even thinking about sex would annoy her. If she thought for just one minute that he was assuming... it would be the basis for another row. Whatever choice he made could be used against him if she so chose. He shut the bedroom door. Next, he vacuumed, retrieving the odd used plate from under the sofa as he did so. Finally, he plumped up the cushions. Everything had to be perfect for Emily. Everything had to be perfect, and he did not have any milk! Emily would not be impressed. He would have to go out, but if he did that, he might miss her. The longer he left it though, the more likely it was that would happen. Quickly he wrote a note and pinned it to the door. Hopefully, he would be back before she arrived. He had to be.

* * *

This week, Emily was in good time for church. She found herself an empty pew in the centre of the church and slid along to the middle of the row in the hope that someone else would join her. It wasn't long before a couple did so. One of them was the woman, she recognised from the book club, whose name she couldn't remember. She just that she thought of her as glasses woman, there being large gold-coloured decorative swirls attached, somewhat distractingly, either side of her blue frames, which made the woman's eyes look even smaller than they were, and that she had a son called Harry who was a recycling operative, much to Emily's amusement. She must remember to tell Lou that one. The woman introduced her husband as Tony, and asked Emily if she had started reading 'Crime and Punishment' yet. Emily hadn't even bought it let alone started reading it. "You'll really enjoy it," she whispered. "If you give me a couple of days to finish it you can borrow mine."

"Oh, right. Thank you," said Emily as the people behind shushed them. Emily and glasses woman smirked at one another like naughty school kids, as they stood to sing the first hymn.

* * *

Just after midday Carla's phone rang. The caller was in a high state of conspiratorial euphoria. She couldn't wait to tell Carla what she had just done and bask in the praise that was sure to come. As she was walking along the high street, on her way to church, minding her own business, she had spotted *that Jessica* skulking in the alley next to the café having a filthy cigarette, most probably *can-a-bissss*. When Jessica had seen her looking, she had quickly stubbed it out against the wall and flung it into the gutter, before disappearing back inside the café. The woman had then – oh, how clever she had been – put her hand to her left ear in alarm – oh, no, her ear ring – she had scanned the pavement for it – my, where could it be - oh, relief – there it was in the gutter – she had bent down pretending to pick up her lost ear ring – palmed the cigarette butt – she was wearing gloves so Carla needn't worry about any DNA evidence - stood up and clipped her ear ring back in place. Oh, oh, oh and then, and this was the best bit, Carla would never guess what she had done next... Carla waited with baited dread. The woman was a moron. She could just imagine the dramatic non-subtlety of her street performance. The woman was well known for her unconsciously comic acting. The Greater Blessing amateur dramatic society had learnt to tolerate her inclusion in their ranks because audiences thought her hilarious; she was so seriously intense. She herself seemed oblivious to their amusement and appeared to genuinely think she warranted her popularity. The woman was still speaking – apparently, she ought to be a secret agent – and as she went on to tell Carla what she had done Carla had to admit, it was genius, she just hoped that she got to hear about the consequences; it would be a real shame to miss that…

* * *

After church Emily e-mailed Grant to say that all being well, she would be with him about 3pm. She remembered to take a screwdriver with her to unfasten the screw holding the spare key in place under the MG's wheel-arch. Having retrieved the key, she folded the hood down and climbed in. After a couple of tries, the engine fired up and she pulled away from the kerb. As she passed the café she spotted Jessica, arms folded, scowling at her. What was she upset about now? That girl was so moody. Every time Emily had met her she had been miserable but then, when Emily had asked for help with her nails, she had unexpectedly 'come up trumps'. Though thinking about it, Becky hadn't done a brilliant job, her nails were more of a mess now than they had been before. The uncharitable thought crossed Emily's mind that it may have been deliberate, but why? No, Jessica might be moody, but she had no reason to be spiteful and why would a professional business-person ruin her reputation by deliberately making a mess of someone's nails. It didn't make any sense.

The drive to Grant's gave Emily plenty of time to think. She had no idea what she was going to say to him. She still didn't really know how she felt about him. He genuinely wanted her back and all his actions indicated that he felt terrible about how he had treated her. He had gone to such impressive lengths to get her back and she hadn't even given him a chance. She parked the car and leant across to pick her bag out of the floor well where it had landed when she stopped. As she picked it up, her eye was drawn to something lodged against the curled-up corner of the floor mat. Delicately she picked it up and studied it.

* * *

Jessica wasn't happy. Grant had phoned to tell her that Emily would be driving the car back for him. He had explained that she was still on the insurance. She had expected Emily to come for the key, but she hadn't. Grant obviously hadn't told Emily that she had it, which meant that he had either given Emily another or she still had one of her own. Either way Grant hadn't seen fit to tell Emily about her key. Why was that? It would have made sense for him to get his key delivered along with his car. Did he not want Emily to know about him and her, if there was a 'him and her'? If there wasn't a 'him and her' then there was no reason why he couldn't tell Emily about the key. Did he fancy her and not want Emily to know, keeping both his options open if he couldn't get back with Emily? Did he want an excuse to come back and see Jess when his arm was better? Agitated, she put the kettle on.

* * *

As Emily rang the doorbell, she suddenly felt a stranger in her own life. Was it only 3-4 months since she let herself in here? Three months since that awful day when she found the note taped to the wall and she'd slid down the wall to the floor, shocked to her very core. Now she was ringing the doorbell, and this was no longer her home. As the chimes faded there was the sound of footsteps stampeding towards the door. Emily's heart thudded in her chest. The door flew open, and Grant was standing there beaming nervously. "Hi, come in, come in. Please let me take your coat. How are you, you look marvellous, beautiful, but then you always did. Can I get you a coffee? Please have a seat."

Nodding she let him take her coat and sat, saying nothing and feeling awkward, the new, strained familiarity inhibiting them both. Grant looked the same, a little thinner maybe and drawn round the eyes but essentially as she remembered him. As he busied himself making coffee, she studied her surroundings. It was the same room, but different somehow and smaller. All the familiar items were there, moved slightly to compensate for the gaps where her things had been. Had she really lived here all those years? It was like a dream to her now, like someone else's life. Was it really her that had lived it? Grant was chattering inanely, obviously nervous and trying to fill the silence, trying to get Emily to respond. She said nothing, making him struggle, observing his discomfort, enjoying the control.

As he put the coffee cup down in front of her and a plate with one of her favourite buns on it, from the bakers down the road, she took in the neatly pressed napkin and the small vase of flowers on the table. He was obviously doing his very best to please her. She had to smile to herself; it wouldn't do to let him see she'd noticed.

"How are you?" he ventured, finally asking a question that she had to respond to.

"I'm fine, really good actually. How are you?"

"I'm miserable, Emily. I love you so much. You're all I think about."

"Really!" said Emily, "Are you sure about that?"

"What? Of course!" He looked stunned, genuinely stunned.

"Then, what's this?" As he watched she removed a scrunched tissue from her pocket and opened it, tipping its content onto the coffee table. Grant stared in puzzlement looking alternately back and forth at Emily and at what turned out to be a cigarette butt.

"What's that?" he asked.

"That was in the floor well of the passenger seat. Miss me, huh? It didn't take you long to find another woman stupid enough to put up with being frozen to death for the pleasure of being driven round the countryside by you. Strange taste in lipstick! Getting desperate?"

Grant stared at the mark on the filter. It was orange. Realisation dawned and he flushed scarlet.

Emily expected some begging apology and excuse, how it didn't mean anything, it was just a one off, it was just a drive, one of the women at the motor club, and anyway nothing happened. Really, he swore it hadn't, but she was wrong.

"That little bitch. How could she! I trusted her. How *dare* she!" Grant was furious and it didn't seem to have anything to do with his relationship with Emily. There was no apology; he didn't appear to need to hide anything. He was just furious at this woman and he didn't seem to feel guilty at all. "How dare she smoke in my car? If she thinks she's getting a ride now she can forget it." Then he remembered Emily was there and explained about finding Jessica sat in this car when he had been thrown out of the well blessing, how she had helped him into the café and given him a cup of tea and stopped him driving home with a broken hand and how he'd promised to give her a ride as thanks. Now, she'd been sitting in his car smoking. Did Emily actually think that he would have let anyone smoke in his car? No, she realised that he wouldn't and now had no doubts that he was telling the truth, and Jessica – really not Grant's type. Besides, what was it to her if he had found someone else, hadn't she come here to break up with him once and for all? She looked at him. He seemed so dejected and exhausted now that he'd proved his innocence. He looked quite shrunken and hurt. She felt the sudden urge to put her arms round him, to run her hands through his hair again and feel the freshly shaved skin of his jaw, slightly shiny with aftershave, and feel his strong arm wrap itself round her shoulders and pull her to him. Instead, she just said, "I'm sorry."

"Emily, there is no one else. How could there be? It has always been you. Please, let's start again. I know I can make it up to you if you'll just give me a chance. How about we go away together, just the two of us. We can stay at that little hotel on the lake you always wanted to go to. What was it called? Something like Ferndene Hall, wasn't it?"

"Oh, Grant, no. I'm sorry. We want totally

different things, you and me. If we got back together, sooner of later we'd be back where we started. I want a family Grant. Here's your key," and she started to stand.

"No, wait, wait there," and with that he rushed off into the bedroom. He soon returned and knelt on the floor at her feet taking hold of her hands. Emily was struck dumb. His touch was tender and slightly shaky, and he appeared to be having difficulty forming what he was about to say. She waited. Was he looking at her nails? Flakes were still coming off. She resisted the urge to pull her hands away.

He swallowed and finally said. "I planned to do this when I came to your house, but I totally messed that up, and I was now hoping to do this on a romantic weekend away but here goes... Emily, I love you, would you please do me the honour of marrying me and making me the happiest man alive and yes, if you want children, then that's what we'll do. I'll do anything for you Emily, please, just say yes..."

She couldn't believe it. Grant had proposed and he was willing to have children, all to make her happy. How long had she waited and prayed for this? How many times had she wrongly thought that he was going to suggest they got married, but never had? And, children? This was what she wanted, what she'd longed for, for so long. Why wasn't she saying anything? Why wasn't she throwing herself into his arms and saying yes, yes, yes? Grant was staring at her, willing her to answer. He was staring deep into her eyes as if his very life depended on maintaining the connection, hanging on to this moment, aware that his happiness was now in her hands and desperately aware of its fragility.

"Grant, I..." She saw it. He mentally withdrew. It was as if something inside him shut down. The light in his eyes which, moments before had shone brightly, was guttering. He kept looking at her, hope stretching thinner and thinner like an old rubber band. She didn't have it in her, to sever it completely, "I'm sorry, I don't know, I need time to think," and then she said it, "This is so sudden," and felt like a fool, of all the clichés...

Incongruously, 'Who wants to be a Millionnaire?' started up from her handbag. Frantically, she delved into her bag and pulled out her phone, stabbing at the controls to shut it up. It was a text telling her that her taxi had arrived and was waiting outside. Thankful for the excuse, she plonked his key on the table, mumbled that she would have to think about it; she'd let him know, and made her escape. Grant was still kneeling on the floor as she closed the door. She ran down the stairs, climbed in the taxicab, gave the driver Lou and Mike's address and burst into tears.

* * *

It was some time before Lou and Mike

understood what had happened. The story of events, as told to them, had been somewhat jumbled and incoherent. Grant had proposed, Emily hadn't said no, or yes, and as far as Emily knew, Grant was still on his knees clutching a ring. Had there been a ring? She didn't remember but then why had he rushed into the bedroom first? But, most important of all, the main thing that Emily was intent on, was changing her ring tone. She sat desperately scrolling through menus and ineffectually pushing buttons whilst Mike itched to get his hands on her phone, all offers of his help angrily rejected. Finally, she flung it into the corner of the sofa, and he scooped it up. A few seconds later, having rejected, 'Here comes the bride', and a number of others that he would really like to have used, he said, "How's this?" and the mobile emitted a simple melody that was the phone's default setting. "Not brilliant, but also not embarrassing, whatever the company."

"Thanks," said Emily, and started sobbing again, but quietly this time.

"Would you like to stay for dinner?" asked Lou, "Stay the night if you like."

"Oh, could I? Thank you so much."

After dinner, Mike made himself scarce and Emily and Lou were left to talk. Over a glass or two of wine Lou asked Emily more about her meeting with Grant and she also asked her about her date with Alex. She didn't say anything, but she noted how animated Emily became when talking about Alex and how maudlin and reflective she became when talking about Grant. When Lou commented on Grant's sudden willingness to have children Emily grimaced; he was only saying that to get her back, not because he really wanted them. She knew that. He'd made his feelings plain enough in the past. What *was* genuine were his feelings for her. What she didn't know was how *she* felt about him. She obviously still cared about him, and her annoyance at finding the cigarette butt was telling but did that mean she could live with him again, and as his wife. Whenever Lou made a disparaging comment against him Emily defended him. Should she say yes? After all, it was silly to throw away all they had had, all those happy years together, because of what boiled down to one row, albeit a big one. They had both hurled equal amounts of abuse at each other. On that score there was nothing left to be said. The hurts were fading. If they could forgive each other that, and it seemed that Grant had forgiven her, couldn't she do the same? Most of it had been said with the sole intention of hurting the other. Had they really meant all of it? Probably not. By the end of the evening Emily couldn't think of any reason to say no, and she could think of any number of positive reasons to say yes. Why was she even hesitating? Lou knew, but now wasn't the time to point it out. Emily had to come to that realisation herself.

CHAPTER
TWENTY SEVEN

Alex was puzzled and a little worried. He had called at Wishing Well Cottage the day before, to return the periapt which he had mended, and Emily hadn't been there. Now, it appeared that she still wasn't in, or at least she wasn't answering the door. Her car was still in the drive. None of the curtains were drawn and when he looked through the kitchen window there were no clues there, no unwashed breakfast items. He hoped she was alright. What if she had fallen and hurt herself. He tried the doors. They were all locked. He wondered whether he should break in and tried to remember if there was a spare key in either of the other cottages he now owned. Surely the triplets had had copies of each other's keys. Suddenly he felt bad. Why didn't *he* have copies? What if one of *them* had needed help! He should have thought of that. Why hadn't it occurred to him that they may have needed looking after? He should have thought to take care of them. Three elderly ladies, what was he thinking? It was too late now, but he could take care of Emily. He would try phoning her and if he didn't get a response, he would break in. Switching his phone on he was annoyed to find he had a message telling him he was about to run out of credit. Damn, he'd have to go to the store. He needed some milk anyway and there was always the possibility that Carla would know where Emily was, if of course, she was willing to give up that piece of information to him. She was usually relatively civil to him, he being a relatively young, presentable male, but that was as far as it went, him being a Wells. Today however, when he broached the question of Emily's whereabouts, she positively gushed to tell him. Emily was last seen driving off in Grant's car, yesterday. So, Emily hadn't come back. Emily must have stayed the night. This realisation seemed to fill her with deep joy, and she watched with undisguised glee as Alex failed to hide his dismay.

* * *

Emily finally crawled out of bed mid morning. Lou plonked coffee and toast in front of her and waited patiently whilst Emily ate and drank. She topped her mug up for her and eventually asked her how she felt.

"Grim. Why didn't you take the bottle off me? I forgot I was the only one drinking. I'd already had some wine with the meal before you opened that one."

"What are friends for," said Lou. "Alka-Seltzer?"

"No, thanks! It makes too much noise!"

"So, what is the decision this morning? Do I need to shop for a new outfit? Only, I'd like some idea of time scales. Given the choice, I'd prefer it to be *after* the baby is born so I can wear the outfit more than once."

"Oh, I don't know. I just don't know. He was so sweet, and he was trying so hard to please me. You should have seen what he had done to the flat. I've never seen it so tidy and there were flowers..."

"Flowers? You're easily won over."

"If he is willing to get married, and have children..."

"Does he really want children? He was always so adamant that he didn't. I used to think that when his mates started having them, that he would feel differently, but he didn't. *And*, he threw you out. Are you able to forgive him for that?"

"But it's Grant. We have been together for so long. Other people have rows and get back together. Why shouldn't we."

"Em, go home and then see how you feel."

"Why are you being so 'anti' all of a sudden? I would have thought that you'd have been keen for me and Grant to get back together again. You were so shocked when we split."

"I don't know. It's just...well...you seem so happy now, in your new life. I guess I just don't see Grant fitting into it. Do you see him in Greater Blessing, or do you plan on moving back here?"

"Lou, I miss him. That big house is all very well but I need someone to share my life with. I don't want to live on my own."

"What about Alex?"

"Damn it. Don't complicate matters."

* * *

As the morning wore on Carla had time to think. In between serving customers she decided that what she needed was more information. If Emily had stayed overnight with Grant, then things may just turn out the way she wanted without any interference on her part. If Emily and Grant did get back together then most of the problem was solved. If not, then action would have to be taken. She needed to make sure things were moving in the right direction. Whilst the store was empty she picked up the phone and, using the rubber end of a pencil, tapped in a local number.

"Hello?"

"Hi, its Carla, how are you?"

"Fine thanks, and you?"

"Yes, I'm okay. I was just thinking we

hadn't had a proper chat in a while and wondered if you fancied coming round for coffee later in the week?"

"Okay, yes, we haven't had a proper gossip in ages."

"Talking of gossip, I believe that Miss Nuevo *Reeesh* drove off in a certain ex-boyfriend's car and didn't come back last night."

"Really!"

"Yes, and I've just had our soppy blacksmith in here. Most put out he was, that she wasn't there when he called round this morning. Bet he wishes now that he hadn't been such a gentleman after their date on Saturday, saying 'goodnight' on the doorstep."

"You saw?"

"Well, not exactly. I just happened to be drawing the bedroom curtains when they came back."

"I'll bet you've got a really good view of Wishing Well Cottage from there."

"No, not really, not now the leaves are appearing on the trees on the green. I couldn't help noticing the limo drive by though, which is the only reason I looked, of course."

"Of course!"

"Anyway, got to go, customers to serve. Let me know when you can come round. Bye then."

"Bye."

* * *

As she was in the city Emily decided to see if she could get her nails sorted. She phoned her old salon and was told that they had had a cancellation and if Emily could get there in the next 25 minutes, she could have the appointment. She looked pleadingly at Lou who raised her eyebrows and nodded, agreeing to drive her there. Before she knew it, she was sitting in a chair at the salon having her nails 'tutted' over. The beautician couldn't work out what it was, on Emily's nails. She consulted her colleagues who were equally baffled. Whatever the substance was, it had crazed like paint and was curling and flaking. Some of it was coming off but the bulk of it was stuck like super glue. Emily explained what Becky had said, and why she had agreed to have this unknown substance applied without testing it, and felt embarrassed. What a fool she'd been. A number of substances were used to try and remove it, but nothing worked. Finally, they resorted to polishing her nails smooth, but this had to be done carefully as the substance appeared to melt and develop a yellowy black tinge. Consequently, they advised her to let the rest come off in its own good time. They refused to apply anything to the unknown substance and told her to leave her nails natural until it had all come off or her nails had grown out. As she left the salon, she stuffed her hands into her pockets.

As she didn't have anything particular to

do with her day she decided, being near the bus station, to get the bus back to Greater Blessing. She needed to think and staring at the countryside would hopefully help her mood. She plonked herself on the back seat and stared through the grimy glass. The world slid by and gradually the large city buildings were replaced by smaller residential ones as the bus worked its way through the outskirts and out into the countryside. She quite enjoyed riding along studying the world from her elevated vantage point, seeing things that were no

t normally visible from the car. As they wound their way through villages she peered into back gardens and shamelessly through windows. There were so many nice houses in these villages and some of the gardens were really spectacular with topiary hedges and lovely flower displays. The bus drew up on the edge of a village green which was rapidly turning yellow as hundreds of daffodils celebrated in the sun, the odd early tulip, unaware of the dress code, embarrassingly scarlet amongst the partygoers. As the bus pulled away she wondered whether or not there were daffodils on the green at Greater Blessing. She couldn't remember seeing any but then this village wasn't as high as hers so maybe they just weren't flowering yet. Gradually the bus climbed into the hills and then started its descent to her stop. As she stepped down from the bus and headed for the kissing gate, she realised that she hadn't thought of Grant for quite a while, she had been too busy looking at the scenery. Now she was home her decision making began again. As she let herself in at the back door the pros and cons fought for dominance once more. What was she going to do? What did she want to do? Her heart was telling her one thing and her head was telling her another. Then the two would switch.

The two cats were sitting reproachfully in the centre of the kitchen table. She had completely forgotten about them. Since moving into the house, she hadn't had a night away. Never having had a cat or a dog before the responsibility hadn't occurred to her. She went straight to their dishes as the cats glared at her. Bending down she stopped halfway. Scattered about the floor were the remains of a bird. They obviously hadn't been in danger of starving. She picked the dishes out of the carnage, filled them with cat food and placed them in the other corner of the kitchen. The cats tucked in. She then got a carrier bag and turning it inside out, like a large rubber glove, used it to pick up the remains. She then cleaned the floor. By the time she'd finished the cats were happily sitting on the rug in front of the hearth washing their paws. Apparently, her next duty was to set and light the fire. Half an hour later the fire was lit, she had a cup of tea and the cats were curled up asleep on the chair opposite. Could she really move back into the city? She didn't think so. Grant would have to move here.

The doorbell rang. There was a stack of mail on the mat. She gathered it up and put it on the hall table and opened the door. On the step stood a beaming Becky.

"I've got them," she said. Emily stared at her. "Your nails, I can do them now if you like. I thought you'd want them as soon as possible."

"Oh, I'm sorry", blustered Emily, "I got them done in Manchester this afternoon. Well, not done exactly. They said I should let them grow out."

"What, rubbish. Let me see."

Emily held out her hands.

"Hmmm. What have they done? Well, I'm sure we can cover that up. They'll be as good as new in no time. Shall we go in?" and she bustled her way past Emily, more or less pushing her out of the way to do so.

Irritated, Emily followed her down the hall and into the kitchen. Unseen by the women two pairs of eyes peered curiously down from the top of the dresser, four furry ears at attention.

"Shall I set up here?"

"Er, well...no." said Emily assertively, much to her own surprise. Becky stared at her. "No, thank you. I think I will do as I was advised and let them grow out."

"But, we can easily cover that up."

"No, thank you."

"Come on, it won't take me long. I bought these specially and I didn't have to come here in my free time you know. I'm really doing you a favour."

"I'm sorry, no."

"I popped round yesterday but you weren't here. Did you go away somewhere?"

"Yes."

"Oh, really. Somewhere nice?"

"I stayed at a friend's house."

"I see you left your car here."

"Yes, I didn't need it."

"Oh, of course, you probably took your boyfriend's car back for him. I hear he broke his hand. How is he?"

"He's fine. Listen, I really need to get on."

"So, you two seeing each other again then. How long did you live together?"

"6 years. Now I really..."

"Well, it's nice that you are getting back together." She winked, "Make-up sex is always... well, you tell me..."

"We didn't." said Emily, getting annoyed, "Now, I really must get on. I am sorry that you went out of your way to come here but I am going to let my nails grow out. I don't want any more chemicals on them."

"Well, if you change your mind, you know how to find me. I'll be off then. All the best to you and what's his name...?"

"Grant."

"Yes, you and Grant. Do let me know how you get on. Will he be coming here or are you thinking of moving back there?"

"We haven't decided anything yet."

"But, It's only a matter of time. I can see it in your eyes." Becky picked her things up and headed for the door. Again, Emily followed her down the hall. At the door Becky stopped and turned. Smiling conspiratorially, one girl to another she said, "It's always good to have a man about the house, they come in useful for all sorts of things." She giggled and elbowed Emily suggestively in the ribs, "know what I mean?"

Emily was now getting thoroughly fed up and just wanted Becky to leave. Through gritted teeth she mumbled, "Yes, they do have their uses."

"Yes, like getting necklaces out of wells. I see you aren't wearing it, how come?"

"It's being fixed."

"Oh, dear. What's wrong with it?"

"The clasp was broken."

"Where are you getting it fixed?"

"Locally, now if you don't mind…"

"Cos I know a good jeweller who'd do a really good job."

"No, that's alright, it's in good hands."

"Local you say, I wasn't aware that there were any local jewellers."

"He isn't a jeweller."

"So, who would you take it to if not a jeweller?"

"A friend, and I am perfectly satisfied that he will do a good job. Thank you for your time." With that she reached past Becky, pulled the door open and shepherded her out onto the step. "Once my nails are back to normal, if I want them ruining again, I'll call you." As Becky stood there aghast, Emily shut the door in her face. Shocked at her own rudeness she retreated down the hall slightly and watched through the stained glass as the blurry shape of Becky disappeared from view. With a huge sigh of relief Emily heard Becky's car start, back out of the drive and fade into the distance. She found she was shaking slightly but energised by the fact that she had actually stood up for herself. She spent the next hour replaying in her head what she had said, embellishing it, coming up with all sorts of witty put downs. Then she started to worry that she had made herself another enemy, after all the woman had gone out of her way to help her, coming to her house, out side of work time. But, on the other hand Becky had behaved unprofessionally and as a result Emily's nails were a right mess and could be that way for another six months. Also, she had been extremely pushy asking so many questions when it should have been obvious that Emily didn't want to answer. It was as if she was completely insensitive to Emily's feelings, ignoring all clues, solely intent on dragging information out of her, or, was that her intention? What exactly had she told her? She didn't think she had said that much. She certainly hadn't elaborated on anything. How did Becky know that she had taken Grant's car back? Then, she supposed, this is a village, people talk. Everyone knows what everyone else is doing. Feeling the need for a friendly voice she considered phoning Grant but then realised that she would need to give him some response to his proposal, and that was a conversation she wasn't ready to tackle. Instead, she phoned Lou.

* * *

CHAPTER TWENTY EIGHT

After tossing and turning for what seemed like hours, worrying about what to do, weighing the pros and cons of marrying Grant, an exhausted Emily finally fell asleep. So, it came as quite a shock to be woken at 2:15am by the shrill ringing of her doorbell as someone stabbed at it and pummelled furiously on the door, screaming her name. Heart thumping, she stumbled out of bed, struggled into her dressing gown, and headed for the stairs. The large dark house seemed emptier than normal, and she found as she reached the bottom of the stairs she was shaking slightly. Through the glass she could see an animated figure silhouetted by an eerily flashing light, multi-coloured through the stained glass. The assault on her door had now stopped, but the shrieking continued. A number of other voices appeared to be trying to silence the attacker who was being led away from the door. Peering through one of the least distorting panes of coloured glass Emily could see several figures, including two police officers, all of whom were remonstrating with a hysterical Carla.

Wrapping her dressing gown around herself against the chill and feeling uncomfortable at being seen by the villagers in her nightwear, Emily opened the door. At the sight of Emily, Carla broke free and hurled herself at her, shrieking unintelligibly. Richard, being nearest to Emily, stepped forward and enveloped Carla in a bear hug, pinning her arms by her sides. As she struggled, he lifted her feet off the floor and turned her round. The police officers, deciding enough was enough, arrested her. They told her that anything she said may be written down and used in evidence against her. As James related later, this was a very impressive claim, especially as most of what she'd said had been in a pitch only canines could hear. Once Carla was safely locked inside the police car one of the officers came to speak to Emily and the little group of villagers that had gathered by her door.

It appeared that, at just after 2am, Carla had run into the street in her nightie and bare feet, screaming her head off. When Richard, who had been first on the scene, the pub being the nearest residence to the store, went to her aid,

Carla had pointed up at her bedroom. With some effort she had managed to stammer, "Bats, bats!" As others arrived on the green Richard had gone into the store and up to her bedroom where he found two bats frantically trying to find a way out. He had opened the window and with some encouragement managed to get them to fly out. The room was a bit of a mess. The magnolia-coloured walls were now smudged with soot and there was the odd bat dropping or two to be seen on Carla's duvet and dressing table mirror. The two bats had obviously come down the chimney. Her room now free from bats and, having had a bit of time to calm down from the initial shock, Carla's mind had started to work. Rapidly she'd deduced that there must be an explanation. One bat would be surprising enough, but two…! Two was too much of a co-incidence and she quickly came up with two culprits. Muttering about Kevin and Angelica she had set off for Emily's getting angrier and more hysterical with each step. By the time she'd reached Emily's front door she was incensed beyond reason.

"Who are Kevin and Angelica?" asked the police officer.

"Emily's cats," said James.

"Cats? What have they got to do with this?"

"Carla believes that they put the bats down her chimney."

"What makes her think that?"

"Well, Kevin put mice through her sky light," said one of the crowd.

"She claims he did, she's no proof," said Richard.

"And pee'd in her doorway."

"Yeah, her entrance stinks," added someone, and they all laughed.

"She seems to think," said Richard, "that since Angelica died, she and Kevin - 'ave got it in for 'er."

"Just a minute. Angelica died? I thought you said Angelica was a cat," said the officer.

"Yes, she died then came back as a cat, like Kevin. He used to live here too."

"Nooooo!" screamed Emily, shocking everyone. "Don't say that, I can't stand it. They are just cats. Ordinary cats!"

At that moment, and for no explicable reason, the now silent group turned as one and looked through Emily's front door. There in the shadows, calmly watching proceedings, were two pairs of eyes, clearly visible every time the police car's blue light flashed. Aware that they had been seen, the cats strolled forward into the porch and sat side by side at Emily's feet. Kevin started nonchalantly washing an ear and his companion rolled on her back and playfully waved her paws in the air.

"So, this is Kevin and Angelica, and they are *your* cats," said the officer.

"No...yes. He came with the house. She

just turned up," said Emily giving the cats an 'I'll speak to you later' look.

"So where were the cats when the bats were allegedly dropped down the chimney?"

"Oh, c'mon officer", said James, jumping to Emily's defence. "You can't possibly blame Emily for what the cats did. In law, owners can't be held responsible for what their cats do, unlike dog owners. Besides Angelica was the sweetest, forgiving old lady I have ever come across. She would never do something like this."

"And you are, sir?" asked the officer.

"James Meacher. I'm the vicar"

"Look," replied the officer, scrutinising James and looking somewhat dispirited at this revelation of united insanity, "is this some kind of elaborate April Fool? You people all believe that those two cats are the reincarnation of former occupants of this house and that they are deliberately playing practical jokes on an elderly storekeeper to get revenge for... what exactly?"

At this point several people started speaking at once offering up various explanations. Angelica's herbs had made Carla's husband ill. Myrtle had driven her husband away The periapt was rightfully hers. Carla had evidence that Angelica had used her powers to steal it from her.

After ascertaining who Myrtle was, and that the periapt was a pendant, the officer asked,

"So Angelica had stolen from Carla and Carla had proof. What proof?"

They all looked at one another. No one wanted to say anything it seemed. Then, an elderly man with a tartan dressing gown and matching slippers stepped forward, "She claimed that Bill Dudley told her that Angelica had given her great grandmother a potion that had made her bequeath the periapt to her, Angelica, but Carla claimed that she had been promised it as a child when she used to berry pick for the old woman."

"And who is this Bill Dudley?"

"He was a despatch rider. He told Carla, back in 1992 that, just before the old lady died, Angelica had visited her with one of her special herbal brews. After that the old lady quickly changed her will."

"How was it known that the will had been changed?" asked the officer.

The man shrugged, but another villager chipped in, "Bill's daughter was a secretary at the solicitors. Bit of a gossip she was. Got sacked for it in the end."

"Yeh, she liked to talk. Just like 'er father. Quite a character 'e was... one o' the first people to be killed on't M6...smashed into a concrete bridge column...made a reight mess of 'is sel'... no open coffin for 'im."

The police officer sighed deeply and weighed up the crowd. "When, exactly, was this?

When did he die? The M6 was opened in the 1960's."

"Oh, I think it was '68. It had been really icy and then it warmed up, so it took everyone by surprise when it was frosty again one morning and even though the sun was out it hadn't reached the patch under the bridge."

"So how, if he died in '68, was he able to tell Carla about something that happened in 1992?"

As one, the crowd replied, "In a séance!"

At this, the officer decided it was time to wrap things up and leave. He noted a few names and addresses and put away his notebook. "If we discover that a crime has been committed, one with evidence and witnesses capable of testifying, we'll be back. Is there anyone we should contact to inform them that Mrs Grimshaw is in custody?"

"No, I don't think so," said Richard, "but I'll get my wife to get her some clothes and we'll lock the store up and follow you down to the station."

As the police car drove away, Carla wrapped in blankets in the back, the crowd slowly dispersed. James lingered to see if Emily was alright. He could stay a while if she felt she needed company. She said she was fine but yes it would be nice if he dropped by in the morning, but not too early.

As she closed the door and walked down

the hall, she gave the cats a wide berth, 'had they really put bats down Carla's chimney? If they had, then how, that building was three stories high?'

* * *

In the morning when Emily finally got up, at the cats' insistence, she wondered if she'd dreamt it all. She quickly got washed and dressed and went down to feed the cats. The doorbell rang as she reached the bottom of the stairs. It was a police officer come to see if she wanted to press charges.

"For what?" asked Emily.

"Well Mrs Grimshaw did try and assault you and we understand that there have been other alleged threatening incidents."

"Oh, well yes but..."

"So, she has threatened you before...?"

"Yes, but..."

"In what way has she threatened you?"

"Well, there was the vegetables...she'd put aside some vegetables for me for the well blessing hotpot, but I'd ordered them on-line. She was annoyed when I didn't take them. The morning after, there were a lot of perfectly good vegetables in the recycling behind the store and everyone thought she might have been trying to ruin the hotpot, but then no-one believed that she would poison the whole village."

"Who is everyone?

"The people at the book club."

"...and was there actually anything wrong with the veg?"

"Well, the veg went with the recycling so we have no idea. It's just that we couldn't understand why she didn't just put them back on the shelves and sell them."

"And you are certain it was the same vegetables?"

"Well, no."

"So, it is just speculation?"

Emily nodded. Realising how ridiculous all this must seem.

"Was there anything else?" asked the officer.

Emily couldn't think of anything else that he wasn't already aware of.

"Would you be happy if, on this occasion we just gave her a warning?"

"Yes," said Emily wondering if, to say otherwise would mean she'd have to go to court and testify.

As the officer left, James appeared. Emily invited him into the kitchen. Seeing Emily looking glum he sought to reassure her that she had done the right thing. Carla needed help, not prosecution. He promised to go and have a word with her, try to convince her that neither Emily nor the cats meant her any harm. Secretly he felt the former was achievable, but he didn't know what he could say to convince her of the latter, especially when, try as he might, he couldn't really convince himself. How embarrassing was that! Perhaps the two of them could go together and convince Carla that if the cats really were to blame it wasn't at Emily's bidding, and that Emily really wished Carla no harm and would like to be friends. Emily thought that was a great idea. James to act as intermediary to help bury the hatchet. It probably wasn't the best choice of words but the right sentiment.

As Emily made them both a coffee James asked how things were with her and Grant? She was surprised that he knew. He told her that Alex had said he'd called three times to return the periapt and had been so worried when there was no sign of her that he had been about to break into her house. Then Carla had told him that Emily had been seen leaving the village in Grant's car the day before. Now it looked like she and Grant were getting back together. "Well, that is what the local gossip is," he confided apologetically.

She confessed that she was seriously thinking about it. She told him how Grant had surprised her by proposing but that she hadn't as yet given Grant an answer. She didn't want to throw away all the history they had together. She gave James all the reasons she had given Louise.

Well, you need to tell Alex something. He hasn't said anything, but I think he is quite upset that you haven't responded to the note he left, especially after he thought that you had both enjoyed your date.

"Note, he left a note?"

"Yes, he pushed it through your letter box yesterday morning."

Emily rushed to the front door. There on the hall table was the stack of mail she had picked up when Becky called to do her nails. She scooped up the pile and quickly sorted through it. In the middle was a folded sheet of paper. Opening it she read, 'Was worried when I couldn't get an answer, but I understand that you took Grant's car back for him. Hope you are okay. I have mended the periapt. Either call round for it or let me know when you are back, and I'll bring it round. Regards, Alex.'

"Regards!" Emily stared at the words, so formal after their date and with a possible hint of reprimand, but then he had every right to be annoyed. They had had a wonderful evening. They had laughed and joked together. She had given him every reason to think there was a future to their relationship. Then, only the day after, she had run off back to her ex-partner, and stayed away overnight without a word. Alex must think she'd spent the night with Grant. How insensitive could she be! She hadn't even replied to his note. No word of thanks from her that he had mended the periapt. No, 'sorry I worried you, but I am back now'. No, 'sorry I went off without telling you and made you worry'. No acknowledgement. No nothing! She hadn't even given him a thought. What was she going to tell him? She wandered back to the kitchen. James was pouring himself another cup of coffee. He glanced up as she approached.

"I'm a good listener..." he smiled ruefully.

So, bit by bit, she told him about how Grant still wanted her back, how she had decided to return his car so that he wouldn't have an excuse to return to Greater Blessing, and how she'd planned to tell him it was over between them. Then he had surprised her by proposing and agreeing to have children. Unable to deal with the situation, she had run away to Lou and Mike's, stayed the night, and now didn't know what to do. Grant was offering her all she had ever wanted. She had had a really good time with Alex, but she and Grant had lived together for 6 years. Wouldn't she be stupid to throw all that away? Shouldn't she give them another chance? They had been so happy before. Why couldn't they be so again? Why was life so complicated?

James topped up her mug with more coffee. She took a sip. Grant had looked so forlorn when she left. Why had she run away? She should have stayed and talked it through. Said something! Instead, she had panicked and left him kneeling on the floor. She didn't know what to do. What should she do? She looked at James for an answer.

"If you are looking to me to tell you what to do, I can't give you the answer. This is something you have to figure out for yourself, but whatever your decision, you need to communicate with both of them soon, because this isn't fair on either of them."

"I know and I feel terrible, but I just don't know what to do."

* * *

When James left she decided to go and see Alex and at least apologise for not replying to his note or contacting him after their date. She walked down the alleyway by the side of the Three Wells and along the back of the buildings fronting the high street, taking the short cut to the forge. As she passed the back of the store she looked up and noted the stepped roof-lines of the out buildings and extension and realised that it was perfectly possible that the cats had made it up to the chimney pots. She walked on, deep in thought, until she found herself standing in Alex's yard. Looking round, she saw that all the doors were shut and apparently locked. She mounted the stone steps at the righthand side of the yard that led up to the first floor and what looked like living quarters. She couldn't believe that she hadn't actually been here before now. She took a deep breath, then knocked on the door and waited. No answer. She knocked again. Had he moved into one of the cottages he had inherited from the sisters? He hadn't mentioned it if he had. She waited but no one came. Partly relieved, but also annoyed that she would have to put off speaking to him and still have the encounter hanging over her head, she wandered down the steps. Then she noticed the plastic covered paper pinned to the forge doors.

Away on business
If urgent please contact Albert Dewhurst
tel. 621315

Finding a piece of paper and pen in her bag she quickly wrote a note to let him know that she had called, climbed back up the steps, and pushed it through his letterbox.

* * *

For the rest of the week Emily struggled with her emotions, unable to decide what to do. Alex remained elusive. No-one seemed to know where he was or how long he would be away. Twice she went back and left notes. She considered phoning Grant, but every time she started to dial she chickened out, uncertain what she was going to say. She spoke at length to Lou who listened patiently and miraculously kept her opinion to herself, despite Emily's pleading. The cats kept their council but kept her under surveillance. Wherever she went at least one of them, if not seen or heard, could be sensed, observing and waiting.

James popped round on the Friday to see how she was and to give her an update on Carla. He had been to the hospital. Carla was suffering from nervous exhaustion. She spoke to him, in a distracted way, refusing to be drawn on the subject of the cats. He had sought to reassure her that, whatever the part played by the cats, Emily wished Carla no ill will and would like to be friends, if Carla would just give her a chance. Carla remained to be convinced, as did the staff, of Carla's lack of paranoia. It seemed they also had their doubts about James as, when attempting to soothe Carla, he had backed her up by voicing his opinion of the cats' involvement. He had then proceeded to incriminate the entire population of Greater Blessing by claiming that the cats, Kevin especially, made no secret of the fact that they didn't like Carla. When the hospital chaplain turned up and engaged him in rather unsubtle questioning about his professional credentials, he decided it was time to leave.

By the time James had finished relating his story Emily was grinning. His animated description had cheered her up no end. As he headed down the hall he hesitated, then turned and said, "I don't suppose I could persuade you to come to my performance, could I? There's a Comedy Caravan night at Barnlees Working Men's Club a week on Saturday. I'm third on the bill. I don't like asking only, well..."

"Try and stop me."

"You can bring Lou if you like, or whoever..."

"I'll get on the phone right away. She'll be

347

thrilled. I am. Thanks, I needed cheering up."

CHAPTER
TWENTY NINE

G rant knocked again, but there was still no reply. Emily was out, or she had seen him coming and was hiding. Then again, maybe she had just gone to the store. He could wait. A quick trip to The Little Teacups Cafe would pass the time and he could tell Jessica what he thought about her abusing his car. He headed back down the drive and climbed into his mate Pete's Spitfire. Together they drove off and parked further down the street. Pete was going to stay in the car, but Grant insisted he come too.

Jessica was delighted to see him. Her face lit up, but her broad grin quickly sagged when she saw the expression on Grant's face. Unnerved, she quickly handed change and a paper bag full of rock cakes to a lady in a blue skirt, orange anorak and Wellingtons, standing at the counter. To Jess's discomfort, instead of going, the woman spent ages rearranging items in her tartan wheeled shopping bag trying to make room for the rock cakes. Then, just as Jessica thought the woman was finally leaving, she stopped to hunt for her purse, which was now buried somewhere in her trolley. As the clock on the wall over the counter ticked ever louder, Grant continued to glower at Jessica. Jessica had no idea what could possibly be wrong. Oblivious to the atmosphere in the shop the woman finally strolled to the door, trolley wheels crashing into chair legs as she went, and bid a cheery farewell. With the door chimes still ringing, Jessica couldn't contain herself, "Grant ...what's wrong?"

At first, he didn't respond, wanting to make her suffer. He just stared at her, rapping his fingernails on the tabletop whilst scrutinising her discomfort. He was so angry; he wasn't certain how to put it into words.

"Grant, please..." begged Jessica, now close to tears, her mind racing trying to think what could possibly account for this change in his attitude towards her. She looked at his friend. Why was he here? Why two of them? Now she was feeling a little alarmed. Of course, don't be silly, with his broken arm Grant couldn't drive himself, but...

Pete was growing increasingly uncomfortable as Grant deliberately prolonged the agony. Observing the multitude of expressions crossing Jessica's face and seeing that she was now starting to look frightened he took pity on her. Lightening the atmosphere he smiled, stuck out his hand and introduced himself.

"Hi, I'm Pete, Grant's friend and chauffeur." Glancing at Grant, who still wasn't showing any sign of saying anything, he continued, "Grant is rather upset at finding a cigarette butt in his car." Noting the lack of comprehension on her face, he added, "He thinks you have been smoking in his car."

At this point Grant found his voice, "I trusted you with that car. How dare you!"

Jessica stared, "What, I never. I would never do anything like that. Apart from walking round and checking it every day I didn't even open the door. I know I was sitting in it when you found me, and I can see you don't believe me, but I swear I never so much as touched it after you left. I know how much that car means to you, please, you've got to believe me..."

"Oh, so a fag end, with *orange* lipstick, just appeared out of thin air, did it. Who else wears *orange* lipstick? Tell me that!"

Just then the door opened, and their voices were drowned by the door chimes. A couple of people walked in, hesitated uncertainly, obviously sensing the atmosphere. Jessica mustered a smile and they settled themselves at a table in the far corner, leaning their rucksacks against the wall. As Jessica took their order, mind racing, she could hear Pete and Grant whispering earnestly together. Pete was obviously trying to persuade Grant that she was telling the truth. As she threw tea leaves into a teapot and placed cakes on floral patterned plates, she trawled her brain for an explanation. Suddenly, the memory of standing outside the café, cigarette in hand, and looking up to find she was being glowered at disapprovingly by one of Carla's cronies, came into vivid focus. She had deliberately flicked the butt into the gutter, knowing it would infuriate the woman. Had the woman then picked it up and put it in the MG? It wouldn't have been too difficult to pop one of the studs of the soft top or get a hand underneath enough to slip a cigarette butt inside. She wouldn't put it past her. Who knows what that evil little bunch of scheming witches were capable of?

As the couple tucked into their cakes, Jessica went and sat down with Pete and a still frosty Grant. Obviously, Pete hadn't fully convinced Grant of her innocence.

"Grant, it wasn't me, but I think you are right; it was my cigarette." His expression softened, judgement now reserved, awaiting her explanation. She told him about standing outside the café, of finding herself being disapproved of by the elderly busy body who took delight in making trouble, of retaliating by throwing her cigarette into the gutter – she would have picked it up later, but she forgot – she wasn't a litter lout – he could check - there weren't any other cigarette butts out there – and how easy it would be to slip the butt into the MG under its cover. She swore she would never have smoked in his car. He had to believe her. Supposing she had, did he think she would be stupid enough to leave the evidence behind?

Grudgingly Grant mustered an apology and had to admit that, considering her obvious enthusiasm for classic cars, it was unlikely that she would have smoked in his. Somewhat chagrined now, he asked for the menu. They might as well have lunch as it was time. Continuing to peace-make, Pete offered to show Jess his Spitfire once they'd eaten.

* * *

"Grant!" Emily blushed down to her toenails. "Hi...I was going to call you..."

"It's okay. Can I come in?"

As she stepped to one side, Grant turned and waved at Pete, who appeared to have Jessica sat beside him, indicating that it was okay for him to go. With a salutary roar of the engine, the two of them drove off together.

"He's giving her a drive. Apparently, she hadn't been smoking in the car," and Grant explained what they thought had happened. At the mention of Carla, Emily sighed knowingly and explained about the bats and the Police, and it

353

wasn't long before the two of them were talking animatedly together, the awkwardness of their last encounter forgotten.

She asked him about his arm, and he explained that it didn't really hurt much anymore, but that he was finding life pretty difficult washing and dressing etc. and that he was living off microwave meals. They chatted about the well blessing and he apologised again for embarrassing her. Now, she realised that she was able to laugh about it and wanted to know if Mike had shown him the video clip. No. It seemed that it would take a little longer for him to be able to laugh about it, but the fact that Emily could, was obviously a step in the right direction for him. To change the subject, she suggested giving him a tour of the house.

"Wow, this really is great, Em," he said as they stepped into the front sitting room." Have you decided on a style yet?"

"What do you mean?"

"Well, all this old furniture. I thought you'd be out shopping, swatches at the ready."

"Actually, I quite like it as it is. I wouldn't have thought I would, but it fits the house. It's comfortable. Besides, I haven't had time."

They moved through the house room by room working their way up to the attic. At the top of the stairs Grant tried to remove his jumper. The warm day and the climb had made them both hot. As he struggled one-handed Emily automatically went to help him. As she slid his jumper over his head, she got the sudden urge to run her hand over his back. Distracted she forgot about his cast and inadvertently tugged at his bad arm as she pulled the sleeve off. He gasped and she automatically put her arms round him as he cradled his arm against his chest. Then quickly let go, having hurt him again.

"I'm sorry, I'm so sorry."

"It's okay. Don't worry."

Avoiding his arm, she reached up and held his face in her hands, watching, until she saw the pain ease. Suddenly she found herself overwhelmed with the urge to care for him. "Oh, Grant, you can't manage like this! Why don't you stay? I've got loads of room."

Noting the last sentence but not wanting to push his luck, and silently acknowledging that this was a step in the right direction, he looked down at her, "Well, I have been finding it hard..."

"When Pete comes back, we'll go and get your things." He looked so grateful that before she knew what she was doing she had reached up and kissed him, just like she used to. He responded, wrapping his left arm round her waist and pulling her to him. It was incredible. The touch of his lips, so soft on hers, his increasing urgency: it had been so long. She felt herself responding to the comfortable familiarity and overwhelmed by the rush of desire heightened by 4months of abstinence. She clung to him, straddling the thigh that was separating her legs and lifting her off the ground. They staggered back so that her hips were pressed against the banister and her back arched. Grant nuzzled her neck then, meeting no resistance, his lips traced the 'v' of her sweater down her cleavage to meet his left hand which was now teasing her right nipple. As he took her into his mouth millions of tiny sensations met in a synchronised rush lifting her to another plane. She got the sudden urge to bite him, her need was so great. Sinking her teeth into the shoulder of his 'T'-shirt she reached down and unzipped his jeans.

CHAPTER THIRTY

G rant and Emily had a wonderful evening together apologising for the things they had
said, agreeing that they had both been in the
wrong; that they hadn't meant the things they
had said. They had been and collected clothes,
toiletries etc from the flat and, on the way back,
bought a bottle of wine and a take-away. By
the time the bottle was empty they were both
laughing at how stupid they had been. Grant was
magnanimously saying that he had been selfish,
and she was saying that she had been too. If
they had only just been sensible and discussed
solutions that would have suited them both instead of accusing each other of 'neglect' then
none of this would have happened. Then again, if
they hadn't, she wouldn't have won the lottery
and they wouldn't be sitting in this wonderful

house. They clinked glasses, "Here's to us", said Emily.

* * *

They spent a luxurious night together, getting to know one another again. When she woke, it was to the gentle rousing touch of Grant's hands. She rolled on top of him and grinned as she ran her fingers through his scrunched hair, watching his face as she moved back and forth. Grant gasped, a spasm drawing his knees to his chest and lifting Emily into the air. Wow, that had never happened before. She grinned, feeling smug, only to discover that Kevin had landed on Grant's foot startling him, and making him jump. Kevin did a circuit of the duvet to ensure that he had their full attention, and then deftly, and very disgustingly, deposited a fur ball on Grant's pillow. As Emily and Grant leapt out of bed spitting expletives, he hopped onto the rug and headed for the door, brushing affectionately against his feline friend who was observing from the doorway.

* * *

After breakfast Emily took Grant for a walk up through the woods to the crag. She wanted to show him the view, keen for him to like it as much as she did. As they approached the top, she realised that he was struggling to keep up. "Gosh Grant, you need more exercise. I come up here quite regularly. It gets easier." He didn't look convinced.

At the top they sat on the rock and Emily pointed out the church and roof of the store and the chimney pots of The Three Wells Pub, all that remained visible now above the green expanse of leaves. She told him about meeting James out training for his charity running, saying how funny he was and that she would have to introduce the two of them. She prattled on about being invited to attend his stand-up act with Lou and that she would ask if it was alright with James if Grant came too, although she doubted James would mind, in fact he'd no doubt be pleased, the bigger the audience, the better.

"It's getting a bit chilly. Do you mind if we go back down?" asked Grant.

"Oh, okay. I can show you the tree with squirrels on the way and if we are lucky, we might see a deer," enthused Emily.

As they descended through the wood, they strolled arm in arm, only separating where the path made it impossible to walk side by side.

"Look, a squirrel…and another…up there."

Grant looked, and smiled at Emily's delight. Yes, they were cute, but they were vermin after all. Still, if they made her happy.

* * *

Carla wasn't happy. Too many people were asking her too many questions and all delivered with the wrong sense of concern. It was like being on stage with a cast of really bad actors placing emphasis on all the wrong words. She studied their faces as they studied hers. In their eyes she saw pity. In their expressions she saw concern, concern for her, not what she was telling them. They didn't believe her. She struggled to articulate what had happened, striving for rational clarity. The gap between herself and her latest questioner widened: she sensed it as he shifted slightly in his chair and, with a "Then what happened", encouraged her to continue damning herself. Hysteria rising again, she struggled to stay calm. Control! Keep control!

* * *

As the week progressed Emily and Grant settled into a routine. She got up first and fed the cats, then helped Grant wash and dress before getting their breakfast ready. Then she drove him to work. At the end of the day, she went and picked him up again and made their evening meal. Grant had to admit that he was quite impressed with the way she had mastered cooking on the range. Having been given the general idea by Anna, when they had made the village hotpot, she had found that chopping veg. and meat, sprinkling on a few herbs and sticking it in the oven for 2-3 hours, worked a treat. So long as she remembered to take it out, give it a stir once in a while, and add some water if needed, they had a great meal. If she made enough, it would 'do' more than once. Add some peas, a chunk of bread, a dollop of brown sauce and a can of stout and Grant was a happy man, which in turn, made her happy.

At the weekend they would go and get his TV and set it up in the living room. Why she hadn't thought to get a proper television when she had the broadband installed, she didn't know. Instead, she had been quite happy watching on her laptop, on the rare occasions she had bothered watching anything since moving into the cottage. She hadn't actually missed television. She had been too busy doing other things it seemed. Grant, however, was insistent that the rugby must be watched in wide screen and forced her to upgrade her broadband package to include it. Irritated, she complied. She had planned on dragging him over to The Three Wells on Saturday afternoon, but he was certain that, if any sport was shown there, it would be football. When she thought about it, she was glad. It would be nice to have him to herself. They would snuggle up together on the sofa. It would be just like old times, shouting at the screen, sharing the highs and lows. She must get some cans in and some crisps.

On the Wednesday, on her way to the store, she bumped into Anna.

"How are the wedding plans going?"

"Oh, er, we haven't discussed it yet, and I haven't actually said 'yes'.

"Sorry, am I speaking out of turn?"

"No, it's just, well, I don't know. Grant and I need to talk," and with that she ducked into the store.

There was someone new behind the counter which was a surprise. A young man, with a mop of brown hair hanging over one eye in defiance of the gel which, by the way he kept attempting to flick it upwards, was meant to hold it out at right angles to his extreme side parting. She had been expecting one of Carla's assistants but thankfully no-one else was in sight. Emily wandered round and filled up her basket. By the time she reached the till a copy of 'Bride' magazine had slipped itself amongst the milk, bread and other items. She went to lift her basket onto the counter and was pleasantly surprised. The young man leapt to her assistance. He greeted her politely and articulately and bagged up her items efficiently. She asked him if this was a permanent position or just temporary whilst Carla was away. Just temporary he hoped. At the moment he was taking any job he could get but hoped to make use of his degree as soon as something came available.

"Well, I hope you find something soon, although I suspect Greater Blessing will miss you greatly when you do. Thank you", said Emily.

Back at Wishing Well she made herself a coffee and sat down with 'Bride'. Flicking through the pages, she got lost in a fantasy. There was so much choice of dresses and accessories, table settings etc. Before she knew it, it was 4:30. She must go and pick up Grant.

* * *

Jessica stared into the bottom of her tea-cup: her fourth of the day. She was going to have to meddle. Emily and Grant were getting on too well. It was good that he was now in the village as it meant he was near. The fact that his car had now been moved here too, she liked, but it indicated that his relationship with Emily was moving up a gear, and that, she definitely did not like. She took a last drag of her cigarette and then stubbed it out in the bottom of her cup, an act which wouldn't grant her any spiritual favours, but then things weren't going her way anyhow. Thoughtfully she watched the tea dregs and ash mingle, forming a sludgy grey mess.

* * *

Emily and Grant were getting on well, but Emily was conscious of the fact that since she'd left Grant kneeling on the floor, his Big Question unanswered, neither of them had mentioned marriage. They had moved back in together and apart from a change of venue, it was as if nothing had changed. Yet every time she tried to bring up the subject, she found she was stuck for words. He hadn't said anything either. Was he feeling uncomfortable about bringing up the subject again? Was he waiting for her? Should she just blurt it out, or should she just assume that they were getting married? One of them had to say something.

That evening, Grant surprised her by suggesting that they went out for a meal on Saturday evening, just the two of them. Emily was delighted until she realised that the meal clashed with James' Comedy night.

"Grant, I'd really love to, but can we go out on Friday instead. We can't miss James' performance."

"What? There will be other comedy nights."

"I know, but I promised. We can eat out any night," replied Emily, wondering whether or not she was messing up his plans to propose again, whilst trying to weigh up who she should favour. James had been really good to her. Besides, it was true, she and Grant could eat out any night. Grant could propose any night. "And Lou and Mike are supposed to be coming. They haven't given me a definite yet, but Lou was very keen."

"Well, I suppose I can cancel the table," he said grudgingly, "If you aren't going to change your mind!"

"No," she was annoyed now, "I'm not letting our friends down."

"Fine! If you're adamant, I'll see if I can book a table for Friday instead."

Realising what might be at stake, that she might be messing up his romantic plans but seeing no alternative, she tried a different tack and turned on the charm, "Please?" She reached out and stroked the side of his face.

Appeased, he grinned, "Okay, Friday. I'll see what I can do, as it's you."

* * *

On Thursday morning, as soon as she had taken Grant to work, she drove round to Lou's. "I think he is going to propose again. He's taking me out for a meal tomorrow night. What should I wear?"

"Go shopping Em. You want to look fabulous, and get those nails seen to."

"You know, I was going to leave my nails, but most of the flakes have dropped off. Do you think if I just get this one done?" and she held up her ring finger.

"It's Grant. Get your nails done."

"Hmm. How's my godson coming along? Started talking yet?"

"Ha, ha. No, and I take offence at having my bump used so blatantly to change the subject. I take it you have decided what your answer is going to be. Are you sure about this?"

"Don't you think I'm doing the right thing?"

"I want you to be happy. Is Grant going to make you happy?"

"Of course. So, are you and Mike coming to see James? Please say you will."

"Yes, we're coming. Wouldn't miss *that*. If we turn up mid afternoon would that be okay?

We wouldn't be dragging you out of bed..."

"Stop it. The cats will have seen to that."

"Yes, how are Kevin and Grant getting along?"

Emily sighed. She related the story of Kevin vomiting on Grant's pillow and how, whilst she was making breakfast one morning, she'd dropped everything to run upstairs when she'd heard Grant's scream followed by several thuds. She had arrived to find Grant wedged in a corner of the room where he'd landed, cursing and glowering at his slipper in the opposite corner. Lying forlornly alongside his slipper had been a dead shrew, its pointy upturned nose mocking Grant's disgust. Then she told Lou about Grant being furious at finding paw prints on the bonnet of his MG. Now, he and Kevin made no pretence of their dislike for one another, Kevin openly hissing and spitting at Grant and Grant shouting and swearing at Kevin.

Lou looked thoughtful, "and Angelica?"

"I don't know. We haven't seen much of her all week."

CHAPTER
THIRTY ONE

D espite frantic shopping, Friday seemed an awfully long day to Emily, who couldn't wait for evening to come. After multiple phone calls she had managed to find somewhere to get her hair done at short notice and, despite what she'd said to Lou, her nails. She'd chosen a classic fitted dress, to show off her figure. It was dark blue with navy lace trim, which showed off her newly acquired 'tan' beautifully. She wanted to look classy without being over dressed for wherever Grant was taking her. Not having worn heels for a while, she knew that her new shoes would pinch a bit, but she wouldn't have to walk far, so that didn't matter.

She went and collected Grant from work and then went and got ready. Looking at herself in the bedroom mirror she was pleased with her appearance. Then she realised that she needed some jewellery. The periapt would have been perfect but of course she didn't have it. Going through her jewellery box she tried on several pieces and finally settled on a necklace that she and Grant had bought, on holiday together, in Amsterdam. It was a little gold and diamond locket on a delicately thin gold chain. It seemed appropriate that it was something that he'd bought her.

Grant was sitting by the fire in the kitchen finishing off a mug of coffee. She stood in front of him and did a twirl, batting her eyelids in an exaggerated fashion.

"How are you going to drive in those?"

"What? I hope you're kidding. There's a taxi booked, right?"

"I thought we could get a taxi back. Then go get the car tomorrow when Lou and Mike are here."

"No, that'll take up half the day. I'm calling a cab. Where are we going? No, on second thoughts, if this is meant to be a surprise, you ring." With that she handed him the phone and stomped out of the room.

Fifty minutes later car lights illuminated the bedroom window frame. She stuffed 'Bride' back under the mattress at her side of the bed and peered out of the window. A taxi was turning round. She drew the curtains and headed downstairs. Determined to have an enjoyable evening, a night to remember for all the right reasons, she mustered a smile and allowed Grant to put her coat on for her, despite his plaster cast. Together they locked the house as if nothing had happened. In the garden, as they climbed in the taxi, four pairs of eyes watched from the cemetery wall.

* * *

By the time they reached the restaurant they were chatting happily. Emily was a little surprised at the venue, but then Grant had had to change his plans at the last minute, so maybe this wasn't what he had intended. For a country pub it was okay, pleasant enough, but nothing particularly special. However, she should stop mentally criticising and just enjoy the evening. She didn't want to become a snob just because she could now afford to buy the place. After all, Grant was paying and there was no shared bank account yet.

Grant was talking. What was he saying!

"I said, sorry about the other table." Pointing at a long table of about a dozen screaming twenty-something's on a hen night, at the other side of the room, he added, "this wasn't what I had in mind."

Trying to ignore the din they studied the menu. They ordered their meal and Grant chose a bottle of Prosecco. The waiter poured the wine, Grant took a sip and nodded, and their glasses were filled. They watched the bubbles settle a little. Then, as they waited for the starter to arrive Grant clumsily took Emily's left hand in his plastered one. Emily was taken by surprise. She hadn't expected him to do it so early in the meal, but then, why not. After a moment, she realised that he was staring at her. She was puzzled; he hadn't said anything, had he? Had she missed it? Had he proposed and she'd day-dreamed her way through it? He was jiggling his glass in her face. Stupefied, she stared at it. Slowly it dawned on her. He was making a toast. Feeling a fool, she picked up her glass and held it in front of her.

"To us," he said, and chinked her glass.

"To us," she mumbled and took a sip. As she did so she caught a distorted glimpse of the hen party through the base of her glass. The bride-to-be was having a whale of a time. She was standing on a chair showing the whole restaurant the pale blue garter adorning her rather chubby left thigh. That could be me, thought Emily, half disgusted by the drunken display but smugly confident that her legs would provide a much better show, despite being a few years older.

Their starter arrived and Grant thanked her for taking him to work all week, saying it had made everything so much easier: that she had no idea how he had been struggling on his own. He was so pleased that she had gone and got his MG. He liked seeing it outside the cottage, knowing that it was safe. Then he started to laugh at how badly he had treated Jessica over her cigarette butt. He couldn't believe that someone in the village could be so malicious. Emily elaborated on what had been going on with Carla and the cats. Although she couldn't really believe that the cats had plotted it all, the evidence was piling up. So many strange things had happened since she'd moved in and all the villagers seemed to act as if this was nothing unusual. Together they laughed, and raised another toast, this time 'to Greater Blessing and its nutty inhabitants'.

As the second course arrived, and with it a bottle of Cabernet Sauvignon, the pair of them talked animatedly and speculated as to what the cats would do next, now that Carla was 'out of the way'. Grant had a number of suggestions, starting with Jessica's nemesis, swiftly followed up by the rest of the twin-set brigade: as they had named the rest of Carla's cronies. Then it occurred to Emily that Kevin, at least, had already found his next victim. Grant wasn't part of the master plan. What would the cats do if she and Grant got married? A small knot tightened in the pit of her stomach. She told herself not to be so ridiculous. They were just cats. The Wells sisters were dead and gone. End of story. The knot in her stomach tightened some more and Emily poured the contents of her glass down her throat.

As the meal progressed, Grant did most

of the talking. Emily made appropriate noises at varied intervals without really listening to what he was saying, and Grant didn't seem to notice, except to keep her glass topped up. Distractedly she noticed that he seemed to be enjoying himself, but then he'd always liked the sound of his own voice. She looked down at her left hand as it stroked the linen tablecloth. How intricate the design of the damask! It was obviously machine made, but how did they do that? Some gravy had splashed off her plate. She stared at the stain. With a feeling of disjointed reality, she tried to tether herself to the present. Inwardly she was aware that she was drunk. She studied the fact. The logical part of her brain told her that she needed to stop drinking. She would regret it in the morning. The sounds of other people echoed round about. Sooner or later, she reasoned, she would have to go to the 'loo'. Better go sooner, rather than later. Delicately she pushed her chair back and stood up. Her chair hit the ground with a crash, and something tickled her knee and ankle. Glancing down she saw that her napkin had fallen off her lap. Oblivious to the chair, lying on its back, she did her best curtsy and retrieved the napkin. Standing upright, she raised her eyebrows at Grant, carefully folding the napkin as she did so. She placed it, badly judged, on the edge of the table and headed across the room. The napkin slid to the floor.

She was quite pleased that her new shoes were a bit tight, otherwise they would never have stayed on her feet. How *she* stayed on them was one of those anti-gravity acts only the drunk can achieve. Humming earnestly, to aid her concentration, she made it across the floor to the bar. Where were the toilets? Looking round nonchalantly, concentrating on casual, she spotted a 'pointing hand' symbol, back the way she had come, with something written next to it which she couldn't read. She turned round, made sure her feet were both pointing the same way, and set off again. Yes, it said 'toilets'. 'Damn', they were downstairs! There was a man coming up. He was dressed smartly in a suit. He was probably old enough to be her father, but she had his full attention. She smiled pleasantly. He looked at her warily. She stepped down, elegantly placing one shapely foot after the other. He hesitated. Emily smirked inwardly. The dress was a hit and so was she. It felt good to 'flaunt it' again. As she descended, he turned as she passed, on the verge of saying something. She very nearly made it all the way down the flight. If it had been three steps shorter, she would have. On the third from last step, her ankle went over and, had it not been for her firm grip on the handrail she would have gone full length. As it was, she arrived at the bottom upright, but with her legs pointing in different directions and her dress up round her waist, lacy hold-ups visible to all. Politely she thanked the gentleman as he helped her to her feet, insisted she was 'owite ankyou' and, clutching her shoes, headed into the Ladies. She sat for a while, head in hands, trying to re-member the route back to their table. Raising her head, she then got engrossed in deciphering the graffiti on the back of the toilet door, mar-velling at the varied use of apostrophes and an-noyed with herself for not thinking to bring a permanent marker.

CHAPTER
THIRTY TWO

T he light through the curtains was blind-
ingly painful. When she tried to sit up to
see what time it was it hit her between the
eyes like an axe. The room swam and her stomach heaved. She waded through her brain, delv-
ing for clues. How had she got home? The last
thing she remembered was, of all things, a gravy
stain and marvelling at how it had turned white
linen threads into spun gold. She reached out.
The bed was empty. Grant wasn't there. Had she
disgraced herself that much! She groped for the
clock. She peered at it through one eye, all she
could risk. It was either twenty past ten or ten
to four. She lay back and considered the possibilities. It must be ten twenty. Slowly the needs
of the day lined themselves up: TV from Grant's
so he could watch the rugby in the afternoon:

make up bed for Lou and Mike: tidy house: shop for Sunday: throw up! As another wave of nausea swept over her she sunk back beneath her duvet.

* * *

The next thing she was aware of was the strident ringing of the doorbell. At first, she ignored it; Grant would get it. As the ringing continued, she grew alarmed, threw on her dressing gown and stumbled down the stairs. Jessica was on the doorstep, sporting a head of newly dyed brown hair, all apologetic.

"Hi, I'm sorry. I didn't mean to wake you. I can come back another time."

"No, no it's alright," responded Emily, not wanting to give the girl an opportunity to come again. "What can I do for you?"

"Well, I went round to the forge and saw Albert, Albert Dewhurst. We got talking about cars and I mentioned Grant's MG. Is he in by the way?"

"I don't know. Don't think so."

"Oh, that's a shame; I had a car question to ask him."

"I'll tell him you called. What did you want?"

"Oh, yes, Albert asked me to give you this," and she held out a bundle of tissue paper.

Emily took it. It was heavier than she was expecting, but then she wasn't expecting the periapt, or the emotion that came with it. Embarrassingly she felt tears pricking her eyes.

"Albert said that Alex had left it with him, in case you went round for it, but you hadn't been, so he asked me to bring it."

"Okay, thank you. I'll let Grant know you called."

Reluctantly Jessica turned and headed down the drive. Watching her go Emily fastened the periapt round her neck and tucked it inside her top, amused. Grant, it seemed, had an admirer. She laughed to herself. Not Grant's type at all. She was about to close the door when a movement at the edge of the drive caught her eye. As Jessica wandered past the church gate a sleek black cat emerged from the bushes and sidled across the chippings and into the street after her. Emily noted that the little knot in her stomach was back, along with the odd disturbing memory from the previous night – stairs, stocking tops. Her head swam. Still, she needed to see that cat. Creeping down the drive, wincing as the chippings dug through her slippers, she stopped at the bottom. Jessica was halfway back to The Little Teacups Café but sashaying along behind her was the black cat. When Jessica turned into the café the cat peeled off to the right onto the green. At the base of one of the oaks it circled once and sat, then turned its head to look directly at her. Rooted to the spot, she stared, as a second cat sat up and scrutinised her. Then she knew. She just knew. Ruby and Myrtle! Shocked, she turned and ran back into the house, shut and bolted the door. Ruby and Myrtle! The full set. Why was she so surprised!

"Grant, Grant!" No answer. She yelled again, "Grant, where are you?" No, he wasn't there. She needed water and a coffee. In the kitchen she found a note on the table.

Gone for TV. Got Steve to come
get me as you weren't fit to drive.
Love Grant.

Brilliant! That was all she needed: Steve turning up and there was so much to do. She felt ghastly. She downed a couple of glasses of water whilst waiting for the kettle to boil, wondering if that was too much for her delicate stomach. No, it seemed okay. At the sound of wheels skidding to a halt on the gravel out front she grabbed her cup of coffee and dashed for the stairs.

It wasn't long before the door bell rang, and it dawned on her that she had bolted the door. She quickly threw on some clothes, went down and opened it to an irate Grant. She tried explaining about the cats but gave up and left them to set up the TV. There was such a lot to do, and she could see that she was not going to get any help from Grant.

* * *

By the time Lou and Mike turned up Emily was feeling somewhat better. She'd managed some toast and her head had stopped banging. It was still a shock to her senses though, when she stepped out of the house to greet her guests and was met with bright sunlight and a fresh breeze.

Lou was eager to know how the proposal had gone, "Well, how's *things*? Gosh, you look awful. Is everything okay?"

Mike was looking expectantly at her. He obviously knew too. Fortunately, Grant hadn't bothered coming to the door. He and Steve were in the front room busy yelling at the TV, which they had obviously got working. It didn't sound like things were going well for whatever team they were supporting. Emily hadn't bothered enquiring. Grant hadn't even asked her how she was, and she had no idea whether or not that was deliberate. Had she ruined his proposal? Had it been a proposal? Had he changed his mind, or just the timing? They needed to talk, and they were surrounded by people.

"I don't know. Come in."

"What happened? You really do look ghastly. You also smell like a brewery." Lou steered Emily into the kitchen, sat her down and filled the kettle.

"I'll go and say hi to Grant," said Mike and left them to it.

Emily explained what had happened and that she really had no idea whether Grant had proposed or not, and if he had, what she'd said, although he wasn't acting like they had just got engaged. It was all such a mess. Was it just a meal, and the rest was in her head? Probably!

"Just forget it. He probably realised how drunk you were. Stop complicating matters. At the first opportunity, just ask him what happened. Tell him you're sorry but you can't remember a thing about last night. Then leave it up to him"

"I know, but..."

"No 'buts'. We are going to have an enjoyable evening together. I haven't been to a comedy club for ages. I'm really looking forward to it. Right, let's go join the others. Who's playing? Who are we rooting for?"

* * *

Not wanting to be tempted to drink again Emily had volunteered to be the second driver, the pregnant Lou being the first. Steve, it seemed, much to Emily's annoyance, was also staying the night. She hadn't been asked. As Steve was a little on the large side, squashing all of them into one car would have been a bit ridiculous. Despite her protests Grant had persuaded her to phone James for an extra ticket and, much to her annoyance they weren't sold out; he'd leave one at the door.

Grant and Steve sat in the back. Over the noise of the radio, she caught snatches of their conversation, mainly about cars. As she approached Barnlee town centre she handed Grant the piece of paper with the address of the club and asked him to put the post code into his phone and direct her.

"Where are we going?" asked Steve.

"Huh, some working men's club," she heard Grant mutter.

"Oh, pie and pea supper and a warm pint then."

"yep, should have brought your flat cap."

The two men laughed, and Emily gritted her teeth.

* * *

Emily was pleasantly surprised when they got inside. What externally was an ugly 1970's prefab with pebble-dashed walls and a corrugated roof, turned out to be a super venue. There was a proper stage which jutted out into the audience in a 'T' shape and the five of them had their own table with only another table between them and the stage. There were about twenty tables in all and at the back of the room was a bar, one end of it labelled 'Food orders'. Having had nothing but one slice of toast all day Emily was ready for some food. Grant, Steve and Mike headed straight for the bar leaving Emily and Louise to get themselves settled at the table and study the food menu and the programme. Halfway down the bill they spotted James – The Irreverent Reverend – all money to St Peter's Young Disabled Unit.

The room quickly filled up and it wasn't long before the lights dimmed. There was a tinny fanfare over the speakers and the compare, in a red velvet suit and frilly shirt, stepped

out from the wings. As he launched into his pat-
ter their food arrived. A couple of late arrivals
caught the compares attention...

"I'm sorry, very rude of me to start without you. No, it's okay, I can wait whilst you get
yourselves seated. Will you be getting drinks, or
shall I carry on?" The audience laughed and the
spotlight swung away from the compare to illu-
minate the two men. To Emily's horror she saw
that one of them was Alex. Dressed in a light
blue 'T' shirt and jeans he looked radiant in the
spotlight. Unfazed by being the centre of attention he stood, looked round at the audience as
if to say, who me, am I causing a problem. Then,
putting on a show of mock graciousness said,
"No, no please, in your own time, do carry on."
The audience laughed. Her heart skipped a beat
and she flushed crimson. Lou put her hand on
Emily's arm. She'd noticed too and seen Emily's
response. Mike was a bit slower to recognise
Alex but then he immediately looked at Emily.
Grant, thankfully, was back at the bar with
Steve, getting in a second round. By the time he
returned the compare was introducing the first
act.

It wasn't long before Emily was laughing, forgetting that Alex was there. Then, intermittently, she'd remember, and her dread of
the interval would return. She couldn't possibly
avoid him. If he didn't know already from James
that she was going to be there he was bound

to notice her. Without realising it, her fingers sought out the periapt.

All too soon the interval arrived, and the house lights came back on. As the audience stirred, she and Lou headed for the sanctuary of the Ladies.

"What should I do? I can't just ignore him, but what do I say?"

"Well, you could take the bull by the horns, so to speak…"

"What do you mean?"

"Go straight to him, say that you are sorry that you haven't been in touch since the meal together, you tried but he wasn't there. He deserves an explanation, but here isn't the place and this is James' night. Can you get together some time next week?"

"Great. Brilliant. Yes, that's good…sorry, deserves explanation, James' night, talk next week…Right, how do I look?"

"Red faced! Here, slap a bit more foundation on."

Heart pounding, she headed straight for Alex's table. To her surprise, he wasn't there, and neither was his friend. She checked the bar, but they weren't there either. Of course, they could both have gone to the Gents or, perhaps he'd spotted her and left. She began to relax although she didn't like the thought of him being upset, if that was the case. Then she spotted him. He was sitting at their table! He and Mike were deep in conversation. Grant was looking on in stony silence and Steve was looking bewildered. As she hesitated, he turned and saw her. Then he got up and came straight at her. "Hi, I've been away. Sorry I missed you, but I see you got the periapt back." The lights dimmed again signalling the second half of the show. "Oops, best get back to our table, James is due on any minute," and with that he left her. Bless him. She hadn't needed to say a word.

To an enthusiastic round of applause James arrived on stage. A number of people in the audience had obviously seen him before. The room settled down to listen.

"Hi, good evening, good evening, thank you, it's great to be here. Yes, yes, I know what you are thinking, (*fingering his dog collar*) but it is real...I am...a real...vicar, which can be a bit of a problem on the Comedy Circuit. The old dog collar has a strange effect on people... as soon as they find out I'm ... 'of the cloth'... they get all apologetic and start calling me father, which is wrong 'cos I'm not, on any front. Firstly, I am C of E not Catholic, so just call me James, not father, and secondly, I've no kids, I am single. So ladieees, you can caaaall me... (*impersonating Bond*) the name's Meacher, Jaaaames Meacher." They all laughed.

Through the comfort of the darkness Alex's laugh repeatedly drew Emily's attention. In the relative privacy of the audience, sitting slightly behind and at an angle to both Alex and Grant, she was able to study the two men. Grant was whispering intermittently with Steve. The pair of them seemed to have their own show, feeding off the headline one, belittling it, or so it seemed. Alex, on the other hand, was totally focussed on the stage, generous in his appreciation and totally comfortable with his surroundings.

"For a long time, *(fingering his collar again)* I didn't wear it socially, but I began to feel like a spy. I had this whole other, secret identity. *(A quick furtive look to both sides of the stage – then, scrutinising the audience, one eyebrow raised)* They think I'm just plain Meacher, quiet, unassuming Jim, pathetic, wimpy Jim, when little do they know – *(taking a super hero stance)* I have the power...to save...their...souls, ... or *(mimicking a silent movie villain, eyes flicking left and right)* ... no, we won't go there! *(slapping his wrist)* Naughty vicar!"

When the audience settled again, he continued, "But, there was always this dilemma of when to tell people that I'm a vicar. The longer I left it, the harder it got, and the guiltier I felt ... which ... for a vicar, was a tad awkward ... especially at gigs like this. Backstage, I can really kill a joke. It's not fair. I never get to hear the end of the dirty ones; I have to make up my own. I'm still trying to work out what the actress said to the bishop. In the end, I had to ask him. He didn't know either."

The final act followed and then the compare wrapped up the show by thanking all the comedians for providing such great entertainment, and the audience for being such a terrific audience.

The place began to empty, and they headed for the door. Emily looked, but Alex was no where to be seen. He and his mate had made a quick exit.

CHAPTER
THIRTY THREE

In the morning Emily woke to find herself on the edge of the bed. If the bedding hadn't been tucked in, she would have fallen out. Grant was laid spread eagled on his back in the middle of the mattress, snoring loudly. She crept out of bed, threw on some clothes and crept downstairs. She was the only one up and about. The cats, it seemed, were absent.

She wasn't sure what she was going to give everyone for breakfast as yesterday she'd been in no fit state to go to the store before it closed, and it hadn't occurred to Grant to volunteer. He'd been too busy getting and setting up the TV and adding to the guest list. Hopefully, cornflakes and toast would suffice until the pub opened and they could get lunch. Sitting there in the silent house, feeling the heat radiating from the range, she fingered the periapt thoughtfully.

One by one people appeared and by mid-day everyone was dressed. She suggested that they have a stroll round the village and then amble into the Three Wells for Sunday lunch, a plan which met with everyone's approval. First, they headed round the church yard, enjoying the floral displays. Then, as they passed the church porch James stepped out on his way home from the Sunday service. Feeling guilty at not having been to church Emily gushed out praise for his comedy performance, hoping it didn't sound false, which it wasn't. The others joined in, asking where he was appearing next. He looked suitably pleased. They invited him to join them for lunch, but he planned on visiting Carla again so declined.

* * *

Kevin strolled round the black marble base of a tall cross shaped headstone, his hot pads leaving tiny evaporating paw prints that disappeared as stealthily as he did. Only the flight of the odd bird out of the shrubbery along the path to the church gate, gave any clues as to where he had gone. At the gate he stopped and peered round the granite pillar, checking the direction of the departing noisy humans. His gaze then switched to the nearest two trees on the green. Just visible, if you knew exactly which places to look, were two pairs of yellow eyes.

* * *

The humans continued their stroll down the high street, chatting about this and that. Lou and Mike, it seemed, where keen to look in the estate agents' window. They read the details of several properties, but there was nothing in Greater Blessing that was suitable for them.

"I wouldn't have thought this was your cup of tea," scoffed Grant. "There's not much going on here. One pub lunch and an afternoon tea and you've done the lot!"

"Lou and I think this would be a great place to bring up kids," said Mike his arm round Lou. "And it would be great with you two here."

"What do you mean?" said Grant looking puzzled.

"Well...I, we...thought, as you'd moved in...," Mike looked at Lou. Lou looked at Mike. They both looked at Emily who was staring at Grant open mouthed...

"Well...," Grant started, as everyone waited expectantly. But he took too long.

The pent-up emotion of the past few days, all the uncertainty, suddenly became too much for Emily. "Yes, exactly what to do you mean Grant? What is this? What are we doing here, you and me?"

He stared at her. "Well, I thought we could find somewhere, nearer the city."

"What! I meant us. Friday, was that a proposal? Did I mess it up? Are we getting married?"

"If you want, yes. I didn't know. You never

gave me an answer. There's no rush is there!"

Emily was seething. "You don't get it do you. You never did. I want to get married Grant and I want to have children, and THAT WON'T WAIT!"

Lou tried to shush Emily, aware that she was getting louder and drawing the attention of passers by on the opposite side of the street, but Emily was beyond caring. Unnoticed, a window above the Little Teacups Café opened. Not completely concealed by the curtain the odd lock of auburn hair was just visible.

"On Friday, I thought you were going to propose. I thought you were making a commitment, but NO, instead you prattle on about everything and anything but our relationship. I thought we could make it work Grant. I really thought we could. Instead, I find I am waiting on you hand and foot because I thought you needed help, but your arm is okay I see to carry a TV and move MY furniture about. Everything is focussed on you. You invite extra guests without even asking me, sorry Steve, but do nothing to help cater. Then, you spent last night making snide comments about the venue and didn't even shut up when James was on stage. Now, I find you don't even like Greater Blessing. Well, I'M NOT LEAVING, but YOU ARE. I am going to the pub for some lunch. When I get back home, I WANT YOU GONE!

Grant looked bewildered, and momentarily Emily's heart went out to him, but he just stomped on it, "What about my car? How am I going to get my car home?"

Emily shook her head and looked to the heavens. It was then she spotted Jessica at her window and pointed, "I'm sure SHE'D be DELIGHTED. Got a driving licence Jessica? Yes? There you go Grant, she's even dyed her hair a nice conservative brown for you, all your problems sorted." With that she turned and marched across the green. If she had been wearing Wellingtons she would have gone straight through the pond. She didn't notice Angelica sitting on one of the pub windowsills.

* * *

Lou and Mike caught up with her at the pub door. Together they went in. Emily headed straight to the bar. As soon as she had ordered them drinks, she launched into an animated monologue, "So, now what am I going to do. I should have known better. You were right. I should have listened to you Lou. Grant is never going to change. He never wanted children and he doesn't now. Then there is Alex, wonderful Alex. What am I going to do about him? I have treated him so badly. We had a really good time together. I was so stupid. How do I explain...?" Neither Lou, nor Mike, was paying her any attention. They were both looking behind her. Irritated, she slowly turned and saw what they were looking at. There, at a table in the corner, all by himself, was Alex, smiling and gesturing at the seat next to him. He was beckoning her over. It appeared that he had heard every word. Lou steered Emily over and sat her down. Then she and Mike made their excuses and left her and Alex together.

As Emily started to splutter out excuses, and to impress upon him how she had tried to contact him, Alex caught Richard's eye and made a couple of hand gestures which produced two glasses and a bottle of red wine. Alex plonked a full glass in front of Emily and when she finally stopped stammering and took a mouthful, he took her hand, "Emily its okay."

"No, I treated you so badly..."

"Shush, sshhh, really, it's okay."

"But..."

"Sshhhhh...I know you tried to see me, James told me all about it, but when I heard you had gone back to Grant, I was devastated. I could not stand the thought of the two of you together. I just had to get away."

"But if you'd been around...Why didn't you fight for me?"

"Emily, dear, don't you know? I would fight, with every fibre of my being, to the very last breath in my body for you, but this, this was something you had to decide for yourself."

"But..."

"No. Deep down I knew all would be well, that you would come back to me, but it was important to me that, if possible, you decided on your own."

"I don't understand."

She saw the strain on his face. "Emily, my whole life has been mapped out for me, manipulated, not in any way you could prove, but, well, you must know how it is here..." then he reached out and took her face in his hands, "Please..." then his hands slid down to the chain round her neck, "please, take this off. The periapt, take it off. Please. I need to know that you want me for me, and not because of some plan cooked up by three, three...deceased nutty old wi... wi... women!" Expertly he reached round and unclipped the clasp. Collecting the periapt and chain in the palm of his hand he laid it out on the table in front of them.

"Then why did you fix it and leave it for Albert to give me?"

"It was yours. If you wanted it back, then you needed to be free to come and get it. It had to be your choice. I didn't anticipate Jessica's interference."

Emily looked at the periapt. Was she being influenced by it? She didn't think so. She and Grant had been falling out before she got it back, hadn't they?

"Emily, I really enjoyed our meal together. I haven't been able to think about anything else but you, since. I would be delighted if you would come out with me again, see if we can

make a 'go' of it … the two of us. It just seems so…
right! Unless you need some time…"

"No, I don't need any time Alex. Please,
I would love to go out with you, just tell me
when."

14 months later

Reclined on a faux leather couch, blue
paper roll scrunched up underneath her, Emily
stared at the screen as Alex held her hand. The
probe slid across the gel and felt cool on her
belly. The radiographer wasn't saying anything,
checking and rechecking her findings. The room
echoed to the sound of the electronic thumping Doppler whoosh which seemed to be getting
louder.

"Is everything okay," asked Alex, a slight
edge to his voice.

"Well, yes, everything is fine. Very fine!
Very… healthy! This might come as a bit of a surprise to you though."

Emily and Alex looked at each other and
sighed resignedly, "Probably not!"

"If you look at the screen… there, yes…
that is a head…." She moved the probe, "…and
so is that, and…," she moved it again, "and that.
Three babies! You are having triplets! It is a bit
difficult to tell the sexes at this stage, that is… if
you want to know…?"

"They wouldn't be all girls by any chance,

would they?" grinned Emily.

"Mrs Wells, as I said, I can't be certain, but I think so, yes."

* * *

Lou and Mike were delighted when they heard. Mike laughed and stroked Ruby's ginger head as she settled on his lap. The Wells and the Parkers would be able to baby sit for each other. When Alex had found out that Lou and Mike were looking to move to the village, he suggested they look at Bode Well Cottage, Ruby's old place. Three months later, when they moved in, they found a large and fluffy ginger female cat in residence. Lou was delighted. "We got our own fairy godcat!" When Emily found out she threatened to resign as godmother if Lou insisted on calling the cat Ruby.

Emily and Alex had been married by James in All Saints Church and nearly the whole village had turned out. It was a lovely sunny September day. Lou was chief bridesmaid. Anna and Karen, Emily's friends from the city, were the other two bridesmaids. A mate of Alex' from school was best man. Mike and baby Nathan had watched from the back of the church in case a quick exit was needed but Nathan had behaved himself and slept soundly through the service.

Carla wasn't there. Despite their troubled history Emily was a little sad that they had never had the opportunity to make friends and that Carla hadn't fully recovered. She never returned to the village, deciding instead to sell the store and retire, moving to Scotland to be near relatives.

Nothing was heard from Grant, but it was rumoured that he had handed in his notice at work and set off around Europe in his MG midget. The Little Teacups Café closed suddenly around this time and it was strongly suspected that Jessica had gone with him, or after him.

Alex and Emily decided to keep Fare Well Cottage, Myrtle's old place. With James' help they turned it into self-catering accommodation for relatives of St Peter's YDU residents. They used their money to ensure that each bedroom was en suite with its own TV, phone and internet connection, and that there was a well supplied kitchen and a comfortable communal lounge. They also ensured that there was wheelchair-accessible ground floor accommodation. They landscaped the grounds, leaving quiet private areas for reflection. A cat flap was fitted in the back door.

When the Well Blessing came round again Emily approached it with enthusiasm. She could not wait. This time she planned to enjoy it. This time she had a ready team of helpers who all knew what they were doing. This time she organised it so that she could take in the whole procession. Together, she and Alex, Lou and Mike, James, Anna and Richard had again decked out all three wells. Marching through the village at the front of the procession lead by James, she couldn't help feeling elated. This village, these people, this community, and a legacy left by three extraordinary old women, had changed her life. This was where she belonged.

* * *

Emily, at Alex's bidding, never wore the periapt again. After careful thought it was taken down into the cellar of Wishing Well Cottage and placed round the base of the stalactite from which it had been carved, which seemed fitting. Had she been influenced by it? She had no idea. Whether she had, or had not, it didn't really matter. She was happy with her life.

The cats continued to come and go as they pleased, keeping watchful eyes on events. They seemed content with the way things had turned out between Emily and Alex, Lou and Mike. Kevin, it was certain, approved of these people.

FAIRY RINGS

Coming Soon - The Sequel To Wishing Wells

Something is not right in Greater Blessing. Someone is interferring with the very fabric of its existence. Can the Wells family fulfill their ancestral role as guardians, and save the village? The cats hope so.

Chapter One

It was on the triplets third birthday that the white cat first appeared, on the wall outside Wishing Well Cottage. Emily became aware of it as she strapped the three children into the back seat of the car. The cat sat, unblinking, scrutinising activity. Emily busied herself, trying to ignore it. Unusually the children settled quickly, all eyes on the cat. Straps secure, she too felt compelled to look. As her eyes met those of the cat, Emily knew. Things were about to change. There was no going back. The feline stood, its glossy white coat glistening in the early morning light. With a couple of flicks of its white tipped black tail it turned elegantly and slipped off the wall out of sight.

ABOUT THE AUTHOR

Pauline Potterill

The author grew up in the northwest of England, on the edge of the Lake District, but has since lived in many other parts of this wonderful country. She particularly likes the quirkiness of life in its villages, its traditions and folklore. She is currently working on a sequel to Wishing Wells, called Fairy Rings.

Printed in Great Britain
by Amazon